KELLY DEVOS

RAZORBILL

RAZORBILL

An imprint of Penguin Random House LLC, New York

First published in the United States of America by Razorbill,
an imprint of Penguin Random House LLC, 2022

Copyright © 2022 by Kelly deVos

Razorbill & colophon are registered trademarks of Penguin Random House LLC.

Visit us online at penguinrandomhouse.com.

LIBRARY OF CONGRESS CATALOGING-IN-PUBLICATION DATA
Names: deVos, Kelly, author.
Title: Go hunt me / Kelly deVos.
Description: New York : Razorbill, 2022. |
Audience: Ages 12 and up. |
Summary: Follows teenager Alex and her horror buff friends
as their dream trip to a remote Romanian castle turns into
a nightmare when they begin to be killed one by one.
Identifiers: LCCN 2022011397 | ISBN 9780593204856 (hardcover) |
ISBN 9780593204870 (trade paperback) | ISBN 9780593204863 (ebook)
Subjects: CYAC: Vampires—Fiction. | Horror stories. |
LCGFT: Horror fiction. | Paranormal fiction.
Classification: LCC PZ7.1.D48915 Go 2022 | DDC [Fic]—dc23
LC record available at https://lccn.loc.gov/2022011397

Book manufactured in Canada

1   3   5   7   9   10   8   6   4   2

FRI

Design by Rebecca Aidlin
Text set in Gazette LT Std Roman

For all us unlikable female characters

You're safe here.

That's what the nurse told me when I arrived at St. Constantin's.

But still.

Every time the wheels of the hospital cart squeak on the freshly mopped tile floor. Each time the orderlies whisper to each other in the hallways. When someone drops a lunch tray or coughs or clears their throat. I flinch and the heart monitor beside my bed beeps frantically.

I can't sleep.

Can't close my eyes for a second.

Every time I do, I see Jax's face.

It's the details that give me nightmares.

The castle turrets that were the same scarlet color as the dried specks of blood I can't pry out from underneath my fingernails. The thin branches of the gray alder trees that twisted around my limbs like endless tentacles. The rustling leaves that concealed a conspiracy of whispers.

I can't stand to be in the dark. For the dead travel fast.

When they found out where I'd been picked up, a look of understanding crossed their faces. They'd heard stories about Castle Prahova. The doctor who spent all morning digging shards of

1

glass out of my scalp told me the private estate about fifty kilometers north of Braşov was a place that inspired legends. It had been the home of medieval warmonger Vlad Dracul, the real-life inspiration of the fictional character Dracula. The locals believed that the monsters of Prahova were more terrifying than what made it onto the pages of Bram Stoker's novel.

Of course, I already knew that.

It was Dracula and his legends that drew us to Romania in the first place.

But we didn't know that the castle had a more recent history of unsolved crimes and unexplained accidents. People went missing. Bodies washed up on the bank of the river that cut across the countryside and ran along the base of the sharp cliffs that bracketed the castle. For years, the place was owned by a drug dealer who used it for storage and operations. The Romanian police spent the better part of two decades relentlessly chasing a cartel across the always foggy, dense forest.

But even the farmers who knew the castle by reputation were shocked when our flaming utility cart crashed into the wooden fence outside of Rupea and I dragged Reagan's bloody body out into the wet, muddy road. Six dead American tourists. The Poliția Română sent a team to recover the remains. I don't know what there will be left to find.

Anything left of my friends.

My hand always feels empty. As if it will always be trying to reach out and pull Hazel from a pool of dark black water. I force my eyes open and stare at the greenish hospital lights.

You're safe here.

Dr. Fieraru says that my mother caught the red-eye from Phoenix. The police will send a car to the airport and she'll come to take me home. When I'm able to check my phone, I see all the alerts about Justin Bloom. In LA, the police are hunting for the famous film director.

Wanted for questioning.

A while later, as I am reading the same page of the hospital magazine for the hundredth time, a short woman wearing a floral-print dress and with her long, dark hair in a neat braid knocks lightly on the open door of my room.

"Alexandra Rush?" she says in a calm, pleasant voice.

The chirps of my heart monitor increase in pace.

I nod.

She enters with soft footsteps and says, "Please do not be alarmed. I am Police Inspector Ana Skutnik. I understand you already spoke to the police yesterday after you arrived at the hospital. Do you feel up to answering some additional questions?"

Truthfully, I do *not* feel up to it. I'm not sure I will *ever* feel up to it. But everyone will want to know the story of what happened, and I am the only one who can tell them. Our families deserve answers. From me.

Again, I nod.

Inspector Skutnik offers a comforting smile and takes the beige leather guest chair to my right. She leans forward, placing a small device in front of me on the overbed table. "If it is all right with you, I will be recording this interview. May I call you Alexandra?" she asks.

"Alex," I croak out. "My name is Alex."

I pick at the cast covering my broken arm and try to avoid scratching at the jagged, crisscrossed black stitches that bind the cuts all over my legs.

She nods. "I have a copy of your statement here. But I am hoping to get a fuller, more detailed picture of what happened. Particularly to gather information that might help the team at Prahova as they search for . . ." Her smile falters.

As they search for bodies.

Don't close your eyes.

I shiver.

"Okay," I whisper. My heartbeat slows. I'm so cold. So almost dead inside.

She smiles again. It's a motherly expression. "Let us start at the beginning."

I notice that the policewoman has a soft leather case she rests on her lap as she pulls out a handful of papers. For a minute her eyes glide over the printed pages.

"What do you want to know?" I ask.

Her eyes linger on the marks around my neck. "Only the truth."

"The truth is messy," I say with a sigh.

Inspector Skutnik reaches for the water pitcher on my table and refills my Styrofoam cup.

"Okay, Alex. Tell me. What brought you to Romania?"

153 days ago

EXT. PARADISE VALLEY—NIGHT— ALMOST HALLOWEEN

Mummy Mountain was silent and still and dark.

I was late. Nothing new about that. Since Dad got sick, I was late all the time.

For everything.

The enormous silver punch bowl on the seat next to me vibrated and bounced up and down as I took the turn from Lincoln Avenue onto the single-lane Hummingbird Road. I had to drive slow in the old Ford Taurus to take the tight turns. Once I passed the country club, I had only the sliver of a moon to light my way. The tip of a white crescent rose slowly above the rock formation that was said to look like the head of an Egyptian mummy.

It always struck me as odd that these narrow, poorly lit mountain roads were the access point to the houses of the richest people in Arizona. But Kenna McKee told me, "We can't make it easy. We don't want just *anyone* to get up here."

During the day, delivery drivers and landscapers and construction crews created a flurry of activity. But after dark, the one-percenters stayed out of sight, hidden behind their private gates and dense landscaping. Me and Kenna and the rest of our friends were supposed to be setting up for the McKees' epic Halloween party. But helping my dad had taken longer than I thought, so it was almost ten when I crept along, alone on a Friday night, my phone no longer buzzing with messages from Jax and Reagan checking up on me.

I should have been focused on my application to film school. USC's Cinematic Arts program admitted around 2 percent of its applicants. I had script pages to polish, a personal statement to write, a short film to make, and reference letters to beg for. Plus, since my family was out of money, not only did I need to be better than 98 percent of the thousands of applicants who wanted to walk in the footsteps of George Lucas, Shonda Rhimes, and Jon Chu, but I also had to find some combination of grants, scholarships, and loans to get me to California.

But tomorrow was *Halloween*. Of senior year. It was the last time that all my friends would celebrate our favorite holiday.

Together.

I didn't know what the future held, but it probably wasn't too many more parties with Paradise Valley Catering's famous ravioli and Mrs. McKee's epic skeleton-themed charcuterie boards. Hopefully someday I'd be a famous director, but that Halloween might be my final chance to sneak a Diplomático rum cocktail and steal sips while gazing at all the twinkling lights of Phoenix's sprawling suburbs.

Halloween. The one day of the year when you got to choose who or what you wanted to be. When you weren't at the mercy of the hand life had dealt you. A prince without a birthright. A witch without magic. A vampire who never has to hunt their friends. You could be anything. And you were allowed to talk about the things that scared you. To experience fear from a position of relative safety. To *sort of* confront the monsters that lived underneath your bed. I think that's what attracted me to horror

6

films. The best scary movies were about people who faced their demons and emerged as something different.

Something better.

The McKees lived in the *middle* of Mummy Mountain. Not in the more "affordable" homes near the base where doctors and lawyers put out their custom doormats, but not at the very top either. A few retired rock stars and film directors and the heir to the Campbell's Soup fortune lived in the handful of homes near the peaks that overlooked all of Scottsdale. I arrived at the long, steep ramp that led to Kenna's house and stopped in front of the closed iron gate with the massive metallic 52, Shane McKee's jersey number, welded onto it. Leaning out the window, I punched my code onto the keypad mounted to a pole.

After the gate creaked open, I had to shimmy the old Silver Bullet up the drive and parallel park it between stacks of tables and chairs waiting to be set up for the party. The truth of it was that I was one of the people who didn't belong on the mountain. Our family business teetered on the edge of bankruptcy. Bills piled up on Mom's desk. Even with us all pitching in to help Dad through his last round of chemo, dirty dishes always filled the sink, and the refrigerator was always almost empty, and the yard was always in need of a mow.

Nothing like the manicured, gated properties up here.

Grabbing the punch bowl, I slid out of the car and into the warm night.

McKee Manor, as they called it, was an odd mishmash of architectural styles. Most of the yard lights were off, so I couldn't quite make out the white columns near the front door or the Southwestern-style patio that I knew was on the east side. Resting the punch bowl on my hip, I pulled out my phone and turned on the flashlight. Half of the front yard was full of gravel and saguaro cactus, and the other contained rows of withered rosebushes. The whole place was surrounded by a ring of tall, funereal cypress trees and a concrete-block wall.

I was supposed to give the punch bowl to Mrs. McKee, but the main house was dark and things were quiet. After listening to the crickets chirp for a few seconds, I continued on.

Kenna had her own little suite on the west side of the property. She had it decorated to look like a house was smashed up against another house. There was a dramatic black-and-white-striped awning and tons of dusty yellow and light green walls. She had done a ton of work to make the place look like perpetual Halloweentown, and it had paid off. Kenna had become a social media star. Her videos on everything from how to choose the right black eyeliner to preparing your own horrors d'oeuvres kept going viral, and she had more than three hundred thousand followers.

I knocked on Kenna's door a couple of times. Where was everyone? Reagan, Jax, Carter, Maddie, and Hazel were nowhere to be found. Maddie was supposed to be setting up her face-painting station, and the rest of us had party jobs that ranged from assembling favor bags to blowing up pool floaties. I imagined my friends off somewhere without me. Carefree and normal. At the midnight movie or having late-night shakes at the country club. Jax was the perfect boyfriend. Reagan could do things with computers that should have been science fiction. Maddie was one of the best artists I'd ever seen, Carter's band was profiled by the *Phoenix New Times*, and Hazel was the genius who had it all figured out.

Where did that leave me?

My armpits grew moist and clammy. It was October in Arizona. In other parts of the world, leaves were changing colors and people were out shopping for sweaters. But in Phoenix, people were debating which Halloween costumes we could wear without getting heatstroke. It was about four million degrees outside. After nearly letting the punch bowl slip from my sweaty grip, I tucked it under my arm and wiped my palms on the legs of my jeans, almost dropping my phone in the process.

I should have worn shorts.

My footsteps crunched in the gravel as I moved past Kenna's green wrought-iron patio furniture and toward her window in the back. There was a light breeze and the tops of the cypress trees swayed as I walked.

This side of Kenna's house was almost its own little world. The trees blocked the neighborhood from view and created long shadows across the rocks as the moon continued to rise. Several patio tables were between me and the wall about twenty feet away. Yard decorations, most still in their boxes, were piled up everywhere. There were fake tombstones, plastic skeletons, an oversize inflatable pumpkin, and a giant, bloody rubber snake. This was probably all the stuff Mrs. McKee wanted us to set up. Off in the distance, the backyard's pool light was on, and tiny waves in the crystal-clear water lapped and sparkled.

Hoping to see my friends inside watching a movie or clustered around Hazel, going over one of her infamous checklists, I turned the corner to the backyard and neared Kenna's large, square window.

Someone else was back there.

9

A man.

A tall and thin man. Partially concealed in a series of bougainvillea bushes to the side of Kenna's window. Clad in a long black coat with a fur collar and wearing a white porcelain mask that suggested that some phantom or specter was underneath.

There was something kind of familiar about the scene.

Like from one of my dreams. Or nightmares.

Kenna's blinds were open, and she was sitting on her bed typing on her laptop the way she usually did on school nights. There was no sign of the rest of our friends. The man leaned out of the bushes, watching her work.

Like he was waiting for something.

The man moved forward, and the moonlight that managed to break through the tree canopy glinted across the blade of a long knife. Or a sword. A dizzy panic threatened to overtake me, and it took all of my concentration to stand. I covered my mouth with my hand to stop myself from screaming or maybe to muffle my heavy, panicked breathing. Some armed maniac was staring at Kenna through her window. I *had* to call the police. My fingers trembled as I tried to unlock my phone.

But the punch bowl.

My arms and hands dripped with sweat, and I could barely keep myself upright. Slowly, slowly, I lost my grip on the antique Edwardian silver bowl. The one Mrs. McKee wanted to borrow and probably fill with some weird pink sparkling wine.

It fell to the ground with a *bong*, kicking up a small dust cloud and rolling along the gravel until it collided with the base of a patio chair. With a smack I felt in my bones, the punch bowl hit the side of the McKees' house.

The man's head jerked up, and I found myself staring into the dark, sunken, and vacant eye holes of the creepy, bejeweled mask that covered most of his face.

I spun around, intending to make a break for my car, but my Vans had little traction on the brown crushed-granite gravel, and I found my feet sliding in opposite directions, refusing to carry me where my brain wanted to go. Bracing myself with one hand on the wall, I made it around the corner. But I skidded ahead, crashing into one of the patio tables and face-planting into a box. The edge of the cardboard sliced my neck.

Warm, gooey blood dribbled down my neck and onto my shirt.

I had seen every horror movie ever made, and people didn't survive these kinds of situations. They had their bodies shoved into fifty-five-gallon oil drums. The maniacs always won.

Footsteps echoed behind me.

The last seconds of my life ticked away.

I would never hug my mom again. Or see my sister.

The last time I kissed Jax was the very last.

Breathe.

Breathe.

I could barely fill my lungs with air.

My feet slipped and my arms waved in the air. I dropped my phone and it traveled, gliding across the asphalt toward Kenna's house. Two seconds later, I collapsed onto the ground.

All I could think about was how some maniac was going to carve me up into a billion little pieces.

The footsteps came closer and closer.

This is how it would end. I'd die here. On Mummy Mountain. I wouldn't even be able to take the punch bowl back to my mom.

Soon the man would come for me.

I closed my eyes.

Finally, with every ounce of energy and courage I possessed, I sucked in a deep breath.

And I screamed.

General Directorate for Criminal Investigations

Pending report—EXHIBIT 81

Rush, Alexandra. *Dead Boys Don't Bite*. Short film pitch.

Attachment to REVISED admission application

University of Southern California; USC Cinematic Arts

Imagine a castle that rests on a jagged cliff overlooking a forest perpetually filled with a fog that hovers close to the mossy earth and never seems to really dissipate. It is a place of legends—said to have been the home of Vlad Dracul, the very real historical figure whose bloodthirsty exploits in medieval Romania inspired the fictional vampire Count Dracula. Imagine that a river twists around this castle and once ran red with the blood of Dracul's many victims. Today, a beautiful girl named Lucy comes to this castle in the company of two boys who claim to love her. When she can't choose between them, she sees masked phantoms everywhere and finds herself attacked in a courtyard. Can she escape a terrible fate and uncover the identity of the real monster?

152 days ago

EXT. MCKEE MANOR—NIGHT— HALLOWEEN

"Oh! Cut! Cut!" yelled a familiar voice.

Followed by: "Alex. Come on. Are you really scared? You wrote this stuff."

I blinked a few times and then forced my eyes to stay open.

Someone had turned on the patio lights, and I found Jax standing over me with a ring of bright yellow creating a halo effect around his face. Behind him, Reagan had pulled off the black hood and removed the white porcelain mask, and was staring at me with a perplexed grimace.

Jax extended his hand and helped me up. "Are you okay?"

I stood there for a second trying to catch my breath.

"Alex, you're bleeding," Reagan said in alarm.

And I had another problem. Even though we had been dating since junior year, my stomach still did a little flip-flop every time I saw Jax. That night, he was actually wearing a pair of white jeans and a half-untucked black polo shirt and loafers that should have looked too goody-goody and too clean-cut and too much like a Ralph Lauren ad. But it worked for him. He hadn't gotten his hair cut in a while, and he probably hadn't even bothered to comb it after swimming, but that too was working. His brown hair kind of puffed up in a James Dean pompadour.

As he pulled me to my feet, and with the lights on, I got a better view of what was really happening. A few of the larger cameras from the school's AV department were perched on tripods, partially concealed in the bushes. Through the window, I could see Kenna and Maddie and Carter inside the bedroom. Maddie wore her makeup tool belt, and Carter held a boom mic on a long pole over the bed where Kenna was frozen in confusion. Hazel had a handheld camera and was positioned in the corner with the lens pointed toward the action.

I noticed that someone had moved the whiteboard from Kenna's room to one of the patio tables. It was covered in blue marker, and at the top, I found the familiar words.

Dead Boys Don't Bite

They were filming my script.

My. Script.

Someone, probably Hazel, had filled the rest of the board with planning information, including a big square that said *ROLES AND RESPONSIBILITIES*. And underneath:

Kenna McKee—"Lucy Westenra"
Reagan Wozniak—"Dracula" and visual effects
Maddie Oliver—Makeup and art
Carter Ricci—Music and sound
Hazel Beckett—Lighting and cinematography
Alex Rush—Writer/director
Jax Flannigan—Producer

I felt myself tensing up all over again. They were making my short film.

Without me.

I bet no one ever started filming before Christopher Nolan showed up on set.

I tried to stay calm. We all needed to get this project done. I wasn't the only person with college application deadlines. Jax was planning to use our film to apply to USC's production program. Reagan wanted to get a visual effects internship. Maddie was up for a bunch of scholarships for art school. But I also kind of wanted to roll my eyes. Hazel was so super freaking literal that she'd put "Dracula" in quotes.

Like, obviously, Reagan, my best friend since first grade, wasn't the actual Dracula, but Hazel had taken the time to note that fact on the whiteboard.

Jax put a warm hand on my arm. "You're not mad, are you? We weren't going to really film anything until you got here to direct the action, but I thought I could get things set up. The lighting out here is exactly what we talked about, and it just seemed like the perfect time to do some tests . . . maybe some B-roll . . . We thought we could shoot for a couple of hours and still have time to do our party stuff. You've just been so busy and I . . ."

My skin sizzled under his touch.

I hated that my hormones kept trying to overpower my brain.

Okay. Okay. I needed to remember to be nice. These were my friends. They were only trying to help. There wasn't any point in losing my shit. "This is awesome. You knew I was worried about having enough time to get my stuff together before the deadline in December and this is . . . this is . . ."

Maddie hurried out of Kenna's room carrying a first aid kit. She saved me from having to come up with a way to finish my sentence. Which was lucky because I probably would have gone with "bullshit." She was wearing an almost-see-through V-neck T-shirt and a pair of fraying jean shorts; she looked like she was about to star in an art deco music video. Her long, dark hair hung in shiny waves. She handed the plastic box to Jax, who opened it and dabbed the long cut on my neck with an isopropyl alcohol wipe.

My neck burned, but I made myself stay still.

Reagan turned his attention to the bush and dug the punch bowl out. Tucking some kind of sword under his arm, he grinned as he stepped forward and handed the silver bowl back to me. "Maddie really came through with the mask, right?" He took it off and held it up to inspect it. "It's original but also kind of *Phantom of the Opera* meets *The Scream*. And it really scared the crap out of you."

I tried to make a casual face, but I could feel my cheeks getting warm. Reagan *had* scared the living shit out of me. Still, I needed to focus on the work. *I* was the director after all.

"What's that?" I asked, pointing at the sword.

My heart continued to pound, and I hoped no one else could hear.

Reagan shrugged, his bright red hair going kind of carrot orange under the yellow patio lights. "My grandpa's ceremonial sword from church. He mainly wears it at the Knights of Columbus pancake breakfasts."

Jax dug around in the first aid kit until he found a few Band-Aids. He put one on my neck.

Carter came out then. Clad in a grungy old Dillinger Four tee, a shirt he probably got at a concert and had washed a zillion times since then, he looked more like a kid Maddie would hire to park her vintage white Mustang than her boyfriend. "We didn't know what you would want to use as a weapon," he said as he smoothed his scraggly dark hair.

Um. Of course not. Because I wasn't there when you planned the shot.

"We need to find something wood," I said. My pulse had finally returned to something like normal. But I still was a bit unsteady on my feet, so I moved to one of the green patio tables and took a seat. "It's supposed to be a stake. That's the big vampire trope."

Maddie took the chair next to me and nodded. "I brought some other stuff. A few wooden crosses and crucifixes. Um, a couple of broomsticks. I actually snatched a few wooden swords from the prop department that were used in last year's production of *Hamlet*. But they just don't look that . . . threatening."

"My grandma has a couple of knitting needles that will take your eye out," Carter commented, taking the seat next to Jax.

Maddie shot him a withering stare, and the rest of us at the table tensed. At the Scottsdale School for the Performing Arts, their bickering was the stuff of legends. Kenna said that they were a terrible couple because they lacked a good #ship name. They could be #Marter or #Caddie. Or something really terrible like #Martie.

Jax sighed and sat down too, placing the first aid kit on the table in front of him. He spoke before an argument could develop. "We've got a bigger issue. We're having a bit of trouble with our leading lady." He jerked his head in the direction of Kenna, who remained in her room, watching us through the window.

Reagan bit his lower lip, like he was trying not to laugh. "She says she doesn't really understand the material. She wants to know what her motivation is."

My boyfriend and my BFF could not have been more different. Jax was the all-American jock. The student council president with an innate talent for shaking hands and kissing babies. The golden boy with a dash of disaffected guitar player thrown in. The lacrosse player who was going to stick check his opponent but write an emo poem about it on the bus ride home. Jax's muscles always rippled and his hair fell the right way and he never lost his summer tan.

But Reagan Wozniak. Well, it's like he would be voted "Most Likely to Become a Supervillain's Capable Henchman." His skin was the color of white eggshells, and he was built like he was assembled from a game of pick-up sticks, all long, skinny limbs that jutted out awkwardly in every direction. He could never keep his legs tucked under his desk. Or his arms relaxed in his lap. His bony elbows were always flapping all around. I think even he was afraid of being jabbed with their sharp edges. The Dracula cloak dangled from his gaunt frame the way it might off a clothes hanger as he slid into the seat on the opposite side of Carter.

Kenna emerged from her bedroom, pausing melodramatically in the doorway to allow the satin fabric of her gothic black maxi dress to sway and shine. "Jesus, Alex! Are you trying to wake the whole mountain?"

"I'm sorry," I told her, trying to clear my throat. "I'm sorry. I guess I panicked. But that means the setup is really good. I mean, the mask—"

Before I could come up with a way to express the terror I'd felt at the sight of the mask, Kenna waved her hand. "I still don't understand why the killer is even wearing a mask."

Hazel was a few steps behind Kenna. "The mask is a problem. It reflects everything. It's also causing lens flares." There was always something sort of businesslike and transactional about Hazel. She dressed for school like it was her job. She had shirts that could be accurately described as blouses. She wore slacks and hardly ever jeans. She ironed everything. That day, Hazel had put on a short-sleeved houndstooth suit with capri pants and had a bit of white silk poking out from the center of the jacket. She remained standing, staring at the whiteboard full of shot lists and instructions.

Reagan sat up in his chair. "I told you. I have that under control. I think I can adapt the reflective floor tool in Final Cut Pro to—"

Kenna almost fell into the last unoccupied chair at the table, heaving out a sigh. "The point is, what's the point? Last semester, Maddie got an A in Wig and Makeup Production. She could come up with something *way* scarier than Reagan in a long coat and a Halloween mask. Remember that zombie she did for Phoenix Fan Fusion? These masks are—"

"I sculpted those by hand, Kenna," Maddie said with a frown.

These were exactly the kind of things I would have explained in a production meeting.

I reminded myself, again, that there was no point in being pissed.

Kenna was hoping to leverage her social media status into a career as an actress. She definitely already had an A-list attitude. And I knew directors and actors sometimes had issues. Bill

Murray told *Entertainment Weekly* that he wished that he could stab the director of *Charlie's Angels.* Shelley Duvall was so terrified of Stanley Kubrick that her hair fell out while filming *The Shining.* But I needed Kenna. She *was* a modern Lucy Westenra. A rich and beautiful socialite whose veneer hid a more ambitious person. I needed her to make this work. She was a good performer. The camera loved her, and having someone sort of famous in the starring role could only help me when I submitted my film to USC.

I brushed some dirt off Mom's punch bowl. "The point is that any man could be behind the mask."

Kenna brushed her brown bangs out of her face. "But—"

That time, I interrupted her. "Kenna, look, everyone knows the story of Dracula, right? That is the tale of *one* very scary monster. Count Dracula is a vampire, and he wants to move to England where, I guess, he'll have more people to eat than he does in his creepy castle in the middle of a forest in Transylvania. He hires this lawyer to help him. From reading Jonathan Harker's mail, Dracula finds out about the lawyer's fiancée, Mina, and her gorgeous friend." I paused to smile a Kenna. "Lucy. That's you. When the count gets to Whitby—"

"Yeah, I know," Kenna said with an eye roll. "We had to watch the old black-and-white movie and the one by Francis Ford Coppola during the horror unit in The History of Cinema. Dracula, like, hunts Lucy and Mina. They get some weirdo doctor, Van Helsing, to treat them."

"Right," Reagan said. "And even though Harker and Van Helsing *know* that Dracula is a vampire, they don't bother to tell Lucy. Or her family. They let her get attacked every night and get half her blood sucked out, and then when she finally turns into a vampire herself . . ."

When Reagan trailed off, I picked up the rest of the story. "Lucy's fiancé hunts her down, puts a stake through her heart, stuffs garlic in her mouth, and cuts her head off. On what was supposed to be her wedding night."

Kenna sighed. "Okay. But. I still don't get why—"

"What if Lucy had been really free to tell her own story? Would it look anything like the one all the men tell?" I bit my lower lip, trying to figure out how to explain Lucy's issue. "She's the only female character in the novel who expresses any kind of sexual desire and who makes any choices in her own self-interest. How many episodes of *Buffy the Vampire Slayer* have we watched in class? Maybe all of them? Buffy stakes all those vampires in the heart with Mister Pointy. But in *Dracula*, did you know that Lucy Westenra is the only character killed that way? Count Dracula is actually beheaded and disintegrates. The stake is an entire trope that's all about silencing women. *Lucy* was a vampire. But who was really the monster?"

Maddie snapped her fingers. "A golf tee! It can be sharp *and* wooden."

Jax shrugged and didn't acknowledge any of my points. "The symbol of the white man's game of privilege. But as a weapon though?"

I was supposed to be the director of this film, and they were all ignoring me.

Carter's face settled into a frown. "I think it would be tough to stab someone through the heart with a golf tee."

Maddie scowled back at him. "In Alex's script, the Masked

Counts don't actually kill Lucy. The whole thing is about how they *can't* kill her. She doesn't die and *she* stalks them."

I waved my hands excitedly at Kenna. "That's when you get to give your big monologue."

Actors loved to monologue.

"Okay . . ." Kenna murmured, looking a bit pacified.

"Yeah. But . . . I'm supposed to pull a . . . golf tee from the folds of my satanic cloak?" Reagan asked with a skeptical frown.

I kept my focus on Kenna. "Picture this. You're at a fabulous party, but everywhere you turn, you see a monster in a mask. He follows you to your room. Attacks you. Leaves you for dead. But he can't kill you. You've become too powerful. So, you give your speech and . . ."

And . . . maybe stop being such a diva all the time?

I couldn't say that out loud. I told myself to stay calm. As Mom liked to say, *You catch flies with honey.*

Hazel neatened her short-sleeve jacket. "What if there's a set of clubs near the window? Kenna, is your dad's golf bag in the garage?"

Reagan ran his hand through his red hair. "It's not menacing enough."

Jax reached out and squeezed my hand. My pulse fluttered, and it took all my willpower to keep my concentration. "I think we're getting too stuck on having a wood prop. We don't need to be *that* faithful to the original Dracula story," he said.

My neck still hurt. I brushed the Band-Aid on my neck with my free hand. When I returned my hand to the table, a few drops of blood covered my index finger. The cut was still bleeding. These storytelling choices should have been mine. But I knew

Jax was right. It was more important that the prop look scary in the shot than be made of wood.

"The speech is good. The speech is good," Kenna murmured. "It will make a good video clip for my feeds."

"Okay," Jax said in his most producer-like voice. "Let's get back to it. We'll shoot until midnight. Get what we can."

"Then we have to deal with the pool toys for the party," Kenna said in a tone of warning.

Of course, Jax was able to get everyone back to work when I wasn't. He was a natural leader and people followed him. But, at least, it did seem like I'd convinced Kenna to give her best performance.

Hazel was busy scribbling some notes on a small pad. "I'll get some good crowd shots of the party tomorrow. And some B-roll stuff of the DJ, food and catering, Mummy Mountain, the moon . . ." She trailed off, continuing with her shot list. As much as Hazel got on my nerves sometimes, the truth was that I was lucky to have her behind the camera. She kept us all organized, and because of her, Reagan and I would have plenty of footage to work with when we sat down to edit.

"We'll get it done, Kenna," Jax said with a smile. He pushed himself up from the table. "Okay. You're up, Alex."

I stood up too. "Okay. Who has the clapper?" A new kind of adrenaline filled my veins; there was something thrilling about directing a scene.

"I do," Hazel answered.

They all returned to their places, and I moved over to stand next to the camera partially concealed in the bushes. "All right. Quiet on the set."

Which was unnecessary because it was already so quiet that you could have heard the cactus needles rustle.

And then, "Action."

We focused on doing two scenes. The first was Reagan standing at Kenna's window. The second was the big speech that Kenna would give on the patio. We had to film the attack sequence later because we hadn't worked out the props or how we'd handle the blood.

At about a quarter to midnight, we had all the cameras focused on Kenna, who was lying faceup on the limestone tiles of the patio outside her suite. Maddie had done an incredible job with the makeup. She's given our Lucy Westenra a black-blue, kind of bloody eye and a gouge on one of her cheeks.

Hazel had the handheld camera and she knelt down.

Kenna stared directly into the lens. "What if the real monsters in this world are not hiding underneath our beds? What if they're out there in plain sight? The nice guys who offer to carry our books and drive us home after dark. And what they expect . . . what they want in return—"

I found myself leaning forward. It was the best take. By far.

A series of squeals and metal slams and shouts drowned out Kenna's voice.

"Cut," I said in an accent of frustration.

Reagan helped Kenna up, and as a group we followed the source of the noise, walking through the side yard and to the front of the McKees' property. The racket was coming from the street. Or rather from the house next door, where an enormous truck was backing into the driveway and a few guys with dollies ran all over shouting instructions at each other.

A splashy logo on the side of the truck read GOOD GUYS MOVING.

The house was a huge, modern teak thing with a stainless-steel sculpture of a giraffe that fell over after every monsoon positioned near the street. It had been vacant for a while. The seven of us inched into the bank of gravel that divided the McKees' property from the empty house. Getting closer and closer to the side entrance, hoping the McKees' floodlights would come on so we could catch a glimpse of what was going on.

Two of the movers pushed a series of large black trunks that looked exactly like the ones we used to store film equipment in at school. There were smaller cases that I recognized. They contained high-definition cameras. Another guy pushed a dolly full of computer towers and monitors. Whoever was moving in was a filmmaker.

"What kind of a person *moves* in the middle of the night? On Halloween?" Jax asked in an exasperated voice.

"The kind whose life is a nightmare," answered a woman's voice with a slight, clipped Eastern European accent.

We all turned around.

Silhouetted by the moonlight, a tall, elegant figure lounged underneath the portico near the side door of the modern house. A tiny pinprick of red light glowed as the woman took in a dramatic inhale. A second later, plumes of cigarette smoke rose, a blue-silver cloud against the night.

She stepped forward into the beam of light provided by the moving truck's headlights.

Good actresses always know how to find their light.

I recognized her instantly.

It was Catrinel Bloom.

Alexandra Elaine Rush—Transcript—Tape 1 [CONT.]

Inspector Skutnik: What did Ms. Bloom mean by that?

Alex: She meant [inaudible] . . . I mean . . . Well . . . She was getting divorced. And her husband . . . I only really know what I saw on Twitter . . . He was being sued by, like, twenty women. Things were so bad that she was dragging her Louis Vuitton luggage up Mummy Mountain in the middle of the night.

Inspector Skutnik: Did she mention Mr. Bloom? He was in a great deal of trouble to begin with. And now . . . with this matter . . . [noise] I imagine things are worse.

Alex: She didn't say anything about him. No. Not until later on. I thought she wanted to help us. And for a while, she did. She's from here, right? From Brașov?

Inspector Skutnik: From Dacia, yes. It is a very small village. Not far from Castle Prahova. She is considered quite a . . . um . . . success story. What happened after that night?

Alex: Nothing. For a while anyway.

46 days ago

INT. RUSH FAMILY BASEMENT—DAY— VALENTINE'S DAY

Okay. What are you?

A specialty item, a replacement, or scrap?

I stared at the dusty stack of mismatched shoe boxes and plastic containers that Mom had collected from garage sales and piled next to my table, wondering what I would find inside. Jax was supposed to pick me up in about an hour, and I had to get through a whole pile of sorting and also try to make something out of my bird's nest of a hairdo. The first box contained dozens of forks. All with different maker marks and different patterns. That one lot would take me at least half an hour to get through. And I had ten other packages to open.

Artificial green-yellow fluorescent light flooded the basement. We used to have a game room down here. But when Dad couldn't afford his office space anymore, Mom converted the downstairs into a workspace for our online business, Silver Rush. Instead of a foosball table and a flat-screen TV, the wide, open room was full of folding tables. Instead of family game night, we bought, sorted, and sold silver. Steel racks full of silverware sorting trays lined the wall opposite the stairs. Mismatched bookcases that held metal punch bowls and goblets and vases covered the other sides of the room. A desk with several computer monitors sat in the corner where we once had a Pac-Man arcade game.

Dad liked to say that life sorted people the same way we sorted sterling silver.

There were the specialty items. Old vases, Victorian calling card holders, candlesticks, and water pitchers. They had intrinsic beauty and a purpose and appreciated in value. Specialty items were easy to sell and almost always made us money. Special people were like that too. They could be polished up to perfection. They were destined to be successful. To be on display.

Then there were the replacements. Did you inherit Great-Grandma's antique silver service set but couldn't find the gumbo spoon? No problem. We scoured estate sales and yard sales and eBay, looking for popular patterns and styles. We could sell you a replacement. Replacements *could* come in handy. Or they could remain in our sorting trays forever, waiting for someone to need them. I liked to believe that replacements had the potential for the happiest lives. If you understood your role, if you found the set of people you matched with, you'd have it made.

Finally, there was scrap. Silver that had to be melted down to be useful.

The cheering crowd at a basketball game. Fans singing along with their favorite band. The audience munching on popcorn during the showing of the latest slasher flick. Scrap was valuable. But only when molded into a collective.

In my jeans pocket, my phone buzzed with an alert. I pulled out my phone and glanced at the screen. It was already after five, and I had a new message from Jax.

He was checking in on me.

See you at seven, gorgeous.

There was a winking-face emoji. Like it was supposed to be cute. And not a reminder that he hated to be kept waiting. Jax didn't offer to help me or even ask much about what I was doing. While I was up to my elbows in silver, he was probably at Carter's house playing *Red Dead* or something. Or watching *The Hateful Eight* for the billionth time and murmuring to himself about the glory of filming in 70mm.

But. Reality check. Did I really want a guy from Arcadia's richest family down in my basement trying to determine if that fork in the decrepit teal Tiffany's box was real sterling silver? And . . . I was lucky to have Jax. He was one of the hottest guys in school. I had to be grateful because he was a specialty item and I was . . .

Scrap.

I shivered in spite of myself.

After carefully inspecting the next fork, I put it in the replacement pile. On the other side of the room, my little sister, Meredith, polished silver and placed items in neat rows on the table in the corner where we had set up the makeshift photo studio. That used to be my job. I used to take pictures of the silver and get them ready for Dad to load on our website.

Heavy footsteps thudded down the stairs, and a couple of minutes later Mom's face popped into my field of view. She held up the fork from my replacements pile. "This is a reproduction," she said. "I told you to check the stuff from Tiffany's *very* carefully. Forgeries are extremely common." Her ponytail swung from side to side as she sniffed the fork. "Did you do a silver test?"

My shoulders fell. If I was unsure of the maker or quality of the silver, I was supposed to do a test. Real sterling silver had to be 92.5 percent pure to even be scrap. But I already had a ton of scabs on my fingers from the nitric acid we dabbed on the edges of suspect metal.

Mom glanced from my hands to the fork to the stack of boxes. She used to be some kind of hippie artist, but after Dad got cancer she lost her chill demeanor. "You need to wear gloves. You're going to need to get much faster at this if you want to take over for . . ."

Behind me, Meredith sighed and coughed. I didn't want to take over for Dad. She didn't want to take over for me. Mom didn't want us to lose our house. Mer was supposed to be getting ready for auditions. I was supposed to hear from USC any day. I'd been waiting for my early decision notice since I sent in my application and short film back in December.

Don't get me wrong. I was *so glad* that Dad was going to be okay. The doctors caught his cancer early and he got treatment. Every day he was getting better. He was able to take short walks around the neighborhood. Mom even let him work a couple of days last week. But since my parents owned their own business, our health insurance was crap. Everything they had set aside for Meredith and me to go to college was gone. Everything we needed to live off of was also mostly gone. And it would be months before Dad could work like he did before.

My phone buzzed again. This time I ignored it.

Sometimes I wondered if our relationship was . . . well . . . normal. I had friends who went on dates and always packed condoms in their purses and were way worried about whether their bras and panties matched. But me and Jax . . .

Even though we'd been dating for a year and Maddie kept scrunching up her nose at me and Kenna kept asking if I was aware that Jax was the hottest guy in school, we weren't hooking up. Both of our families were super Catholic. Our dates generally ended right on time because Jax's dad usually paced around their foyer making sure his son came home by curfew. My mom kept picking up "The Case for Chastity" pamphlets at Mass and leaving them all over our house for me to find. Sometimes she circled certain lines with her pen.

A sense of warmth ran through me. I did my best to ignore it.

I'd almost gotten my shirt off this one time when we thought Mr. and Mrs. Flannigan would be gone for a while at the movies. And once at the lake, Jax kind of fumbled with the ties of my swimsuit bottom. Both times we stopped. Maybe Jax was reading the pamphlet too.

Sex may deceive young couples about the quality of their relationship.

Based on her use of orange highlighters, I'd have to guess that line was Mom's favorite.

I opened the next box, and my heart sank at the sight of a motley mess inside. A chocolate muddler. Grape shears. An ice-cream slicer. A butter pick. It was the kind of weird stuff that required a ton of research to value and would take me forever to process.

And yeah, duh, Kenna. I've seen Jax in his boxer shorts. I know he's hot.

Mom plucked the box out of my grip, put a light hand on my shoulder, and tried to smile. "I can handle these boxes. You should get ready."

"No, I can finish," I said, trying to take the box back from her. Mom already had too much on her plate. "I promised you I'd get through today's arrivals."

Putting the box to the side of the table, Mom pulled me into a hug. "It's okay, Alex. Go. We've got all the rest of our lives to sort silver."

I knew Mom meant to be reassuring and make me feel better, but Meredith turned around. She pushed a piece of her stick-straight bob out of her face and stared at me with eyes that were exactly the same as mine. Same round shape. Same boring brown color. She pressed her lips into a thin line, making the same face as I did when I was terrified. I could tell we were both thinking the same thing.

Is this what we'll be doing for the rest of our lives?

"Um. Thanks," I said.

She nodded and put the box back into the stack. "I'll tackle that bunch in a second. Right now, I need to check on your father." Mom left me alone in the basement with my sister.

At the table behind me, a flash went off as Meredith took a picture. I walked over to her table and put an arm around her stiff shoulder. "You almost finished?"

She shook her head. Then shrugged my arm away. Then opened her mouth like she wanted to say something. But she stayed quiet as she reached for the next item in the line of silver waiting to be photographed. There was a trash can to the side of the photo table. A flyer advertising the open auditions for the Arcadia Ballet's production of *Swan Lake* rested on top.

"Why did you throw this away?" I asked, reaching for the green paper.

Meredith snatched it from my hand. "I'll never get cast."

"You don't know—"

She glared at me as she wadded the flyer into a tight ball and tossed it like a basketball back into the trash can. "I *do* know. They give all the best parts to dancers who did the Summer of Ballet program. *And* I had to quit my private lessons. *And* I don't have access to a practice space. *And* we can't afford new shoes. Or wardrobe."

My heart sank. Meredith was only thirteen, and all this stuff was really hard on her.

I sighed. "Meredith, you should at least go to the audition. If you get cast, we can figure out something. Maybe we could ask Uncle Steve . . ."

Meredith snorted. "I heard Dad tell Mom that we already borrowed a hundred thirty thousand dollars from Uncle Steve for medical bills." She plunked a silver vase down on the table in front of the camera. "Do you really think that you're going off to USC? That I'll dance at Juilliard? If this were one of your scripts, do you think it would have a happy ending?"

My stomach twisted into a hard knot. "Dad had tacos for dinner last week. Pretty soon he'll be back to work and things will be . . ."

Normal. I wanted things to get back to normal.

Meredith rolled her eyes and fidgeted with the fraying hem of her green T-shirt. Her clothes were coming apart at the seams. Literally. "You can lie to yourself, Alex. But you can't lie to me."

"Meredith, I'll get into film school," I said. "Business will pick up. Everything will be fine. You'll see. We have to hang in there."

I smiled at her. But she didn't smile back.

My phone buzzed again. And again I ignored it.

Casting one last look back at Meredith, who had begun polishing a small cigarette case, I took the uncarpeted steps up and left the basement. On the way, I passed Mom's desk and couldn't help but see papers stamped with FINAL NOTICE peeking out from the edges of a manila file folder. My parents were trying to keep it quiet, but on top of everything else, we were on the verge of losing our house.

Upstairs, I tiptoed around as quietly as I could. Dad might be sleeping, and I didn't want to wake him. Our whole life seemed to be vanishing right before my eyes. Every time I went into the living room, something else was gone. And we never talked about it. Like we were never going to acknowledge that, all of a sudden, Grandma's Hummel figurines had all disappeared from the display case or that the antique road signs Dad used to collect were being sold off one by one. I passed into the kitchen as I headed for the stairs to the second floor, which were on the opposite side of the house. There always used to be snacks piled up high in the center of the marble-topped island, and we would crowd around laughing and chomping on granola bars. But just then, a single orange sat all alone in a cheap wire basket. Outside the sliding glass door, Mom had covered the pool with a black tarp.

We couldn't afford chlorine for the water.

Upstairs in my room, I sat on my bed for a few minutes wondering what to wear. I considered calling Jax to see what he was wearing because he always looked perfect. Trying to match him was always a good strategy. And then I sat there silently cursing myself and wondering what kind of person couldn't even get dressed on their own. Anyway, I only really had, like, three good outfits left, so how hard was it going to be?

In the end, I went with my black baby-doll dress, some tights, and my Mary Janes.

The doorbell rang right at seven, and I almost ran down the stairs so Jax wouldn't have to stand in the doorway while my mom asked him about his grades, college plans, and how late we would be. He hated that small talk.

I called, "Bye!" and, without waiting for an answer, swung the front door open and jumped out into the night.

General Directorate for Criminal Investigations

Pending report—EXHIBIT 7

Personal statement by Jackson Flannigan

Skutnik's note: Submitted online via the Common Application used by American high school students to apply for college.

I remember reading this article about Quentin Tarantino. It talked about how he wanted making movies to be fun, how he wanted his cast and crew to be disappointed when they had to work with someone else. As a producer that's what I want to do. Obviously, I need to make sure that the production runs smoothly. A budget has to be made. A schedule has to be maintained. But I want people to enjoy themselves while they work. Because I think that translates to what the audience sees on the screen. With all of Tarantino's films, the passion is there and can be seen in every frame. People line up to work with him. That's the spirit that I want to bring to the production program.

46 days ago

EXT. RUSH FAMILY DRIVEWAY— NIGHT

Jax snorted in surprise. He stood there on the mat in his chambray shirt and khaki slacks looking like he might be waiting in the queue to audition for a part as Brad Pitt's younger self in a flashback scene.

"So, you're ready, I guess?" he asked with a smile.

He handed me an oversize bouquet of what was probably at least two dozen expensive roses. I pressed them to my nose, inhaled their fragrance, and smiled.

"Roses are red, violets are blue. There's never been a rose as beautiful as you," he said.

"Happy Valentine's Day," I said, and kissed him on the cheek. I would have liked to really kiss him, but my mom was peering through the blinds of the living room window.

I followed him across our empty driveway to where his father's Mercedes SUV waited at the curb. Kenna's family was rich, but Jax's family was *wealthy*. They lived in one of the old, original neighborhoods of Arcadia, in a historic home that had been in their family for at least three generations. Jax's brother, Luke, was already off at Princeton, and there was always a new German car parked in front of their stately brick house with white pillars and trim.

Jax put his hand on my back as we walked.

I swooned a bit in his direction, getting a whiff of his cologne.

Something that made him smell like he'd spent all day roaming a pine forest.

Mostly to distract myself, I said, "What's Fred Flannigan up to tonight?"

Jax unlocked the car and held the passenger-side door open for me. "I'm sure he's on his second martini and midway through a little lecture that I like to call 'Pay No Attention to My Trust Fund.'"

I tried to match my boyfriend's wry tone. "I always enjoy his speeches about how character builds wealth."

"Of course," Jax said with his usual polish.

We lived right on the line that separated Phoenix from Paradise Valley. Just a few miles from Mummy Mountain, we might as well have been on another planet. Jax drove us past the rows of beige houses that were identical to ours, out of our subdivision, and onto the main street. The world outside was twilight blue, and the streetlights popped on as I watched.

We came to the long, saguaro-cactus-lined drive that led to the Montaña de Luz hotel. Jax had made reservations at the fancy restaurant called Pradera inside the resort that overlooked the mountain. He even did valet parking, which kind of amazed me because that whole kind of thing gives me low-key anxiety. When do you tip? What if you forget to leave the keys? What if you hit the valet with your car?

Jax held my hand as we entered the resort. It was designed to look like an adobe fort and make people feel like they were maybe in some sheltered cove in Majorca, returning home from an afternoon of sailing around on their catamarans. Everywhere I looked, my eyes found stone arches and bright Spanish tile and giant paintings framed in gold.

We entered the restaurant. The hostess smiled at Jax and led us to a small table in the corner of the patio. It was totally dark outside by that time, and I could make out little of the mountain other than its general shape and a few dots of home lights. After we ordered, Jax took my hand and rubbed my palm with his thumb.

"So. It's time," Jax said with a smile.

My fingertips tingled, and I could feel the slight breeze run across the tiny hairs on my neck. Wait. What? Was tonight *the night*? We'd finally do it, and Maddie and Kenna would stop giving me crap. Maybe Jax got a room here. But how? Where would we tell our parents that we were?

My face grew warm. I was thankful that the table was lit only by a single romantic candle that flickered. Having a face as red as a stoplight probably wasn't sexy.

"I thought we could do it together," he said with an oddly enthusiastic nod.

I frowned in confusion.

Obviously. I mean, we had to be together to do *it*.

Frantic thoughts raced through my brain. Maybe he meant we should check into the hotel together. How do you do that? I had something like eleven dollars in my bank account. I glanced at the table next to us, where a waiter was busy uncorking a bottle of wine with a label in French.

I couldn't get a room here with eleven dollars.

"Oh . . . um . . ." I muttered. I was wearing a black bra and white panties. I should have done my laundry yesterday so that I could at least wear something that matched.

When I didn't say anything else, Jax went on. "Did you already look?"

"Look?" I repeated. It kind of felt like I was sinking in my chair. We weren't talking about the same thing.

He made an impatient noise. "I was hoping that we could check the portal together."

We *weren't* thinking the same thing.

My face continued to burn, but from embarrassment.

"Check the portal?" I couldn't keep the disappointment out of my voice.

He released my hand, pulled out his phone, showed me his email. The top message had the subject *You have a new message from USC Cinematic Arts.*

I froze. It was our college decision letters.

My heart began to pound again, but for a different reason.

I tossed my small bag on the table and dug out my own phone. The alert I had ignored had been my email. "I was too busy getting ready. I didn't check."

"Okay," he said with a wider smile. "Let's check together."

We both ignored the server as he dropped off two iced teas at our table. I tapped the link in the email, typed in my username and password, and waited for the results to load. Jax and I held our phones up together.

Waiting.

His letter came up first. *Congratulations! You have been admitted . . .*

He grinned at me and took my hand again. My knees bobbed up and down in excitement. It was working. My whole big life plan. Jax and I would be a director/producer team. Like Ryan Fleck and Anna Boden, sometimes making cool documentaries. Sometimes making *Captain Marvel*. I would find a way to help my family. Things would get better.

Then my message loaded on my screen. *Thank you for your application to the USC School of Cinematic Arts (SCA). We are pleased to offer you a place on our waitlist. To learn more about our waitlist process, <u>click here</u>.*

I was waitlisted.

Basically rejected.

The message went on with a bunch of stuff about how many applicants they'd had, how few they were able to admit, and how I should be proud of my accomplishments. It was like being punched in the gut. And I watched what I was feeling inside register on Jax's handsome face. *Confusion.* I mean, we'd submitted the same material for our project. *Fear.* What was going to happen if I couldn't go to USC but he could? More confusion. Because this was supposed to be a happy moment for him. I should celebrate Jax's success. He should commiserate with me. What were we supposed to do if we were happy and sad about the exact same thing?

"Congratulations," I said with as much enthusiasm as I could muster.

His mouth sank into a deep frown. "Alex. This has to be some kind of a mistake. We made the movie together. On Monday, we can talk to . . ."

Okay. Right. A mistake. I nodded. "Yeah . . . yeah. I mean, we submitted the exact same film. We're a director/producer team."

Jax hesitated. "Well . . . um . . . I didn't want to take anything away from you and your vision . . . so I . . ."

The world spun beneath my chair. "You recut the film," I finished. "You submitted a different version." I hesitated for a second. "You . . . you think my version isn't any good?"

"Alex, of course I think it's good," he began. "I just wanted it to be *your* version. I thought it would look better if we didn't submit the exact same thing. So, yeah. I recut it. Shortened a few of the sequences. I . . . mean . . . um . . . I thought that it would showcase my skills as a producer to have more action . . . and less . . . um, speeches . . . and . . . I wanted you to . . ."

I tuned out the rest of what he was saying.

My whole life was falling apart.

"I'm glad you got in," I said. It was barely above a whisper. "I'm proud of you. You . . . you deserve it."

"We'll figure this out," he said, rubbing my palm with his thumb.

I yanked my hand away and let it drop into my lap. I wasn't sure how much longer I could sit at the table without bursting into tears. Snatching my clutch, I murmured, "I . . . I need to . . . go to the bathroom."

Before he could respond, I jumped up from the table and took enormous steps in between the tables full of couples on dates, following the sign that pointed to the restrooms on the other side of the restaurant's open kitchen where fires burned bright in several pizza ovens. My heels clicked sharply on the Spanish tile floor.

Arriving at an oversize carved wooden door, I pushed it open to reveal an opulent lounge area. The large room contained lit makeup mirrors on one wall, a plush set of beige sofas on the other, and what might have been a writing desk in the corner. Beyond that, I could see a tiled arch that led to a more normal restroom with a series of stalls with wooden doors that ran all the way to the floor.

It was quiet. I could hear the slow tap of a leaky faucet.

The bathroom seemed empty.

I wilted onto one of the velour stools in front of the makeup mirrors.

Pulling out my phone, I typed, *Will I get off the USC film school waitlist?*

The first result read, *Top universities typically admit only a small percentage of students off their waitlists. Applicants should make alternate plans.*

Inhaling a deep breath, I prepared to let it all out. All the sobs for all my dreams that were disappearing right in front of me. It was stupid. So stupid. I couldn't help my family. I couldn't help myself. All the hours I spent writing and revising. I ate, slept, and bled movies.

And it was for nothing.

All. For. Nothing.

I didn't *have* an alternate plan.

The spot in my chest where my heart was supposed to be literally throbbed and ached.

I jumped at the sound of a toilet flush. An elegant woman in a loose-fitting T-shirt dress left one of the stalls and went to the sink to wash her hands.

It was Catrinel Bloom.

I had seen her on the screen so many times. As a Bond girl. In those Marvel movies. But most of all, in *Island of the Dolls*. The horror movie that made me want to become a director. In real life, Catrinel was even more beautiful than on the screen. She had her icy blonde hair effortlessly rolled up in a bun at the nape of her neck and wore no makeup. Other than a few thin lines around her mouth and the corners of her eyes, she hadn't aged much since her *Doll* days more than a decade ago.

After Halloween, I was hoping that we'd run into her. I mean, we were filmmakers, and Kenna lived next door to one of the world's most famous actresses. A couple of times, Kenna tried to take a plate of brownies over. But we hadn't seen her. Jax said that she was deliberately keeping a low profile. Jax said that's what you had to do when your husband was way #canceled for bullying and sexually harassing actresses on his sets.

The world expected his wife to hide.

I dabbed at the tears forming in my eyes and tried to sit up more normally. This was the opportunity I wanted. This was where I was supposed to pitch her a script idea or ask about her agent. But I couldn't even pull myself together to ask for her autograph.

Catrinel Bloom left the sink, walked into the makeup room, and approached the counter a few feet from where I was seated. She leaned into the mirror and applied a new coat of red lipstick. "What is your name? Why are you crying the bathroom?" she said in her light Romanian accent.

"I'm Alex . . . Alex Rush. And you . . . you're Catrinel . . . *the* Catrinel Bloom." I checked my own reflection in the mirror. My mascara was still in place, and I didn't look that messed up. "What makes you think that I'm—"

She made an impatient noise. "I have spent enough time having breakdowns in bathrooms lately that I can certainly recognize someone doing the same. What is wrong?"

The last thing on earth that I wanted was to tell a screen legend that I was a total major loser, but the words spilled out anyway. "I was . . . I applied to film school. I was . . . wait . . . wait . . . waitlisted. And people don't get off the waitlist."

As Catrinel turned to face me, the expensive fabric of her dress swished. "You are that girl from next door? You and your friends were making that little movie on Halloween? But you are not the basketball player's daughter?"

No. I was not.

My heart sank even farther into my stomach.

Kenna planned to move to LA after graduation and do auditions.

She had a life plan. And rich parents. I was me.

Catrinel nodded. "The McKee girl posted some of your stuff on the internet, yes?"

". . . Yes?" My mouth fell open. Kenna had a ton of followers, and *yes*, she had posted part of the *Dead Boys Don't Bite* monologue in her feed. But I had no idea that someone as important as Catrinel Bloom might have seen it.

She pulled up a stool next to mine and took a phone out of a small clutch. She continued to talk as she stared at the screen. "You are very talented. I remember the days when I was like you. When I thought talent would be enough."

A sense of confusion pushed against my urge to cry.

Catrinel tapped on her phone screen. "I grew up in a small village in Romania. Too small for you Americans to even note it on your maps. My father was a good man. He made me believe that I could be whatever I wanted to be. And then I came here. I became an actress and I *could be* whatever I wanted. As long as what I *wanted* was to be sexy. Yes. A sexy murder victim. A sexy nurse. A sexy pirate. Some cop's sexy wife. Yes." Her gaze snapped back to me. "Your work is good. Remember that."

I bit my lower lip. "It wasn't good enough for USC."

Catrinel sighed. Her voice grew sultry and hypnotic. "My dear Miss Rush, who do you imagine runs that school? My husband and his . . . friends . . . sit on the committee that evaluates student work. Do you believe these monsters in masks want to be exposed? Do you think they even want to permit a level of dissent that would brand them as monsters?"

"Um . . ." I muttered. Her cynicism hit me hard and left a lump in my throat.

She was essentially saying that talent didn't matter.

She stood up and tucked her bag underneath my arm. "My husband went to that university. His grades were poor. His portfolio . . . nonexistent." Catrinel stared right into my eyes. "There were people who had more talent. But Justin's father had a checkbook, and an admissions officer golfed at the same club as he did."

I sniffled. My pulse slowed and cool dread ran through me. "You're saying Justin Bloom . . . Academy Award winner Justin Bloom . . . bribed someone to get into film school?"

She didn't directly answer me, and her pouty lips formed a

hard pucker. "In Romania, we have a saying: a man without money is no man at all. But nowhere is that more true than in Hollywood."

Catrinel Bloom turned her back to me as she headed to the door. "Men like my husband, they break us. These men. They think we need them. They are careless. They smash everything because they think *we* will always be there to pick up the pieces. Well. Perhaps *we* will not."

"What . . . what do you mean?" I asked.

But she was already gone in a red blur.

Leaving me alone in the bathroom with my tears and the feeling that things were, somehow, even worse than before.

General Directorate for Criminal Investigations
Alexandra Elaine Rush—Transcript—Tape 1 [CONT.]

Inspector Skutnik: Then your friends set up the online fundraiser to pay for the production of a student film?

Alex: Yes. And it was a mistake.

Inspector Skutnik: [papers rustling] [inaudible]

Alex: Right from the beginning. A terrible mistake.

44 days ago

INT. SCOTTSDALE SCHOOL FOR THE PERFORMING ARTS—THE HISTORY OF CINEMA CLASS—DAY

Ms. Weiland was midway through a lecture on film noir when I slipped into the darkened room and took a seat at a table in the back. I dropped my backpack on the floor next to the chair where Reagan sat waiting for me. As I took my seat, he turned his attention away from the clip of *The Maltese Falcon* on the large screen at the front of the amphitheater-style classroom.

He leaned over and whispered, "Did they have any ideas?"

I shrugged.

They were the counselors in the student advising center, and I had spent most of Monday morning with all four of them huddled around a desk murmuring to themselves. Checking and rechecking the letter I had received.

She has so much talent.

And.

Jax Flannigan used similar footage for his application.

And.

Maybe they had fewer applicants for the production program than for film direction.

Mrs. Shelton suggested that I film something else. Another project, and submit it to USC along with a letter of continued interest. "Something that really shows your range, dear. Perhaps . . .

something less . . . controversial," she suggested, pulling a pencil out from her gray bun. "You might check out Jimmy Lewis's film."

Jimmy Lewis had made a movie about a British mime whose wife had a baby. It was a one-man show, and he was in the freaking film, in black-and-white, in full-on mime makeup, pretending to rock an invisible baby in his arms.

He was accepted to Columbia.

That's what kind of world we lived in.

The counselors all tried to tell me that I had a good shot at getting off the waitlist.

But Mr. Ramirez spoke for everyone when he said, "It might be time to look at your other options. In-state schools. Less competitive programs . . ."

They all promised to meet with me and make calls, and I knew that I should have been grateful. And, like, yes, insert my mom's lecture here about how your choice of college isn't your destiny. But I felt like E.T. after he realized that the spaceship had left without him.

I tried to focus on the lecture in front of me where our teacher was busy scribbling *GERMAN EXPRESSIONISM* on the board. "They said I should make something different," I whispered to Reagan. "And send it to USC."

"*Dead Boys Don't Bite* is fucking awesome," Reagan said with enough force that Ms. Weiland stopped talking for a moment. When she resumed her lecture, he added, "We're not making something different. We have a better idea," in a quiet tone.

The dismissal bell rang. Some kid sitting near the door turned on the room lights, and there was a collective groan at the sudden fluorescence filling the space. The History of Cinema was required at SSPA, so it was held in the school's largest classroom. About a hundred students were seated at long, curved gray tables and were busy shoving notebooks in their backpacks. Lunch was next period, and no doubt everyone wanted to get over to the Cantina before the line at the coffee cart got too long. A few people waved to me on their way out the door.

I remained, sitting motionless as Ms. Weiland swept away from the classroom.

Reagan stood up and put his hand on my shoulder as the rest of our friends approached us. We normally sat closer to the front so Kenna wouldn't have to put on her glasses. Ms. Weiland hadn't bothered to turn off her computer, so Bogart's snarling face remained on the screen as my friends approached and took seats at my table.

We were all in our school uniform of beige pants, white shirt, and blue tie.

But only Jax managed to not look dorky in his outfit. He picked at the collar of his crisp white shirt. His slacks weren't sweaty or wrinkled. He gave me a reassuring smile. "We've been talking about things that we can do. My dad said he might know someone who—"

"We should all tell USC where to stick it!" Reagan said. "This whole thing is totally sexist. We all worked on the same project. And what? Jax and I get in? And Alex didn't?" He kicked the worn blue carpet with the toe of his Doc Martens.

I hadn't even checked in with Reagan. I had been too focused on myself. "You got into the visual effects program? Reagan, that's great." Even though my stomach tumbled around, threatening to purge the Egg McMuffin I ate for breakfast, I hoped I sounded convincing. Reagan had mad computer skills.

He deserved his success.

"Reagan, you're a guy," Maddie said, crossing her legs. "What do you know about sexism?"

I sighed. "Jax has to go. It's a big deal that he got accepted. Maybe I'll get off the waitlist. Maybe I can transfer in later."

Reagan snorted and ran a hand through his red hair. "Jax attending USC without you is like Ron Howard making movies without Brian Grazer. I thought the two of you were supposed to be a director/producer team." He shot Jax a disgusted look. "I guess you two are more like Joss Whedon and Zack Snyder. Both doing your own versions of *Justice League*."

Carter draped his arm around Maddie's shoulder. "The Snyder version was the best."

"We are a team," Jax said, glaring. "I thought it would be better for everybody if I varied my cut. I was trying to use stuff that showed my production skills. But my future is with Alex."

It was kind of sweet. But also kind of . . . basic. Not really what you should say when you decided to recut your girlfriend's movie without telling anyone. Hallmark didn't make a card for *that* occasion.

And he hadn't even *offered* to show me his cut of our footage.

But he was my boyfriend. "Jax was just trying his best to get into film school," I said.

Maddie looked at me like she thought I was kind of pathetic.

Reagan started to say something, but Hazel waved one of her

hands in the air to silence him. "You guys can fight later. Tell her what we did."

Kenna cleared her throat. "We are gonna fund your movie."

"Um. What?" I asked, trying not to get too excited. Kenna's father played for the Phoenix Suns. The McKees were rich, but she was always talking about swag and perks that never seemed to materialize.

Kenna smiled. "I've been researching horror projects that were crowdfunded and—"

Hazel smoothed her already neat brown bob and cut Kenna off. "Actually, *I've* been researching it—"

"I suggested it!" Reagan said.

"—and I think we should use the *Babadook* model," Hazel went on. "Jennifer Kent crowdsourced around thirty thousand dollars. We could do something similar."

Jennifer Kent was a hero of mine and I already knew all of this. "They had two million dollars in grants. They just ran out of money before they could build all the sets. So that's why they did the fundraiser. You can't make a feature for thirty thousand dollars," I said.

And seriously, Jennifer Kent was a grown woman who'd spent a long time working in the film industry. Who would even give *me* thirty thousand dollars?

Hazel nodded. But she pulled out her laptop, placed it on the table in front of me, and showed me a dense spreadsheet. "I agree. But the running time of *Monster*, the short version of *Babadook*, is ten minutes," she continued in her usual business-like tone. "Because we focused on keeping the length of *Dead Boys Don't Bite* tight for college submissions, it's just under four minutes. Which is too short for most festivals and a lot of contests. If we had a little bit of a budget, we could make a longer version. We could hire some extras. Rent better lights. Carter could do more creepy stuff with the sound. I emailed Ms. Shan. She said if we buy the raw materials, she'd have her Set Construction class help us put the stuff together. If we film during spring break, we'd have time to enter Scream Fest."

Carter was texting someone, but he glanced up. "If I had more time, I could really use audio to amp up the jump scares, Alex."

If I directed a short that got into Scream Fest, USC would *have* to admit me.

I found myself smiling at Hazel. But also feeling a little foolish. This was *kind of* a good idea. At least it *was* an idea, a longshot idea. Why wasn't it *my* idea? Jax's face was, well, blank. He was the producer. It was his job to *produce* these kinds of solutions.

We'd all been busy and under a lot of stress, and it wasn't fair to hold my boyfriend responsible for me getting into college. And Hazel's dad was a CPA and her mom was a retired FBI agent. Her project management skills were almost genetic. She would have made a great producer, but she wanted to be behind the lens.

"You're thinking too small," Kenna said. She was hunched over her phone, twirling a strand of her long, Kim-in-*Edward-Scissorhands* blonde hair, checking the metrics of her last vlog. She'd convinced some fashion designer to send her a black glitter-bombed Ouija board that probably cost, like, ten grand, and her phone was filled with the image of her own pale face making dramatic expressions and moving the crystal planchette. "We should try to get the feature film made. Alex has the script written. So what's the problem?"

The *problem* was we had absolutely *no way* to get millions of dollars. Plus, full-length movies, even low-budget horror movies, took months to film. *Seance* was shot in twenty-two days. But Simon Barrett knew what he was doing and had Suki Waterhouse to work with.

And I had sent the script to USC as part of my application.

The positive energy drained out of me. The school thought the script wasn't even good enough for me to get a dorm room, let alone film financing. What was the probability that I could get something into Scream Fest? Also, there was something kind of odd about the whole situation. Hazel wasn't exactly known for her selfless generosity. Just last week, she had reminded me that I borrowed six dollars for a boba tea back in December.

Before I could ask about that, Kenna turned around in her chair and grinned. A wide Cheshire Cat kind of grin. She grabbed Hazel's laptop and made a couple of clicks. When she turned the computer my way, a GoFundMe page appeared on the screen. It had tons of information about *Dead Boys Don't Bite*, some links to Carter's music, a few pieces of Maddie's art, and our bios. There was no mention of USC and our college applications. Just a link to Scream Fest. My friends must have put the page together over the weekend, and it had already collected a couple hundred dollars.

Reagan grunted. "Jax didn't think we should talk about how fucking sexist the USC thing is."

Jax frowned. I'm sure it was hard to have your closest friends suggesting that you only won because the game was rigged. "Um. We don't *know* that it was sexism."

I nodded. "Jax is a great producer. The personal statement that he wrote was excellent."

"Oh, don't worry, Reagan," Carter said with a smirk. "Before we're through, we'll make sure everyone is aware of your personal mission to smash the patriarchy."

Reagan's shoulders slumped. "I'm just saying—"

"The point is that we're here for you, Alex," Kenna said, clicking her black polished nails on the desk.

"Kenna, you're here for the clicks," Maddie said with a frown. But she let the notepad she was holding rest on the gray table. She had been doodling, sketching the outline of a castle. Hazel had already convinced her. Maddie was thinking about set design.

"I am not," Kenna said defensively. "And anyway, exposure helps all of us."

My gaze traveled over the bulletin boards that lined the walls of the large classroom, where Ms. Weiland had hung posters from her favorite movies. I had always hoped that the art for something I made would be hanging up there with *Moonlight*, *Lady Bird*, *Parasite*, and *Inception*. That a poster would say *A film by Alex Rush*.

"Anywho," Kenna said, with a pointed glare at Maddie. "As I was saying. I'll boost the GoFundMe page on all my channels. We'll collect as much money as we can before spring break. If we only get a little bit of money, we'll make the ten-minute version. If we get more"—she paused to paste a smile back on her face—"and I think we can get much more—if we do, we'll make the feature."

I picked at the sleeve of my polo shirt and tried to ignore the sense of lightness spreading over me. "This will take a lot of everyone's time. Not that I don't appreciate it. But . . ."

"I'm here for you, Alex," Reagan said.

"We *all* are," Jax corrected. "Like Kenna said."

I smiled at my friends. "You don't need to do this."

Hazel had an unexpectedly awkward expression on her face. "Yeah . . . I do," she said slowly. Her shoulders sank, and for a second, she was uncertain and not the person who always acted more like a teacher than a student. "I didn't get in either. I got accepted at CalArts . . . but . . ."

That shouldn't have made me feel better. But it did. Hazel was brilliant. She had filmed tons of projects. She had hours and hours of footage to choose from, and the piece she submitted showed how lighting could change the way an audience felt about a character or a story. *She* didn't get into USC.

"But . . . what?" I asked.

She ran her fingers over her already perfectly flat-ironed bob. "CalArts didn't offer any financial aid. My parents think that the tuition is a total waste of money when I could go to a state school almost for free. They don't even want me to go into cinematography. My dad made an actual fucking slide presentation and gave it at the dinner table. He went on and on about how there wasn't enough ROI—"

"What?" Kenna asked.

"Return on investment," Jax whispered.

"—on tuition to film school and that I could take my *little pictures* just fine in Tucson and I should consider jersey sheets for my dorm room and also isn't accounting a great major and he knows someone at Deloitte who could get me a summer internship."

My mouth fell open in shock. She was talking so fast that I could barely understand her. "Um. Whoa," I stammered.

"I don't want to scan papers for a CPA all summer long!" Hazel jumped up and stood in front of me, waving her arms around in a way that was so out of character that it was scary.

"You should have a sip of water," Carter suggested, jerking his chin at the yellow Hydro Flask sticking out of Hazel's backpack.

She took in a sharp, deep breath, and then she was herself again. "I have to show my parents that my USC tuition *is* a good investment. So, we are going to successfully fundraise enough money to make a quality short film." She grabbed her laptop and returned it to the screen that displayed the spreadsheet. "I will show my parents that this is a valid life plan that I have thought about very carefully." She snapped her laptop shut and picked it up off the table. "I need this," she said as she put her computer in her backpack.

"If you win at Scream Fest, you get a cash prize," Maddie said. Her face went kind of red. "Uh. Mama needs some new art supplies."

"Scream Fest would look good on a grant application," Jax agreed.

Carter adjusted his chair and pulled a giant bottle of red

Gatorade out of his own pack. "My band can totally use the exposure."

I thanked everyone, and we agreed that we'd ditch fifth period and discuss what to do next. With everyone chattering about going to the bathroom or grabbing something from their lockers or hitting a vending machine, my friends cleared out of the room.

Jax smiled and said, "How about if I produce some coffee for my favorite director?"

"So you're taking espressos to Tarantino?" Reagan said with a snort.

Jax rolled his eyes and left.

For a minute it was just me and Reagan. He helped me pack up my stuff. "See, I told you I have a plan," he said with a thin smile.

"Yeah. Yeah," I said, rising, buoyed by a sense of optimism. "Thank you. For suggesting all of this."

When I got to my feet, Reagan drew me into a hug.

I needed a hug. And we were best friends.

Since back in the days of backyard sleepovers and Disney Channel dance parties.

Except. He hugged me a bit too tightly.

For a minute too long.

"Alex," he whispered. "You know I'd do anything for you."

I gave him a light pat on the back and stepped away.

And I realized that only *he* hadn't said why he wanted to help with the next version of *Dead Boys Don't Bite*.

Of course, he was my friend.

But.

What if his reasons for helping me weren't what I wanted them to be?

General Directorate for Criminal Investigations

Pending report—EXHIBIT 14

Bloom, C. [@catbloom] (February 21)

Online statement on Rush/McKee GoFundMe; page administered by Reagan Wozniak

Skutnik's note: Post on Catrinel Bloom's social media accounts led to increased donations.

Alex Rush is a promising young filmmaker who has been denied entrance into one of this country's best film schools because her content challenges male power both behind and in front of the camera. Cases like this are far too common. When I was tapped for *Island of the Dolls*, the studio didn't want to hire my husband to direct. He had no experience. I insisted, and then he went on to make a deal that guaranteed him a percentage of the film's gross. Ten years later, I wanted to appear in the sequel. The studio wanted a younger woman. Justin told me he would cast me anyway. As the main character's mother. I was thirty-two. I am so tired of letting these men get away with this behavior. Please contribute to this fundraiser if you can. We need to show the film industry that it must make space for talented women.

32 days ago

INT. ALEX RUSH BEDROOM—DAY

As it turned out, Kenna was right.

And wrong.

The first week that the GoFundMe was up, nothing much happened. We raised about five hundred dollars. Mostly from people who followed Kenna on Instagram.

Then our page was boosted by Catrinel Bloom. She posted a big statement about how sexist Hollywood was, and that seemed to get the attention of . . . everyone. In the week that followed, our fundraiser got more than thirty-six thousand dollars in donations, which honestly sounded like an absolutely ludicrous amount of money to me.

Not as much as Kenna suggested we would make.

But plenty.

We ended up with enough money to make a new short version of the film.

Hazel was thrilled. We could use all her spreadsheets.

And, seriously, so was I. A bunch of strangers believed in my idea and in our movie. We would get to film more stuff. My belly fluttered with an unfamiliar feeling.

Hope.

It was Saturday and I was in my room sitting at my small writing desk, waiting for Maddie. Her plans for the new sets were due to the Set Construction class on Monday if we wanted everything to be ready by spring break. We would reshoot the early scenes in Kenna's backyard using more extras in Dracula masks to hopefully create more of a sense of panic from the audience. I hoped that the more elaborate sets and costumes, and the fact that we'd have more special effects, would impress the judges at Scream Fest. And the admissions office at USC.

But I worried that it wasn't enough.

The sound of footsteps on the stairs brought me back to the present, and I waved hello to Maddie as she entered my room. She plunked a bottle of water down on the small white wicker nightstand next to my bed.

"Time to hydrate!" she said. She dug around in the fringed purse slung over her shoulder. "Got you a Clif Bar too."

"Thanks," I said, twisting off the cap of the water.

Even though we were just supposed to be working in my room, Maddie was rocking her usual vintage West Coast style. She wore a linen collared white blouse with a black bra and had her hair pulled back by a retro cream-colored headband. A thin layer of sweat glistened on her tan arms. She slid her backpack and purse off, and they landed on the floor with a heavy thud.

"I dropped the masks off at Kenna's on the way here," she said.

I nodded. "How many did you end up making?"

She shrugged. "I got ten that turned out really good and another five that will work as long as they're in the background or out of focus. I had to toss the rest."

My room looked like a dumpster full of clothing had projectile vomited its contents in every direction. I'd been up since six in the morning sorting silver and had spent most of the day getting our new items listed on the Silver Rush website. Maddie moved a pile of old T-shirts and took a seat on my bed. I hoped she didn't notice the pilling and clumping of my pale pink tufted duvet. Of all the rooms in our house, my room and Meredith's had stayed the most normal. My books were stacked all over in the usual way. Pictures of my friends and past vacations covered my mauve walls. My desk still had the antique Corona typewriter that I got when I went through the phase when I was obsessed with Hemingway.

But it had been a quite a while since we'd been able to dry-clean our comforters.

Maddie bent over to pull some stuff from her backpack. When she sat back up, she had half the school library's collection of books on European art in her arms. Her mom was a curator at the Phoenix Art Museum, and her dad was a sculptor. I doubted she needed the books.

"I've been thinking," she said. "I've got lots of great ideas about how to use color and texture to create really interesting interiors."

The last thing in her stack was a sketch pad. She opened it and handed it to me. I flipped through a bunch of gorgeous sketches of sets that were fit for a queen.

"These are lovely," I said, running my fingertips over the pages of Maddie's fancy linen paper that were covered by her gorgeous watercolor paintings of a sitting room with rose-colored furnishings and abstract figures seated at a candlelit dining table.

While I made some notes about the sets, Maddie got up and went over to the bay window that faced the street, mesmerized by something down below. I dropped my pen and joined her at the window. It was only my sister. Meredith was out in the front yard watering my father's withered rosebushes with a silver can. She had borrowed my red sundress without asking, Again. It was one of my last halfway-decent-looking outfits. I reminded myself not to be mad. I was still getting to make my film.

Meredith was doing ballet in our yard.

She moved gracefully among the half-dead tea roses in subtle pirouette turns. Dance lived inside her. She couldn't turn it off.

"What's she doing?" Maddie asked.

"Practicing," I said, hoping my voice didn't betray how difficult things had been for the past year. "She wants to try out for *Swan Lake*."

Maddie played with one of the locks of her shiny brown hair. "Ballet draws a lot of inspiration from birds. Art too. Most of the greats painted swans. Da Vinci. Correggio. Cézanne."

I shrugged. "Swans are beautiful."

Maddie's mouth formed a thin line, and when she spoke again her voice was uncharacteristically hard. "Alex, have you ever studied swans? They're vicious. They can capsize small boats and break bones with their bills. Mute swans are considered an invasive species because they wreck their environment."

It was around two in the afternoon, and even though it was barely March, it was getting really hot inside the house. When my dad got sick, my mom put us on some cost savings electricity plan, and she hated to run the air conditioner during the day. Pulling a hair elastic from the pocket of my shorts, I put my hair in a messy bun.

"I'm . . . I'm not sure what you're . . . talking about," I said with a frown.

Maddie continued to stare down. She was there in the room with me but also not there somehow. She was lost in her own thoughts. "People like us. We're not swans."

I assumed she meant that we weren't elegant the way that swans were. We were average height and had average brown hair. Sometimes I had to be really careful in pictures to tilt my head so that my nose didn't cast a shadow on my face.

"That's a good thing, right?" I asked. Pushing my awkward feelings down, I forced a smile. "I mean, I don't want to go around knocking tourists out of canoes."

She sank onto the seat under the window. "You know what we are? We're dodo birds."

"Dodos are extinct," I said slowly, a sense of dread settling in the pit of my stomach. I went back to the bed and tried to resume looking at Maddie's sketches. My fingers clutched the pad so tightly that they turned white.

"Yeah, exactly." Maddie wrapped her arms around her body and rocked back and forth. "Because they were friendly and curious. They were beautiful and happy and unafraid and they'd walk right up to sailors on the beach, expecting to make new friends. Then the sailors ate them for dinner."

"Maddie, what is the point of this?" I said. "Why are you . . ." I couldn't bring myself to finish my thought.

She continued as though she hadn't heard me.

Why are you acting this way?

"Because when you come from an environment with lots of predators, you get strong. You develop a fight-or-flight reflex.

64

You become a swan," Maddie said. She returned to the bed and sat next to me.

An uneasiness settled on the surface of my skin. Like dust on the carpet.

Maddie leaned even closer and stared into my eyes with the intensity of a leopard about to pounce. Part of me wanted to take the advice they give you on those nature shows. Get up and back away very slowly. But I remained seated.

"Aren't you even a little pissed that your boyfriend totally changed your film and got himself admitted to USC?" she demanded.

Well. Yeah. I mean, I was. But I needed to get over it. I needed Jax. And my friends. And Hollywood didn't take kindly to women with anger management problems. "I can't afford to think that way. There's no advantage to getting angry."

Maddie's head fell back in an annoyed gesture. "Yeah. Okay. That's what I'm trying to tell you. Maybe there *is* an advantage. Maybe if we stop being nice, we won't end up on a sailor's plate. Maybe we could be swans. Not dodos. You're trying to redeem Lucy Westenra. But what about us?"

"What about us?" I said in a tone of frustration. "The reality is that we can't change the world without some cooperation from people currently running the world. And . . . do you know how many girls would kill to have Jax as a boyfriend?"

I scooted a couple of inches away from Maddie. "Is everything okay?"

She twisted her body forward and again forced my eyes to meet hers.

With her crisp blouse and fluffy skirt and crossed ankles, she was the portrait of old Hollywood royalty. "What makes you ask that?"

The intensity of her expression was intimidating. "Well . . . you . . . you . . ."

She hesitated for a moment. But then, for a second, her facade melted away. She spoke in her usual singsong voice. "Alex, I'm worried about the future. About what's gonna happen when . . ."

She trailed off, and I assumed she intended to say *when we go off to college*. And yes, I was worried too. "I know things will be different next year, but—"

Maddie grabbed my arm. "Alex, people do bad things sometimes. Something's happened . . ."

My pulse quickened and I tried to move away without looking like I was moving away. "Mads, what's going on?"

Maddie drew in a deep breath. She jumped up again and faced the window. Like she couldn't sit still. "Do you remember Christmas break? When I told everyone we went to visit my grandma in Wisconsin?"

"What do you mean, you *told everyone*?" I asked. "You *went* to Wisconsin. You brought me back a mug from the Starbucks in Milwaukee."

Her shoulders crept up toward her ears, and her eyes went unnaturally wide. "I know, but actually my father was—" Before she could finish, she sucked in a surprised breath and squinted at something down below.

I dropped the sketch pad and went back to the window as well. Down below, Meredith was no longer dancing. A BMW had pulled up to the curb, and my sister ducked behind the bushes and peeked out at the car.

"Oh. My. God. Is that . . ."

Catrinel Bloom.

One of the biggest movie stars on all the planet was gliding up our unswept walkway, past the brownish walls that needed a fresh coat of paint and toward our front door. Her bright hair glittered in the afternoon sun, and her designer mauve sundress flowed behind her.

Maddie and I both kind of stumbled back.

I couldn't remember what we'd just been talking about.

The doorbell rang.

Once. Twice. Three times. We stood there. Me and Maddie. Frozen. I guess I just assumed that our encounter in the bathroom would be my one brush with fame for a while.

"Why is Catrinel Bloom at your house, Alex?" Maddie said.

I was too dumbfounded to answer.

"Alex? Alex?" Maddie repeated a few more times.

I heard my name again, and this time Maddie poked me in the arm.

It was my mom calling from downstairs. "Alex!" she shouted again.

We took the stairs at a run. Maddie barely stopped herself from crashing into me as I came to a stop on the landing near the front door. From there, I could see Catrinel sitting on our shabby, sun-bleached leather sofa, oddly at ease while my mother fumbled around with a few bottles of water.

Maddie and I tiptoed into the room.

Mom backed away from the couch and yelled, "Alex," one more time.

I was only a couple of feet behind her, and my ears rang. "I'm right here, Mom."

Mom turned to me with a pale white face and pointed to the empty space on the sofa. She made several jabs in the air until Maddie and I squeezed in next to Catrinel Bloom.

"You . . . uh . . . you . . . uh . . ." Mom stammered.

For the first time, I noticed that Dad was also in the room. He sat on the loveseat and leaned around Mom to say, "You have a visitor." He actually had kind of a goofy grin on his pale, thinned-out face. I hadn't seen him smile like that since before his diagnosis.

Without ever taking her eyes off Catrinel, Mom kept on fumbling backward until she flopped onto the loveseat next to Dad. "This is . . . it's . . . you are . . . Catrinel Bloom."

Maddie sucked in a deep breath. "You're so beautiful. Like in real life. That dress is so pretty and . . . your hair . . . and . . . and . . . just can't believe it . . . I can't believe it. I'm sitting here on the fucking couch with you and . . ."

My mom frowned at the swearing.

My parents must have told Meredith to wait outside because she was on the patio sitting at the picnic table peeking in through the sliding glass door.

Maddie's mouth was moving faster than a race car on the track. "Is it true that you suggested using *Woman Reading a Letter* in the movie *Portrait of the Artist's Wife*? It made so much sense to have Aubrey steal that particular painting because—"

Catrinel leaned back, and her bright blue eyes were wide. She held a bottle of water in one of her elegant hands. I noticed her French manicure when she handed the bottle to Maddie.

"You need to relax, my dear," Catrinel said. "Hello again, Alex, my friend."

A movie star just called *me* a friend.

If I was going to be a film director, I had to resist the urge to join Maddie in squealing and asking a thousand fangirl questions.

"How . . . how did you know where to find me?" I asked.

Catrinel smiled. "Your little friend, you know, the girl from Instagram who is always dressed up in a Halloween costume—"

Maddie kind of smirked. Truthfully, it was a little nice to see someone not act like Kenna was the center of the universe.

"Kenna McKee," Mom supplied.

"Yes, yes," Catrinel said, with the air of someone not especially concerned about the details. "She gave me the address."

Mom regained some of her usual composure. "Ms. Bloom—"

"Please, call me Cat. All my friends do."

"—um, Cat was telling us that she met you and your friends when she moved in next door to the McKees. She has an interesting idea about your project," Mom said.

"I have found a place for you to film your little movie," Catrinel almost purred. She had a sharp, dramatic expression on her face. "Near the village where I grew up, there is a castle. A magnificent place. Castle Prahova. It was the home of Vlad Dracul. But he never returned to that place after the death of his first wife. Afterward, they said it was . . . haunted. By her love." She leaned over in my direction, sending a wave of lavender fragrance my way. She pulled out her phone and swiped through a few jaw-dropping photos of forests at twilight, steep gray cliffs, castle turrets, and lush candlelit interiors. Her face returned to a more natural smile. "It is owned by my cousin. Next year, he will turn it into a tourist . . . uh . . . trap. But now, no construction. It is the rainy season, work is slow, and he says you can film there. Over your spring break. At no cost."

"Whoa!" Maddie blurted, completely voicing what I was feeling inside.

"I can arrange for the necessary permits," Catrinel went on.

"We appreciate the offer. I'm just not sure . . . if it's safe for the children to go to . . . Romania," my mom said. She had her teeth clenched in a combination between a scary smile and a scowl.

"Safe? Why not safe?" Catrinel asked. "Travel is safe. Romania is safe."

But I'm not sure that Catrinel had done us any favors by making the castle sound like a fixer-upper haunted house.

"Oh . . . yes . . . of course," Dad said. His gold ASU shirt was way too baggy, and it rippled as he moved. "The kids haven't done much travel. Alex has only been out of the country once. When her class went to Canada for the Toronto Film Festival last fall."

"But we all have our passports," Maddie said.

"*I* will go with the children," Catrinel said with the air of someone doing a grand reveal. "My agent feels that it would be beneficial for me to keep a low profile until my divorce has concluded and there has been a resolution to my husband's . . . legal troubles. I would also very much like to assist upcoming filmmakers."

Maddie was whisper-chanting *ohmigod, ohmigod, ohmigod.*

My dad was enthusiastically nodding, but Mom's lips puckered and her eyes moved back and forth and she cycled through a range of expressions. Worry. Annoyance. Confusion.

"Well," Mom said, picking at something invisible on the knee of her jeans. "Our finances being what they are . . . and Alex wanting to go to college in a few months . . . I don't think we could afford to send her even if we wanted to."

Mom's voice suggested that she did *not* want to.

Catrinel then looked confused. "Their fundraiser has been quite successful."

"Fundraiser?" Mom asked in a tone so sharp it could have cut glass.

Oh, yeah. I didn't tell my parents about the GoFundMe.

That was probably a mistake.

Focus on the film. Focus on the film.

I repeated that in my head over and over. But, like Maddie, I found myself unable to control my enthusiasm. "The castle sounds totally perfect. It would totally differentiate us from other filmmakers who can't film in cool locations. Ohmigod. Ohmigod."

"What *fundraiser*?" Mom said again.

Catrinel cocked her head. But she answered me. Her blond curls bounced up and down. "Castle Prahova. It *is* a perfect location. Yes. You see, Alex, you have a strong point of view. Yes. But your problem is that you have a message that hits the gatekeepers of the film industry too close to home. The movie business is full of men who abuse their power. Monsters who do not wish to be unmasked. The castle . . . well, it is unfamiliar. From another world. By putting the action in a more abstract setting, by creating some ambiguity as to whether Lucy's revenge is real or imagined, you will enable these insecure men to support your creative vision without feeling that they themselves are under scrutiny."

I sighed internally. My guidance counselors at school had said the same thing.

But it was the missing element. What would make our new ten-minute version of *Dead Boys Don't Bite* much better than the original that had gotten me rejected at USC. Catrinel had probably watched my movie once. And this was the analysis that she'd come up with.

It made me wonder how many of her ideas appeared on-screen as credited to her husband.

"Oh. Yeah. Um," I sputtered.

Dad cleared his throat. "That's an excellent point, Miss Bloom." His voice shook with a giddy excitement. My father knew next to nothing about filmmaking. His favorite movie was *Happy Gilmore*. Catrinel Bloom could have been talking about her shoe size, and he would have thought it sounded excellent.

From beside him on the loveseat, Mom shot him a dark stare.

Maddie grinned. "We could use the GoFundMe money for travel. We wouldn't need to build any new sets."

I nodded. Forcing myself to take deep, steadying breaths and trying to ignore the drumming sensation building in my chest, I added, "We would still need equipment though. I'm not sure if the school would let us take their stuff out of the country . . ."

Ohmigod. Ohmigod. What if we could do this? What if it could really happen?

I trailed off because Mom glared at me with the force of a thousand fiery suns.

She clearly didn't like this plan as much as Maddie and I did. But Dad wore a goofy grin, and I got the idea that he would work on Mom.

Catrinel rose gracefully from the sofa. "I have equipment. You come over tomorrow. See Justin's old stuff. And tell me what you decide."

Maddie and I both jumped up in unison and followed the gorgeous woman out of the living room and to the door.

"I wish I could do more to help you, dear Alex," she said. Her purple sundress revealed her perfectly tanned skin. "I would like to have financed your film myself." Catrinel's voice became hard. "But at the present time, my husband has cut me off from our production company. He has not exactly been forthcoming about information relating to the status of our finances."

We were nearly to the door when my mom called, "It was a pleasure meeting you."

"Yes . . . pleased to . . ." Dad said. My guess was that the rest of his sentence was cut off by one of Mom's looks.

Maddie bounced up and down on the entryway as the three of us stood there, clustered together. Her heels clicked on the tile.

"I hope things start going better for you," I said.

Catrinel snorted. "You know what they say about hope?"

"Uh. Hope springs eternal?" I asked.

She smiled again as she opened our front door. But it was a smile without any humor or comfort. "Hope prolongs the torment of man."

She patted my arm lightly. "You come by tomorrow, and we will work out the details."

The instant I shut the door, Maddie and I both pressed our faces into the window that faced the front yard, watching the star float to her silver BMW.

When Catrinel was gone, Maddie and I turned around. Mom blocked our path to the stairs. "Alex. What is that woman talking about? What fundraiser?"

"Um . . . well . . ." I mumbled as I pulled out my phone.

Almost giddy, I sent out a group text.

We need to meet.

A reply came through immediately. From Kenna.

Yes. We do.

Standing next to me, Maddie had her own phone out, scrolling through images of forests in Romania. Mom was talking and tapping her foot and going on about safety and being practical and getting my head out of the clouds. I was trying to nod along.

"Alex!" Mom said more sternly. "What *fundraiser* was that woman talking about?"

Another message from Reagan popped up on my phone.

Have you seen the fucking fundraiser recently?

Maddie made a few taps and opened our GoFundMe page. Her mouth fell open. She didn't seem to be breathing.

She held up her phone so that I could see the screen.

I blinked my eyes over and over, unable to process what I was looking at.

"What the hell is happening?" I asked.

General Directorate for Criminal Investigations

Alexandra Elaine Rush—Transcript—Tape 1 [CONT.]

Inspector Skutnik: And so Maddie was behaving oddly. She mentioned a trip she took with her family. Did she ever explain what she meant? Why did she broach that particular subject?

Alex: No. Not until we got to the castle.

Inspector Skutnik: [papers rustling] Later that day, Kenna McKee informed you that a half-million-dollar donation had been made via your GoFundMe? That is a lot of money.

Alex: Yeah. A lot.

Inspector Skutnik: You had no idea where the money came from?

Alex: No. By the time we figured it out, it was too late. Someone had already stolen it.

Five days ago

INT. PHOENIX SKY HARBOR AIRPORT—NIGHT

It was the first day of spring break, and we were flying to Bucharest.

Our parents spent the week after Catrinel's visit to our house arguing among themselves. No surprise, but Kenna's parents, the McKees, were totally on board with us going to Castle Prahova. They thought it was a big opportunity and felt it would look really bad to refuse an offer from a big-time movie star. My family and the Flannigans were on the opposite side, but Hazel's parents were the most upset of all.

Mrs. Beckett used to be on an FBI task force that investigated drugs coming out of Eastern Europe. She had a lot of opinions about whether it was safe for us to be "gallivanting around" with a movie star. And my mom was convinced that the half a million dollars came from some maniac who wanted to gather us all together and hunt us for sport. Basically, the plot of *Ready or Not*. The two of them acted absolutely certain that something terrible would happen to us. For a while they debated sending a parent with us, but everyone had work and other kids and other issues. No one could go.

In the end, Shane McKee bedazzled most of the parents, and they agreed to let us go. They reached a compromise. We'd use the small donations we'd gathered to film the ten-minute version of *Dead Boys Don't Bite*. Jax's dad, Fred, was a financial planner who had Winona Ryder as a client. He would try to figure out where the large donation came from. Most likely we would have to return the money.

Which was fine, honestly. I was getting to make my short film and getting a second shot at applying to USC. Plus, what if we actually won at Scream Fest?

After that, things moved fast. We went through the equipment in Catrinel's garage. Justin Bloom had left her enough cameras, lights, and computers to start her own movie studio, and we easily found the stuff we needed. She helped us get it packed up. We had to spend a little bit of our money to have it all shipped to Romania, but it was worth it.

The day before we left, I spent almost all night sorting silver. Not only was I trying to get back into my mom's good graces, but I wanted to leave Meredith with as little work as possible. I had successfully identified three replica spoons and found a set of Kirk Stieff Repousse ice-cream forks mixed in with a bunch of junk.

But because I'd been working, I put off packing until the very last minute. So when Maddie arrived to wait for the shuttle to take us to the airport, I was frantically shoving stuff into my suitcase.

Maddie entered my room and made a disapproving snort.

I had a bunch of different piles of clothes, and believe it or not, I had a system.

She approached the mound on my window seat. She inspected a T-shirt on the top. "Are you packing this?"

"No." My face heated at the sight of the tee that was covered in holes and bleach spots. I pointed to a pile next to my suitcase.

"That's the stuff I'm taking. Assuming I can get it into my bag and get it closed."

Maddie made a skeptical face at my half-empty suitcase. "Ohmigod! Alex! We need to hurry. The shuttle will be here in fifteen minutes."

Our plane left a little after nine in the morning, and the airport van was picking us up at six. For a while, we were quiet and focused on folding up my jeans and shirts as neatly as possible. Maddie sat on my suitcase while I zipped it shut.

"Okay . . . there," I said, huffing and out of breath as I dragged the bag to the door.

"Soooo," Maddie said, drawing out the word as long as possible. Her long green cotton maxi dress was probably supposed to be casual, but the way it draped on her was elegant and dramatic. "Are you and Jax gonna, like, do it in the castle?"

"Maddie!" The last thing in the world I needed was for Mom to walk in on this convo.

She grinned. "Oh, come on. Jax might not *be* the perfect boyfriend. But he is the perfect-*looking* boyfriend."

My stomach did a little somersault. "He *is* perfect. He has a lot of good ideas and . . ."

Maddie's smile fell. "Alex," she began.

Lights flashed across the large window, cutting through whatever she intended to say.

The SuperShuttle van was in the driveway, and I heard Dad call me from downstairs.

My dad shouted, "Alex!" again, and outside, Jax, Reagan, and the rest of our crew milled around in our driveway. Kenna was fluffing her hair and checking her phone.

I grabbed my stuff and dragged my suitcase down the stairs. By the time Mom and Dad finished hugging me and basically giving me the safety lecture that Liam Neeson delivers at the beginning of the movie *Taken*, Maddie was already in the van.

I wheeled my bag down the sidewalk, where Reagan and Jax lingered at the spot where our concrete entrance path met the driveway.

"You'll take good care of my girl, right?" Dad called out to Jax.

I cringed, but Jax answered, "Of course, sir."

Sometimes, I thought my parents trusted Jax more than me. I continued on toward the boys. They were . . . talking.

"You are seriously saying that you want to get on a plane with her and not tell everyone else what's happening?" Jax said.

The sun had not yet risen, and it was still dark outside. Under the yellow-orange lights mounted to the stucco near our garage door, Reagan's red hair looked strangely pink. Like raw shrimp. "It isn't going to change anything," he said. "We have to see where this leads."

"Where this leads?" Jax repeated. "After what you found out? People have a right to decide for themselves if they want to be involved or not."

Reagan hesitated. "We're all involved. Whether we like it or not."

"Someone could get hurt," Jax said.

It was the way he said it. It made me glance back over my shoulder. At my house. And wonder if I should have stayed there.

"Alex needs this," Reagan said. "Or maybe you don't care about that."

A scowl fell across Jax's face. But he spotted me and replaced his tense look with a fake smile. "You all set?"

Reagan gave me a curt nod and walked in the direction of the large blue van.

"What was that about?" I asked Jax.

He extended his fake smile into a grin. "I'll explain later."

The fear that must have been etched on my face caused him to soften. His shoulders relaxed and he put his arm around my waist.

"It'll be okay, Alex," he said. "There's just a lot going on right now. And I think Reagan is having some trouble . . . adjusting."

Right.

Jax smiled, ran his hand through his pompadour, and guided me toward the van.

The driver took my bag, and I climbed in the wide-open sliding door. Maddie and Carter were in the very back row. Hazel and Reagan took the middle, leaving the front row for us.

Kenna greeted Reagan with the air of someone addressing an incompetent assistant. "Did you get our financial affairs in order?" Since Reagan was the official organizer of the GoFundMe, he had become the de facto treasurer for our trip. Kenna had him send the money for the plane tickets to her dad.

"How many times are you going to ask me?" Reagan grumbled. "For the last time, yes."

Kenna faced forward again and began using her phone to check her makeup. She was glamorous as always in a lacy black shirt and tight black jeans.

"Are we picking up Catrinel?" Carter called from the back.

I could hear Maddie snort indignantly.

Jax put his arm around me. "Oh, sure. She's going to squeeze into the smelly ShadyShuttle right between you and Mads."

Kenna stretched and yawned lazily. "She's meeting us at the airport."

Finally, we arrived at the drop-off point at the airport curb and climbed out of the van. Jax dragged a black Samsonite suitcase on wheels behind him. It was the perfect amount of beat up and covered with the exact cool number of stickers. He wore an old pair of black sweats and a lacrosse T-shirt, and he was gorgeous. And my stomach did a little flop every time I looked at him. It was always the same. Since that day in tenth grade when Mr. Cork put us at the same table in screenwriting class.

I reached for Jax's hand. He would be right at home in the world of movie stars, and I couldn't shake the feeling that I was counting on him to take me to that world too.

Kenna led us to a group of seats near the large window. Blue lights lit the runways below. "Who's ready for the trip of a lifetime?" she said with a grin.

It was so early in the morning that even roosters were probably still asleep, and she had her lash inserts on.

I scanned the airport but didn't see Catrinel Bloom anywhere.

"She's probably in the Admirals Club," Kenna said.

I had no idea what the Admirals Club even was, but I guessed that Kenna meant that there was a better place for movie stars to wait than out here with the old guy who refused to put his shoes back on after security and the kid watching a singing robot video on his iPad at full volume.

Back at the gate, we continued to wait. Kenna returned with a stack of magazines as the flight attendant made the call for first-class passengers. It was then that we learned that Kenna had upgraded her own ticket. She boarded with Catrinel as the celebrity breezed into the terminal. We would be flying in coach.

"Typical," Hazel muttered under her breath.

Our group boarded last. We had to file past Catrinel, who was slumped over in her seat, mostly covered by a blanket, wearing an eye mask, and apparently already asleep. Kenna gave us a little wave as she fluffed her pillow and took a sip from a fancy bottle of water.

"My dad has a ton of airline miles," she said without a hint of shame.

The rest of us took our seats in coach and tried to sleep on the plane.

It was Monday morning when we landed in Bucharest, which felt strangely natural as we'd lost almost an entire day due to the time difference.

I was heavy with exhaustion.

But still, excitement fluttered within me.

Tomorrow, we'd start filming the all-new *Dead Boys Don't Bite*.

"Has anyone seen Catrinel?" I asked as we walked from the gate in the direction of the baggage claim area.

Kenna shrugged. "They let her get off the plane first and made the rest of us wait."

Jax and Reagan shared an uncomfortable look.

Maddie yawned. "She's probably in the lounge having a drink while someone else runs around to get her luggage."

Kenna's dad had arranged for the transportation to the castle. We were getting some kind of luxury bus. After we picked up our bags, we were supposed to meet a driver. While we waited at the carousel, we took turns calling our parents and letting them know we had arrived safely.

"Is Catrinel Bloom going on the bus with us?" Carter asked.

Maddie glared at him. "You seem pretty concerned about her."

"I'm just asking a question," Carter said. But he gave himself away when he neatened his hair and T-shirt.

Kenna swiveled her head around in all directions. She pointed toward the crowded walkway. "Oh! There she is!" she said, unable to keep the excitement out of her voice. We all turned that way and caught a glimpse of Catrinel in the company of a tall man with thinning dark hair who walked with a hunched-over gait.

Catrinel Bloom bypassed the baggage turnstiles and headed for the exit doors. Everything about her was cinematic. Her long, graceful strides. The way a few elegantly twisted strands of blond hair escaped the bun at the nape of her neck. Her long beige camel-hair coat. The way she kept her oversize sunglasses on even inside the airport. A few people pointed and took her picture with their cell phones. Others called out her name. She appeared not to notice.

She stood outside on the airport curb with the strange man while I struggled to listen to the loud airport announcements being read in several languages.

Kenna was on her phone the whole time, texting someone or staring at something on the screen. She left the rest of us to pull her many matching Louis Vuitton suitcases off the baggage carousel. Maddie and I exchanged a look.

"Kenna," I said. "We're gonna be on the bus to the castle for hours, and we'll have plenty of time to call our parents or post on social media or whatever."

She ignored me as I yanked her duffel bag off the carousel.

Once we had our suitcases, we headed out glass double doors toward Catrinel. She stood right next to the stranger, but the two of them faced forward and didn't speak to each other. It was like they knew each other but would have *preferred* not to know each other.

The boys had most of Kenna's luggage, and she continued to hold her phone right up to her face. She didn't appear to notice, or care, that a long black limousine had pulled up in front of Catrinel. A driver scurried out and held open the rear door.

The movie star apparently wasn't riding with us.

"Ms. Bloom! Cat! Cat," I called out.

We had to close the distance between us and the limo at a full run. The seven of us must have looked ridiculous, and we made a ton of noise as the wheels of our bags scraped along the sidewalk outside the airport.

By the time we reached the car, Catrinel Bloom was already inside. She had to roll down the window to speak to me. "Ah. Yes. Miss Rush. There you are. Good." The way she said it was like she didn't really give a damn whether she saw us or not. She waved a hand with a regal air at the man who lingered nearby.

"There is my cousin Raul Stoica. He is the owner of Castle Prahova and will assist you with your film."

"I'm sorry. Did you say Stoica? Stoica?" Hazel repeated as she
wrung her hands.

That seemed like a strange detail to get fixated on as the only
adult we knew in a foreign country was about to ditch us.

"Stoica," Catrinel repeated absently, and was about to roll her
window back up. "My dear cousin Raul. Yes. He once told me that
the only thing I was good for was milking goats. Yes. Stoica."

A lump formed in my throat. "Wait! Wait. You're leaving us at
the airport?"

Catrinel pressed her red lips together. "No one is being left
anywhere. I was told that the basketball player arranged for a
bus. Raul will assist you at Prahova."

"But . . . but . . . you told our parents you would take care of
us," Maddie said, shooting another accusatory glare at Carter,
like all of this was somehow his fault.

Catrinel removed her sunglasses so we could see her make an
annoyed face. "Young lady, I have taken care of a great *many*
things. I have secured a filming location. Yes? And all the proper
permits. Loaned you thousands of dollars of equipment. Seen to
your safe arrival to my country. Yes. Yes. I have taken care of
many things."

She addressed the man standing on the curb in Romanian.
Raul Stoica had dark eyes, closely cropped dark hair, and tat-
toos with their edges poking out from the trim of his faded black
T-shirt. He lit a cigarette, jerked his head at Kenna, and spoke
to her with a thick accent. "Cousin Cat showed me your little

pictures . . . on Instagram . . . You are always dressed for a funeral . . . a wife of Dracula . . . yeah . . . I like it . . ."

Kenna didn't even look up from her phone.

This was bad. I had just told my mom that everything was fine. If our parents found out we were alone in Romania without our chaperone, we wouldn't be going to a castle, we'd be on the next flight home. The only place I'd be going was back to the basement to sort more silver.

I stepped forward, wrapped my fingers around the window, and shoved my head inside the car. "What about the film? What am I going to do?"

She gave me a little, brittle smile. "Miss Rush, you know what you must do."

Um. Yeah. Okay. But what is that exactly?

"Yeah. But. Where . . . where . . . are you going?" I was still stammering to myself when the shiny limo drove away and a bus pulled into the spot right in front of us. Its double doors opened to reveal a refrigerator-shaped driver with a brown-gray walrus moustache and the general appearance of someone who could have been a villain in a movie about the Cold War. But he grinned at us and bellowed, "Prahova, party of seven," in a friendly voice.

Raul dropped his cigarette and smooshed it with his shoe. "Yeah. All right. Let us go. Time to take the little children to the castle."

"We're not children," Jax muttered.

Kenna remained on the sidewalk. "We'll be right there," she said.

She finally glanced up to find Raul staring at her with a

disgruntled expression. "We just have something to take care of real quick," she added.

"Take care of? What take care of? You have your bags. You called your parents. You went to the bathroom," Raul said. He was wearing an outfit very similar to Carter's. A punk band T-shirt. Old black jeans. They could have been twinning on social media. "Time to make your little movie."

I was close enough to him to see how greasy his dark hair was and how his rumpled clothes created the suggestion that he spent his nights sleeping under a bridge.

"We just need a minute," Kenna said.

Raul rolled his eyes and said, "One minute."

The instant he was on the bus, Kenna rounded on us. "We have a problem."

"Yeah, obviously," Maddie shot back, reaching behind her head to wrap her hair in a bun. "We know precisely one person in this country, and we have no idea where the hell she went."

Hazel tapped her foot on the sidewalk. "What am I gonna tell my mom?"

From behind me, Jax said, "Oh, we know where Catrinel went."

I turned around to find my boyfriend frowning at Reagan, who suddenly seemed very interested in a giggling couple getting into a taxi.

My stomach clenched. "What are you talking about?" I asked.

Jax cleared his throat. A light breeze blew his shirt tight against his body as he waited on the curb. "Catrinel Bloom isn't going to the castle. The computer equipment she gave to Reagan—"

My mind struggled to connect the dots between the stuff Catrinel loaned us and her disappearance from the airport.

"You're not listening to me," Kenna interrupted. She didn't seem to care that the driver was just a few feet away, shoving the last of her massive collection of Louis Vuitton roller bags into the back of the bus. Her face had gone gray as the cloudy sky. She almost dropped her phone. "The money. It's gone."

"What?" Maddie said, whirling around. "What?"

Kenna sucked in a deep breath. "The money from the Go-FundMe. All of it. All. The. Fucking. Money. Is. Gone."

General Directorate for Criminal Investigations

Alexandra Elaine Rush—Transcript—Tape 1 [CONT.]

Inspector Skutnik: Did you have any idea who took the money?

Alex: No. Reagan said he could figure it out. Given enough time.

Inspector Skutnik: This is when Raul Stoica entered the picture?

Alex: Yeah.

Inspector Skutnik: What did you think of him?

Alex: Um . . . [inaudible] . . . he was . . . [inaudible]. He was Catrinel's cousin. We wanted to trust him. We wanted things to work out. But there was something about him. Something that made the little hairs on my arms stand up. Something . . . wrong.

Four days ago

INT. BUCHAREST MINIBUS—DAY

I flinched as Raul Stoica rapped on the window and gestured to a watch on his wrist.

The driver hustled behind the wheel and started the engine.

"We have to get on the bus." I couldn't help but glare at Jax as I spoke. He had lied to me. *Again.* Or kept things from me. I wasn't sure which one was actually worse.

"Alex?" Kenna said through clenched teeth. "Did you hear me? I said—"

"I heard you," I cut her off. I was supposed to be the director. It was about time everyone started listening to me. "We're not gonna figure things out standing in front of the airport. Get on the bus and we'll figure out what to do next."

"Yeah," Reagan agreed, moving toward the curb. "It's not like we'll find the cash in our carry-on bags."

Next to me, Jax nodded, and everyone formed a line to board.

Glancing at my phone, I saw that it was a little before ten in the morning. Whatever his faults, Mr. McKee made sure we traveled in style. Comfy cream-colored leather captain's chairs filled the interior. Each seat had a tablet attached to a tray that displayed a breathtaking image of Castle Prahova at dawn. There were bottles of expensive water for all of us.

As we filed past, the driver told us that his name was Marius. "Okay, okay," he said, standing at the front, near the driver's seat, and speaking to himself. "That is everyone, right? Prahova, party of seven." He read our names off a list attached to an old wooden clipboard. "Hazel Beckett, Jackson Flannigan, Kenna McKee, Madeline Oliver, Carter Ricci, Alexandra Rush, and . . . Mr. Reagan Wozniak. With the red hair!" He grinned and waved his hands. "Make yourselves comfortable. The drive is a little over four hours. We want to make it to the castle before dark, so we don't stop. We have provided meals in a box for whenever you get hungry."

Raul sat in the front row right behind the driver. He turned around in his seat to speak to us. "We need to be quick about our business," he said, squinting at the sky.

I wondered what Raul thought our business *was*.

His dark eyes found mine. "This is the rainy season. We do not approach Prahova at night. Not during a storm."

I shivered.

He looked me over. "You should learn to carry a sweater when you travel. Or perhaps you are one of these American girls who are scared of your own shadow."

I tried to remain calm. So Raul Stoica had greasy hair and rumpled clothes that suggested he spent his nights sleeping under a bridge. So he glared at me like he wished he could bore a hole into my skull. So what? We had bigger problems. The only thing I had to be afraid of was my parents. They would absolutely freak when they realized that Catrinel wasn't with us. I'd be on a plane back to Phoenix before I could say *Bram Stoker*. When I spoke to them earlier, I told them that Catrinel was off getting her bags. My mom made a point to ask.

We kept walking and took seats toward the very back of the bus.

I scooted out of the way to allow Jax to take the window seat of the last row and sank into the leather chair next to him. I expected Reagan to sit across the aisle from me, but he didn't. It was like he couldn't get far enough away from me. He pressed his face against the window.

I poked Jax in the arm. He was going to tell me the truth. Whether he wanted to or not. "What's up with Catrinel?"

His face flushed red, and he didn't immediately answer.

Maddie dropped her bag into the row in front of us and leaned over the headrest. "Screw that. What about the money?"

Carter sat down next to Maddie and faced forward. "The money? Maddie, where in the hell is Catrinel Bloom? She ditched us at the airport!"

"You're really interested in that," Maddie said. Her fingers tightened around the headrest and turned white. "Someone stole half a million dollars from us, but *your* primary concern is the whereabouts of the hot movie star."

Kenna started to pace up the aisle, like she intended to get off the bus. "We need that money."

It was an odd comment. Kenna's parents were super rich, and our trip was already paid for. Our parents told us that we would be returning the large donation. We didn't *need* the money, and we certainly didn't need it right that minute.

"Why were you even checking the fundraiser?" Carter asked, suspicion on his face.

Kenna's face turned red. "I just like to . . . Sometimes I . . .

Oh, who cares, Carter! The point is someone stole our fucking money."

"Maybe it's a bug," Reagan mumbled. "Maybe it will fix itself. I can look into it more when we get to the castle. They have Wi-Fi, right?"

"Fix itself? Fix itself?" Kenna shrieked.

Hazel was the last person to come up the aisle, her perfectly clean shoes squeaking on the rubber mat floor. She blocked Kenna in.

"Will you *please* sit down?" Hazel said.

"Yes, yes," Marius called out in a cheerful, booming voice. "Everyone sit."

Kenna sank into a chair, and the expensive leather puffed out a sigh. Maddie's eyes widened in anger, but she did the same.

Ignoring the driver, Carter stood up. As he did, the bus began to move, pulling away from the airport, and he had to brace himself to keep from falling into the aisle. "Maddie, my primary concern is that we're in a foreign country, and if our parents find out that—"

"They won't," Reagan said, speaking into the window. "They won't find out. Unless we tell them."

"Um. Helllllooooooo," Kenna said. She had smeared a streak of eyeliner across her face. "Our fucking money is—"

"We heard," Jax interrupted.

"I think they probably heard on the International Space Station," Carter said.

"Hello! Jax!" I said, waving my hand in front of his face. It was like he was intent to let that argument go on forever so he wouldn't have to answer me.

Jax swiveled around in his chair so that he faced the aisle. "Alex. Don't me mad, okay?"

Reagan cleared his throat. "Catrinel Bloom isn't going to Castle Prahova. I don't think she ever really intended to."

Jax sighed. "We *know* she never intended to. She's on her way to Switzerland."

"What . . . what . . ." I felt lightheaded.

I glanced at the driver. Marius was humming a song to himself. Between his singing and the noise of the road, he probably couldn't even hear us.

Jax reached out to put his arm around me, but I shrugged it off.

Reagan had his phone out and was clicking around on our GoFundMe page. "Catrinel gave me some of the computer equipment she had in her garage. One of the old laptops was still getting her email, I guess. And I saw a confirmation." He paused dramatically. "Catrinel Bloom is going to rehab for painkiller addiction. To some place called the Kusnacht Practice."

Kenna nodded. "I've heard of that."

Maddie had her phone out and was already googling it. "I'm sure you have. It's in the Swiss Alps, costs a hundred thousand dollars a week, and you get your own personal butler."

Kenna rolled her eyes. "One of my dad's teammates went last summer."

"The point is," Reagan said, "that Catrinel's management team probably felt like it made sense for her to pretend to be with us while she went to rehab in secret. Castle Prahova is so remote. No one is going to know whether she's there or not."

"Unless we tell them," Hazel said, agreeing with Reagan's earlier statement.

Kenna's shoulders hunched up, and red blotches broke out across her skin. "We're going to have to tell them. We need . . . we need . . . help." Her arms fell into her lap.

Hazel smoothed her bob. "Forget whether or not we should tell our parents. The two of *you* should have told us."

Jax and Reagan exchanged a tense look.

I remembered the conversation I overheard between them before we left home.

Someone could get hurt.

But.

My hands grew clammy, and I wiped them on the legs of my pants. "My parents are gonna kill me. Catrinel told them that she'd look out for us. Oh. And. We'll have to go home and then . . . and then . . ."

We were digging this hole, and it was getting deeper and deeper. We were in a country where we didn't speak the language. Catrinel Bloom had deserted us and left us in the care of some random guy who looked like the mob's mortician. Jax was keeping things from me. The right thing to do was to call my mom. And go home.

I put my hand in my pocket, rubbing my fingers over the smooth screen of my phone.

Ready to make the call.

Ready to go home.

Home. And sort more silver. And resign myself to watching

other people's movies and my parents losing our house and my sister dancing only in our garage.

I needed to make my film. Catrinel said Prahova was safe. Anyway, what was the worst thing that could happen?

"We can't tell anyone," Reagan said, facing me. "Not yet."

Jax's composure fell away for a minute. "I'm not sure about that . . ."

Another subtle betrayal.

Marius steered the bus through a scenic route of the city center, past the graying opulence of the Athenee Palace Hilton. He pulled out a square, boxy microphone and spoke into it. "And this, my children, is one of Europe's most notorious dens of spies. During World War II and what you Americans called the Cold War. In the communist times, the government bugged every room. Real James Bond stuff." He put the microphone down.

Carter sat down and rocked back and forth in his leather chair. "You don't want to tell our parents that we're in a foreign country alone?"

"We're not *alone*," Reagan said. "We have each other. The castle has a caretaker. And do we really need one more person getting in our way while we film?"

We were on a street lined with casinos. Marius came back on the microphone to say that Israeli tourists liked to gamble. I spotted a few luxury goods stores before we went through a neighborhood full of more mundane office and industrial buildings.

"If we tell our parents . . ." I dug my fingernails into my palms.

Reagan finished my thought. "We'll go home with no footage. We'll have *no plan* to get you into USC."

Kenna, side lit dramatically by the spring sun streaming in though the bus's large windows, leaned into the aisle and waved her hands at Reagan. "We need to figure out what happened to the money!"

"Our parents weren't going to let us have that money anyway," I said, unable to keep the frustration out of my voice.

"So someone should just steal it?" Maddie demanded. In the window behind her, the gorgeous Romanian landscape whirred by.

Reagan returned his attention to his phone and made a few more taps. "I can't really tell what happened. It looks like an authorized user made a transfer late last night. That could be one of our parents."

"Transferred it where?" Carter asked.

Reagan shrugged. "I can't tell from the app. The beneficiary screen isn't loading."

Kenna snorted indignantly. "The transfer was made by a profile called TheCount1897. Do you really think that Mr. Flannigan or Mr. Beckett would use that name?"

Reagan glared at her. "The point is, I need some time to check things out. While I do that, we can get Alex the footage she needs. Don't you think that's a good idea, *Jax*?"

Jax had been lost in his own thoughts. He reached out for my hand and gave it a reassuring squeeze. He knew that I would go along with what he said. "Yes. Well . . . I think we should just get to the castle. Give Reagan a bit of time to find out what happened. In the meantime, we film what we can. Then we can make a decision about what to do next."

Maddie squirmed in her seat. "That's a lot of money."

Carter tried to take her hand, but she pulled away. "I agree with Jax," he said. "And Reagan's right. It's probably a bug. Or one of the parents. We'll figure it out."

Hazel nodded. She gave me this look, and I understood that she was as invested in *Dead Boys Don't Bite* as I was. "We've come all this way," she said. "Reagan can investigate from here. We don't gain anything by going home right now. Let's at least try to film something."

"This is a bad idea," Kenna said. But she resigned herself to looking out the window.

Jax sat up straight. "Everything will be fine," he said.

That seemed to settle everyone down. My own heartbeat settled into a normal rhythm, and I felt myself relaxing and snuggling into Jax in silent forgiveness.

It was silent for a minute, and only the noise of the road filled the emptiness.

We had made our choice.

We were going to carry on with the trip.

Jax kissed me lightly on the forehead. "Don't worry, Alex."

The city was behind us, and we were mostly surrounded by farmland ahead and on all sides. Marius turned the microphone back on and gave a long speech about Ceaușescu and the Revoluția Română of 1989, and then concluded, saying, "And that is Romania, my friends."

Then turned on the radio and bopped along to Romanian rap.

Outside, the storm clouds were growing thicker and darker.

We continued to drive until the occasional farmhouses or

abandoned buildings were few and far between. I closed my eyes and tried to release some of the tension of the day. Lulled by the rhythmic bumps and the soft whir of the bus, I fell asleep.

It seemed like I had barely been sleeping a few minutes when Jax squeezed my hand.

"Alex, you have to see this."

My eyes fluttered open in time to see the bus cross a narrow wooden bridge over a river that flowed with brisk white water.

I leaned across to get a better look out Jax's window.

In about fifty feet, the asphalt road would give way to a dirt one. A bit beyond that, the yellow grass of the countryside abruptly ended at the perimeter of a dense forest. Tall beech trees that were far too massive to hug rose up and seemed to pierce the dark, cloudy sky. It was like we would collide with a wall of greenery at any second. When I was a kid, my crayon box had a few shades of green, but here I found a million, and as the tree branches swayed, they created their own ballet of jades and teals and shamrocks and of lights and shadows. What must have been the red-topped turrets of Castle Prahova darted out above the treetops.

The bus was slowing down. It had to. The road was being swallowed up by the forest.

"Here we are," Marius called out cheerfully.

I squinted at the dark forest ahead. Where was *here*?

"What do we do now?" Kenna called back.

Raul remained in his seat. "We walk."

Marius opened the door, and as Raul stretched, a loud clap of thunder sounded. It would have been comical were it not for the fact that we were apparently going to have to drag our own bags up a steep hill to the castle. I got to my feet as well and lumbered off the bus.

Raul stood up and spoke into his cell phone in Romanian.

As I passed by him, he ended his call and stared at me.

I wanted to be friendly, so I said, "Do you like it here? At the castle?"

"No one likes it here," Raul said to me.

Jax gave me a smile as he helped me take the steps off the bus. I didn't know how his hair wasn't dirty or his clothes weren't wrinkled or why he didn't look like he had slept on a plane or why he still smelled so good.

I wondered if I had been too quick to forgive him. He hadn't even really apologized. For recutting my movie. For concealing Catrinel's plan to ditch us at the airport. But it wasn't the right time to be having those thoughts.

We all milled around near the back of the bus where our bags were. Carter took a picture of the castle turrets with his phone. "So. Uh . . . do a lot of people go here? To the castle?"

"On and off," Raul said with a shrug. "Depending on the rain. And the construction."

"People say the castle is haunted," Kenna said.

Raul scowled. "People say many things."

Reagan frowned. "What about the locals?" he asked.

"What about them?" Raul shot back.

Marius smiled. "In the country, they are . . . *superstitious*. Prahova is . . . beautiful. Full of history." He opened the luggage compartment and stacked our bags neatly on the dirt.

It was chillier out here than at the airport, and I did wish that I had a sweater.

The land smelled like wet earth and mushrooms and mildew.

Hazel coughed a couple of times.

We waved goodbye to Marius and watched as he put the van in reverse and drove off.

The rumble of the bus engine grew faint, and I reached for Jax's hand.

We found ourselves facing the wilderness.

General Directorate for Criminal Investigations

Alexandra Elaine Rush—Transcript—Tape 1 [CONT.]

Inspector Skutnik: And you arrived at Prahova . . . Did you know anything about the castle?

Alex: We knew some stuff. Like, from Google. That back in the fifteenth century, Prahova was the summer home of Vlad Dracul, the inspiration for Count Dracula. I did a bunch of research about him for my screenplay. But then when we got there, we found out that . . .

Inspector Skutnik: Found out what?

Alex: That locals thought the place was haunted. By Dracul's victims. I mean, he was known as Vlad the Impaler for a reason, right? Kenna tried telling us that Bram Stoker had traveled to Prahova before he wrote his novel, but we knew that wasn't true. I don't believe in ghosts. But there was something dark in that place. Something that I couldn't see through the lens of my camera.

Four days ago

EXT. CASTLE PRAHOVA—DAY

We had shipped as much of our stuff as we could, but we still had a bunch of extra bags full of makeup that might melt or costumes Maddie hadn't finished in time to put in the boxes. There was a ton of stuff to carry, and we divided up the bags. The seven of us clustered behind Raul at the head of the trail where we would enter the forest.

I was the last to enter the woods, and two things immediately struck me. First, everything was wet. It must have rained in the area all the time. And second, it was quiet.

Unnaturally quiet.

Back home, I often went camping with my dad in Tonto National Forest, and the environment had a soundtrack. Birds chirped, bees buzzed, deer moved about, people laughed as they camped and hiked. Here there was only the occasional rustling of leaves and the far-off rush of the river water. And the trees themselves were unlike anything I had ever seen. Their trunks were covered in thick blue-black moss, and their branches twisted up in impossible ways, forming otherworldly knots and creases and folds.

Kenna was up ahead with Raul. The two of them were walking at a fairly fast clip.

The path was getting darker and narrower, and the spindly tree branches overhead no longer created crisscross shadows on the dirt. I dug my phone out of my pocket to use the flashlight and noticed that the screen read NO SERVICE.

Perfect.

The altitude was higher than I was used to and I was dragging my bag behind me and we were going almost straight uphill and I was gasping and wishing that I'd listened to my sister when she told me to do more cardio. Every minute or so, a pebble got stuck in the wheels of the suitcases I was towing, and I had to stop and fix them.

We arrived at the start of a cobblestone pathway that continued on toward a thick iron gate that opened to a courtyard and a steep staircase. My stomach churned. We had a lot more climbing ahead. Castle Prahova rested up on a perch high above.

And it was . . .

A mess.

The lower level consisted of gray brick and masonry with chunks that had been gouged out. Piles of stones had been built up along the castle's perimeter, and long grass grew up to my knees. The upper levels were also gray and weathered and streaked with water damage. We found murals that were peeling off the walls and Latin inscriptions that were barely legible. Many of the old windows were broken or cracked or missing. Most of the turrets were missing red tiles, but one was completely smashed in. From somewhere inside the courtyard ahead, chickens clucked and a goat bleated and water dripped in a way that sounded off.

"This is . . ." Hazel said as her mouth fell open.

"Not what I expected," Carter finished.

Maddie actually laughed.

Clearly, the photos that Catrinel had shown us back at home had been taken very strategically. The eastern wing of Prahova was mostly intact, and its tower had been spared the damage and vandalism of the rest of the place. The sun was setting behind the tower's red roof, creating the picture we'd been staring at on the screens on the bus.

Still, it was obvious why this wasn't a tourist attraction.

"Yeah. Yeah," Raul said. "Under renovation. But there is enough done that you children will be okay." He continued forward and tugged the gate open. Two brown chickens rushed in our direction.

"We're gonna have . . . to be really . . . careful about where we film," I said.

Hazel nodded. She was out of breath too. "In the . . . morning . . . tomorrow . . . I'll come out and take some stills." She scanned the area. "I think the fact that it's . . . rustic might help us. It's a little scarier."

"I know *I* find it terrifying," Carter said.

Jax frowned at him. "We can go over the shot list later."

There were paths of various widths and states of decay. They twisted and curved and disappeared between the castle's far-off buildings. Raul led us into a square garden. The area was overgrown with yellow grass, and a brown goat with a white beard was inside, chomping and chewing, unconcerned by our arrival. When we were all inside, Carter dropped his bags, and I jumped at the thud of the leather on stone.

Raul laughed. "Yeah. You *are* afraid of your shadow."

I clutched one of the suitcase handles, holding on to the lifeline of that normalcy. But I tried to sound cool. "I am *not* afraid of my shadow."

The bags jingled and jangled as I traveled across the cobblestone. Next to me, Jax's face was all sweaty, and I recognized the dread. We were going to have to carry all our gear up what looked like three or four flights of stone stairs. We took slow, deliberate steps across the courtyard, walking by a round stone well. I think we all wanted to catch our breath. A large statue on a pedestal dominated the square.

"Is that . . ." I trailed off, not bothering to finish. I recognized the Suman coat and the long stone fingers clutching a sword from my research. It was obviously Vlad Dracul. Or part of him anyway. The statue was missing its head.

Raul stood next to me. "It is supposed to be Vlad Dracul, yeah," he said. He gestured to the top of the statue, which lay on the ground, surrounded by tall weeds. "Apparently somebody felt the statue would look better with . . . some modifications."

"Jesus. That thing is hideous," Jax said, pointing at the head's bulging, rounded eyes.

Raul nodded and, with an air of resignation, took the stairs at a fast clip. Jax sighed and entered the staircase next. The rest of my friends went up one by one. I remained at the base of the stairs, staring at the beheaded Dracul, desperately tired, still unable to catch my breath.

To me, it looked like the garden was one of several walled spaces between two long, dramatic entrance halls. But that grandeur was in the past. The walls tumbled down, revealing dilapidated interiors full of mold and mud and piles of old bricks. Light streamed in from gaping holes in the roof.

A bang of thunder clapped and echoed off the stone walls.

We arrived at the top of the stairs, panting and exhausted. But from up there, all was well. The staircase emptied us onto a wide terrace that lined the side of the castle. The sun was beginning to disappear behind the treetops. The visible portion of the castle was lovely, and as I tottered up to the edge of the terrace, I found myself staring at a long, steep drop down a dramatic gray cliffside into the rushing river below.

Raul led us toward a rounded wooden door. When he pushed the wood open, we were in for another surprise. We went inside and found ourselves in a large, fairly modern kitchen.

With electricity. And stainless-steel Viking appliances.

Almost exactly like the ones my family was forced to sell after my dad got sick.

My instincts had been correct; the original entrance to the castle must have been one of the wrecked halls on the first floor. We were essentially coming in through the back door or a service entrance. The kitchen was huge and well organized and well lit from clean windows and cheery lightbulbs. More modern dark wood paneling met what looked like the original fourteenth-century masonry. Dozens of copper pots hung over a huge gas stove. They looked so banged up and weathered that it would not have surprised me to learn that good ol' Vlad Dracul had used them to boil blood sausage. Odd antique cast-iron fixtures hung from the ceiling, and the lights flickered. The place smelled of garlic, mint, and dust.

The modern polished beige marble tile clicked under our heels as we hustled along behind Raul. He was mostly talking to Kenna, kind of giving her a status report on the renovations. Like he was the Lurch to her Wednesday Addams.

While I gawked at the odd mishmash of old and new stuff in the kitchen, Jax and Reagan and the rest of our friends were farther inside the castle. I almost had to run to keep up with Raul as he paced down a long, austere cream-and-stone hallway. I joined everyone in what might be described as a sitting room. The room had been completely redecorated such that very little remained of the Transylvanian style. An enormous window ran along the side of the room that faced the forest, and it flooded the room with a grayish light. Dark wood-paneled walls were covered with bookshelves and art. A grouping of furniture—a burgundy leather sofa and several purple velvet striped armchairs—formed a circle in the center. I dropped my bag in the pile of mostly Kenna's luggage that was near the windowed wall.

"Wow," Jax said as his gaze traveled across furnishings and up to the black tin ceilings. "This is an odd aesthetic."

"Kind of like the set of *John Wick*," I suggested.

"Yes," Raul agreed with a curt nod. "It has a certain charm though."

Reagan leaned against the mantel of a marble fireplace with his nose only a few inches from a wooden wall to the right of the door.

I walked in his direction, passing a row of massive dark wood bookcases filled with leather- and canvas-bound books, probably antiques, all with titles in Cyrillic script. My sneakers squeaked on the black Portoro marble tile until I reached the plush red Persian area rug. "This is *really* different," I commented. "I guess I just expected . . ."

Raul snorted. "That the place would be filled with dusty coffins and spiderwebs?"

I cleared my throat.

Maddie was inspecting the walls too. She was to the left, playing with a strand of her long, dark hair, standing underneath one of the wide room's three flickering chandeliers, and staring at a large painting of a nude androgynous man riding a bright red horse in front of a blue pool. "This has to be a reproduction of *Bathing of the Red Horse*. The original is in a museum in Moscow." Moving on to a smaller piece, she said, "But . . . I think this is a real Chagall."

"Is that possible?" I asked. Maddie had dragged me to a traveling Chagall exhibit at the Phoenix Art Museum.

"Um . . . maybe," she said, distracted by a new piece of art. "There are some in private collections . . . and . . . a bunch of them were stolen in the sixties." She flipped a switch on the wall that lit up two crystal chandeliers on opposite sides of the ceiling.

We all turned to look at Raul, who was checking the time on his watch and ignored Maddie's comments about the art. Like it wasn't unusual at all to have museum-quality artwork hanging on the walls.

"Great," Jax said, flopping down on the sofa. "Let's shove that one in my suitcase and take it home with us when we leave."

Carter took a fluffy chair near Jax and chuckled at this suggestion.

Maddie continued to stare at the painting. "But why would a Chagall be here?"

"You will take nothing," Raul almost growled.

"It has to be a fake," Reagan said from beside the fireplace.

"The decor is all Russian colonial," Hazel said, somehow managing to ignore the caretaker. She was walking around, picking up bric-a-brac off the round end tables that punctuated the room. A Fabergé egg. An antique cigarette lighter. A silver ashtray.

Maddie nodded. "I remember. From set decoration class."

"The last owner had fine tastes," Raul said.

"Who *was* the last owner?" I asked, curious about whoever would buy such a place and then furnish it in this way.

"Someone who wishes to remain anonymous," Raul said.

"Maybe it was Catrinel Bloom," Reagan suggested.

Raul actually smiled, and somehow that was more unnerving than his regular expression. "My cousin is the opposite of anonymous."

My friends and I exchanged a series of tense looks. Raul Stoica truly didn't intend to tell us who owned Castle Prahova.

He was still smiling when he went to the corner of the room and pulled a black binder with something that looked like a coat of arms embossed in gold from the drawer of a low oak table. He approached Kenna where she stood by the windowed wall that overlooked the forest below, and handed it to her. "Okay. There is a map inside. Unless you enjoy having roof tiles drop on your head, remain in the east wing. The rain will fall soon. Stay inside. Get yourselves settled. I put your little cameras in the music room. I will be back in one hour."

Hazel's voice was semi-hysterical. "You're leaving us? Where are you going?"

Raul rolled his eyes. He was already halfway across the room, back toward the door we'd entered through. "I go to village for Ana-Maria and Ioana. Unless little children wish to cook their own dinners and make their own beds, then I must return with the cook and the housekeeper."

"We're not little children," Jax said, sitting up a bit straighter in his chair. "And why couldn't we have picked them up on the way?"

"Village is north. We come from south," Raul said with his hand on the wooden door.

"Why didn't they just meet us here?" Hazel asked, her voice even more shrill. "Do you have a car?"

"There is a car in the garage in the north wing. And the ladies . . . they do not like to be alone at the castle," Raul said.

"We don't either," Maddie said, turning away from the painting for a moment.

"What should we do?" Reagan asked. Despite Jax's insistence that we weren't children, we sounded young and silly. I *felt* like a kid. "How do we access the Wi-Fi?"

Raul turned around and rolled his eyes in what was becoming a familiar pattern. "No Wi-Fi. No color television. If you stand in exactly the right place in castle and hold your phone *exactly* so, it may work. You unpack. Relax. Do whatever you want to do. You have map. You go upstairs and you find bedrooms."

The mention of the word *bedroom* sent a jolt through me as I realized that Jax and I might be sharing a room. Like a real couple. Of grown-ups. My face got even hotter at the thought of my boyfriend without his shirt on. Swinging a lacrosse stick gives you great abs.

"You go downstairs, you find smoking room and bathhouse. Locked doors will remain locked," Raul finished with a grim formality.

"Do we need the key?" I asked.

"Map? Locked doors? What? Wait a second. Wait a second," Hazel called.

Raul ignored her, opened the door, and was gone.

As the door slammed, thunder boomed again.

And then we were alone.

General Directorate for Criminal Investigations

Pending report—EXHIBIT 15

Image of article from the *Journal of Romanian Literary Studies*

Translated from Romanian

"Bram Stoker and Castle Prahova" by Hedda Barbu

The first vampires were real. Bram Stoker's novel, while fanciful in some senses, solidifies the historical connection between fact and fantasy. "*Dracula* was the reshaping of four centuries of folk legends that had accreted around the historical Walachian warlord Prince Vlad Tepes (Vlad Dracul)" (Dziemianowicz 11). We know from notes that Stoker had been researching vampirism for some time prior to beginning his work and had determined to write a novel about a fictional antihero called Count Wampyr. But Stoker knew little about the occult. When Stoker secretly traveled to Castle Prahova in 1890, he found the inspiration he was seeking. For Vlad Dracul was an inspiration for terror.

Skutnik's note: Fake article planted by Raul Stoica in sitting room cabinet. Stoker did not visit Prahova.

Four days ago

INT. CASTLE PRAHOVA—NIGHT

My stomach twisted into a hard knot.

Raul Stoica was gone. We were alone, and Kenna looked like she wanted to make a break for the airport.

"Alex, check this out," Reagan said.

I passed Jax on the sofa and made my way over. Reagan was staring at four silver swords that were mounted on the wall. Three of them were old and dull, but one looked different. "What are these?" I asked.

Reagan shrugged, continuing to stare. "Ceremonial swords, I guess."

Hazel sat in a fancy gold chair near the bookcases. She had taken the black leather folio from Kenna. "Okay, here," she said, flipping pages. "There's some info about the castle in here. It says, 'You'll find four authentic kilij swords hanging in the receiving room. These are from the personal collection of Yuri Stoica, acquired during his travels across Romania. The set includes one curved kilij believed to belong to legendary Walachian ruler Vlad Tepes, also known as Vlad the Impaler and Vlad Dracula, and is said to decapitate enemies in a single blow.'"

"Yuri Stoica," Hazel repeated thoughtfully. "That name sounds familiar. I know I've heard it somewhere."

"Yeah, we've *all* heard it somewhere. *Raul* Stoica is the

caretaker. They must be relatives." Carter got up out of the chair and came to the wall. "Think these swords still work?"

Jax glanced at him and said, "Only one way to find out."

"Yeah, but . . ." Hazel trailed off.

The Vlad Dracul sword had to be the one on the bottom, hanging just a couple of inches above the mantel. It was the most curved, and its gold and onyx handle was weathered and marred and worn. But the blade. There was nothing *ceremonial* about it. I'd handled enough silver knives and gotten enough nicks on my hands to recognize a sharp blade when I saw one. The silver's edge was completely smooth and formed a dark, nonreflective, almost black line.

That sword was dangerous.

Reagan reached for it, and I grabbed his hand. "We need to stay away from that thing," I said. My hands rested on the mantel. At a glance, fanciful cherubs were carved into the surface. But I jerked my arm back because concealed in the elaborate curls of the wood were two demons. One grotesque figure on each side.

Kenna hovered near the window that almost covered an entire wall, and we all joined her there. As we pressed our faces toward the glass, we all sucked in a breath and let out a collective *ooooohhhhh.*

It was as if we had our very own world.

The terrace we'd seen earlier extended right beneath the window and all along the side of the castle. A long white marble table and wicker chairs were below, along with a few luxurious chaise lounges that faced the steep cliff that plunged toward a wide river. Beyond that, a green forest stretched on forever, gloomier than before and shrouded in storm clouds. A gray misty fog was rising from the riverbed. It was *Paradise Lost*.

I pointed to a few locations where we might film.

Hazel still had a puzzled expression on her face, but she resumed reading from the binder. "It says that the east wing overlooks the river. It would be really cool to get the rushing water in the shot."

"Now *this* is more like it," Kenna said. And just like that she was in her element again. "Perfect for the movie. Doesn't this make you wonder what Bram thought when he came here?"

"Stoker didn't come here," Hazel said.

Hazel was right. And we all knew it. We all did a bunch of research about *Dracula* when we were planning the movie. Bram Stoker spent his whole life in Ireland. His fictional castle was based on one he visited while on vacation in Scotland.

I noticed that the window didn't open.

Jax looked up. "Why does it seem like that guy Raul is a low-level villain in a Christopher Nolan movie?"

"Why does it seem like he's giving Kenna status reports?" I asked as Hazel nodded along enthusiastically.

Kenna gave us a weak smile. "I can't help it if I'm charming." She paused. "Now, we need to talk about the money."

Carter had meandered over to the corner of the room beyond the fireplace and was hunched over, fiddling with an antique record player on a stand.

Reagan said what we were all thinking. "Kenna, why are you so interested in the GoFundMe money? Your dad is a basketball player and your parents have, like, a zillion dollars."

Kenna sat down in a chair. Her pleasant, dreamy smile vanished. "God, Reagan, you know, sometimes you are so naive. My dad's not LeBron James. He's a forty-one-year-old benchwarmer who will probably be forced into retirement next year. Coke and Nike aren't exactly blowing up his phone. *We* have the attention of . . . someone important in the film industry—"

Reagan scowled. "This would be Catrinel Bloom, who ditched us at the airport? Yeah. It seems like she's super into our film."

"Kenna's right," Maddie said. "We have to find out what happened to the money."

Reagan stepped back from the window. "So there's no Wi-Fi? I guess I'll try to find that one place in the castle with cell service."

"I told you that we should have stayed in the airport," Kenna complained. "We need that money. We could use it for . . . advertising. For marketing the movie."

"Kenna, you don't spend five hundred thousand dollars marketing a student film," Hazel said.

"I'm starving," Jax said. "I hope there's something good for dinner." He was clearly hoping to change the subject.

Maddie had gone back to inspecting the paintings and murmuring to herself while Carter put on yet another record.

"Ah. Duke Ellington," he said. "'Creole Love Call.' Nice." The room filled with andante tempo and Ellington's trumpet.

· I remained at the window. Waiting. Watching. The fog crept up along the edge of the terrace, spilling onto the marble. The forest trees swayed slowly, creating a low moan.

"Kenna, we're in the middle of nowhere." I said, suddenly heavy with fatigue. "Most of our parents want us to return the money, and even if we don't end up having to, it's not like we can spend it out here."

Behind me, Kenna and Maddie sighed in unison.

Hazel squinted at the fog that was on the verge of rolling over the treetops. The room was getting darker and gloomier by the second. Most of the light now came from the crystal chandeliers overhead, which created a yellow glow that shimmered and almost pulsed. "We should look around and get some shots in before our cryptoid caretaker comes back."

Reagan moved closer to the door. "Seriously. What maximum security prison was that weirdo released from?"

I pressed my hand to the cool glass of the window and spotted the tips of the sunken, pockmarked rooftops of the east wing. Considering the ramshackle status of most of the castle, my guess was that the renovations weren't going well.

The glass under my fingertips shook at the loud bang of more thunder.

Hazel returned her attention to the map and took charge, which was probably for the best because someone needed to do something. "That caretaker guy said that our stuff is in the music room. Maybe that would be a good place to shoot scene three. We should choose bedrooms and get settled and then see if we can get something on film."

So we were going upstairs. To. The. Bedrooms.

So I had something else to freak out about.

Hazel picked up her carry-on and mumbled that she'd come back for the rest. The rest of us grabbed our bags and made our way to the right, to the wide, rounded wooden door opposite the way we came in.

The door creaked and released a plume of musty air as it slowly crept open.

We found ourselves in a long hallway in the same style as the sitting room.

Hazel had the map in her hand. We formed a small cluster and trailed behind her up the hallway. Like in the rest of the rooms, we found more expensive black marble. More crystal chandeliers. More dark walls with paintings that probably belonged in a museum. Or were stolen from one. Everything was gilded and had the vague aroma of expensive cigars.

As Raul had said, the hallway led to a massive carpeted staircase. I didn't know what it was like back in the days of Bram Stoker, but now it basically looked like a walkway to the Russian Tea Room. The intricately carved wood banisters had more of the angels and demons from the sitting room fireplace. The blood-red rug had a mesmerizing pattern of small oval medallions.

The hallway ended about ten feet from the stairs at another one of the heavy doors.

Jax trotted ahead and tugged on it a few times. The door jiggled but remained firmly shut.

Locked doors will remain locked.

"What's in there?" I asked Kenna.

"No idea," she said with a bored shrug. She was trying a little too hard to give off a vibe that there was nothing odd about being alone in a remote castle where there appeared to be very few ways in. Or out.

"The map just says *Exterior*," Hazel commented.

I glanced over her shoulder at the map. There were four main wings, east, west, north, and south, and the drawing showed several places that looked like they'd be good for filming. A hedge maze dedicated to Vlad Dracul's wife, Justina, would be a particularly good place for Lucy's speech. There was also an enormous courtyard with an old well where we could set up the scene where Lucy would be surrounded by the men in masks.

We came to the staircase. The steps going up to the second floor, where the caretaker said we would find the bedrooms, were well-worn but polished marble and brightly lit by an elaborate chandelier. According to Raul and the map, if we took the steps down, we'd end up in the smoking room. Those stairs twisted downward before disappearing into darkness. A light fixture covered in dust and spiderwebs hung over them and swung slowly.

Hazel started up. The toe of her shoe tapped on the marble as she put her foot on the step.

Jax hustled back to the staircase from where he was still fiddling with the locked door. "Should we check things out down there?"

I shook my head. The truth of it was that we were all exhausted. We'd been traveling for more than twenty-four hours. I was starting to forget the last time I had brushed my teeth.

So we continued up the stairs. Maddie had her phone out.

"Does anyone have a signal?" she asked, searching for the magic spot that supposedly had cell service.

I pulled my phone from my pocket and shook my head.

"Great," she said.

When we arrived on the second floor, immediately to our right was a long room with enormous double doors that were thrown open at odd angles. It was the music room. One of those places where old-timey people listened to each other play the piano. Hazel reached inside and felt along the wall for a light switch. As she flipped a series of switches, more chandeliers and wall sconces began to glow. On one wall, dusty red curtains were drawn over a series of floor-to-ceiling windows. There were cabinets in the corners and stacks of our boxes in the center of the room.

A small statue of Vlad Dracul, a three-foot replica of the headless version in the courtyard, stood guard outside the music room. He clutched a thin silver kilij that was unusually sharp in his stone grip.

"Creepy," Maddie said.

I nodded. "Perfect for scene three."

Jax yawned, and we continued on.

The bedrooms were to the left.

According to the map, the second floor had twelve bedrooms, and almost all of them had been remodeled to include a bathroom, so there wound up being little fighting over who slept where. Jax chose the bedroom closest to the stairs.

I waited for my friends to pass and then hovered in the narrow doorframe. Jax and I really hadn't discussed sleeping arrangements, and I was pretty sure that Mom had shoved another copy of the "Case for Chastity" pamphlet in my suitcase. But what would Maddie and Kenna say if I got my own room? What if Jax didn't really want me in that way?

Jax approached the door and reached for my hand. "You coming in?"

He seemed uncertain too. I took slow steps into the center of the room

A desk faced the room's window, and I could imagine Bram Stoker, or maybe his alter ego, Jonathan Harker, sitting there writing longhand letters. I walked around for a couple of minutes inspecting a series of little wooden tables in the corners that were covered with expensive doodads while Jax tossed our bags on a leather boudoir bench.

My heart fluttered, and I wondered what adults did in this situation. Okay. We'd be spending the week in this room. Should I let Jax see me change my clothes? Would he want to do it right away? The room suddenly was warm and stuffy. I approached the large window and searched for a way to open it.

This window didn't open either.

Outside, the storm clouds were nearly black. Down below, I saw more of the stone terrace, a few more chairs, and what were probably some small citrus trees in pots. The mist covered the railing, creating the impression that the world beyond the castle had vanished.

Returning to the center of the room, I tried to relax.

Everything would be fine. Jax wouldn't let anything happen to me.

He took slow steps in my direction, and as he moved, he slipped his T-shirt over his head, revealing a near perfect set of abs, toned from lacrosse and tanned from all the afternoons by the Flannigans' pool.

My insides jiggled. I managed to come closer. I let my fingertips find his chest and ignored their trembling as I traced the ridges and valleys of his muscles. Jax leaned in closer, his breath warming my ear. He peppered light kisses along my jawline, and his hands fiddled with the frayed hem of my shirt.

Forgetting that I had been in another time zone and on another continent the last time I had a shower, I arched my back up and pressed into him, my hands sinking lower toward the waistband of his sweats.

Jax's tongue lightly brushed my top lip, and he murmured my name.

It was gonna happen. Here, in a castle.

"Oh, Jax," I moaned as his hands traveled up my shirt.

It was so right.

But he froze. His hands fell away from my body.

And I understood why.

A terrible scream echoed up the hall.

And then another. And another.

General Directorate for Criminal Investigations

Pending report—EXHIBIT 22

Rush, Alexandra. *Dead Boys Don't Bite*. Theatrical script.

Revised March 14

Scene 3; page 3

Lucy Westenra [presses the keys of a piano]: I'm the valedictorian, you know. And also Miss Corona Teen. I think my parents are more proud of that second thing. They want me to go to a good college. But not to learn anything. It's so I could meet a boy. Maybe a nice dentist. Or a stockbroker. My dad keeps saying that I need someone to take care of me. So that I can spend all my days in yoga pants. Driving around in my minivan.

Masked Man [whispers]: What's wrong with a minivan?

Lucy Westenra: I suppose you think it's selfish not to want one. This world acts like it's sickness or a weakness for us to want to decide for ourselves what we want.

Masked Man: Maybe what you want is dangerous.

Four days ago

INT. MUSIC ROOM—NIGHT

Jax quickly tugged his shirt back over his head, and together we ran down the hall, following the direction of the screams. My heart pounded as we moved.

We found ourselves in the music room. It was easy to imagine this room full of ornate chairs, Count Dracula occupying one, watching his next victim play the piano. The filmmaker in me marveled at the setup. The grand piano. The carved harp pushed up against the wall, casting an abstract shadow on the wallpaper.

On the wall to my right, long, dust-covered draperies hung over what I assumed were windows overlooking the terrace. Rain pounded against the thick glass.

I almost ran into Maddie, who had set up a makeup station on top of a few of the boxes we'd shipped in. Kenna sat, hunched over, on a small stool, panting and crying. I couldn't get a sense of what was happening. While the music room was creepy, it was also the same as when we had come up the stairs a few minutes earlier. Empty, dusty, and still.

Putting my hand on her back, I helped Kenna sit up straight. Mascara ran down her face. "What's wrong?" I asked her.

She extended her elegant arm. "There. There." She pointed toward one of the corners.

Heavy footsteps sounded in the hall. Carter burst into the

room. "What? What's happening?" he asked. He too was out of breath.

Jax was already headed in the direction that Kenna pointed. Something fluttered behind one of the curtains in the far corner of the room. Jax's feet were quiet on the room's old patterned rug. He quickly yanked the red fabric back, revealing a tall, narrow window that opened to the stormy night outside.

Something small flew in his direction and almost brushed against his face. It squeaked and chirped as Jax flailed his arms all around, trying to get the thing off himself. When he had gotten it away, he took a deep breath.

"It's just a bat," Jax said in a relieved voice.

We all looked up to see the creature, and Kenna screamed again.

Hazel ran into the room. She now wore a pair of green yoga pants and a beige hoodie that looked like they'd been ripped off a mannequin in the window of a Lululemon store. "What? What's happening?" she called out from the doorway.

The bat's little wings flapped as it circled the chandelier a few times before whizzing in the direction of another oversize wood-and-marble fireplace very similar to the one on the first floor. It disappeared into the wide, dark opening, leaving the room quiet again.

"It's probably a vampire bat!" Kenna shrieked.

"No. No. It's not," Jax said. "We're very close to a forest, and these old chimneys probably don't get used a lot. A tree bat just found its way in."

"What's a tree bat?" Hazel asked.

Kenna sobbed while Maddie rolled her eyes.

Carter patted Kenna's back a few times. "Whatever it was, it's gone now."

While the boys tried to calm Kenna down, I approached Maddie. She had changed into a T-shirt dress and wore her makeup apron.

"What are you guys doing?" I asked.

Maddie led me to a box where she'd set up a makeup station. She had a bunch of lip colors and blushes fanned out and organized by tone. She also had the white Dracula masks out. They were polished and in a neat stack.

I wasn't exactly thrilled to see those things again, but we needed them for the scene.

"I thought I'd get Kenna ready for scene three," she said. "Hopefully, we can get something shot before dinner."

This was assuming that Raul would make it back with the cook. Given the storm outside, that seemed optimistic.

She paused to let her green eyes find mine. "I do want to make the movie, Alex. This thing with the money has thrown me. But I love your script. I hope you know that."

I nodded. "Where's Reagan?" He was supposed to be the masked man in the scene.

Carter glanced up from trying to comfort a still-crying Kenna. "He was looking for the one place in the castle with cell service. He should be back in a sec."

Kenna sat up and wiped away her tears. "Good. Hopefully he'll have some information." The color began to return to her face.

"So, do you feel up to shooting something?" I asked. Part of me hoped she would say no, because part of me wanted to go back to my room with Jax.

But Kenna nodded. "We don't know how much time we'll have to film," she said. "I'll be fine. I mean, once Maddie fixes my makeup."

Maddie rolled her eyes again.

"Okay. Let's get set up," I said. It sounded more like a question than a statement. There was something a little undermining about Kenna's attitude. I got the sense that she didn't plan on working on the movie if we didn't figure out what happened to the missing money.

No one moved until Jax said, "Let's do it."

There was yet another reminder of how much I relied on Jax. I was supposed to be the director, but somehow he always ended up in charge.

Hazel got to work unpacking the boxes, and Maddie fixed Kenna's makeup.

I explored the rest of the room to determine the best place to shoot.

Near the fireplace, I found a teeny yet elaborate piano. It was like the twins from *The Shining* should have been sitting there. Two silver candleholders rested on it top. As I came closer, I recognized the candleholders. They had Vyrzhikovsky's maker's mark on their bases. They were Russian and probably sterling silver, with a pear-shaped design and intricately carved leaves climbing up their sides. Unlike the set we had sold at Silver Rush, these were perfectly polished and extremely valuable.

They held two unlit white taper candles that had wax dripping down their sides.

With a sigh, I pressed down on a couple of keys on the tiny piano. They sounded like a music box playing the *Nutcracker* theme.

"It's a Celesta," Carter said, coming my way. "It sounds kind of like a glockenspiel. It goes along pretty well with the nineteenth-century vibe they've got going on around here."

"I like it," I said. "It's weird and creepy."

Carter smiled. "Yeah, I think it would be cool to play the *Dead Boys* theme I wrote on it." He really loved music, and his excitement began to build. "I can record some effects and some music in here and mix it in later with the audio track."

I noticed that Carter didn't ask me what I thought of this plan.

He, instead, wanted approval from Jax.

We agreed that we'd start scene three with Kenna sitting at the Celesta and then have her move around the room holding one of the candlesticks. While Hazel got the lights set up and Carter positioned the audio equipment, I started looking through the gilded gold cabinets that were in the corners of the room. I opened each one carefully, hoping not to find any more bats or other creepy creatures.

Most of the cabinets were full of small instruments and sheet music. But in the last one, the one in the corner near the Celesta, on the center shelf, between a couple of violins, I found stacks of newsprint. They were old, yellowing, and dusty. *Gazeta de Transilvania.* My gaze landed on a date.

1890.

Underneath a headline written in Romanian that I couldn't read, I found a black-and-white photo of the castle. Prahova was in slightly better shape. The grand first-floor entrance appeared to be intact, and the courtyard wasn't filled with roof tiles and piles of fallen stone. The statue of Vlad Dracul still had its head. But it wasn't exactly nice back then either. The trees and plants were overgrown; paint splotches covered the walls. There were gouges in the stone. Menacing dark shadows. Even back then.

In the article underneath the picture, I spotted the name Bram Stoker several times. And I found another term I recognized from the research I did for my script.

Strigoi mort.

Ghost of death.

Vampire.

"This can't be right," I said. We knew Stoker never came to Romania. That he had never been in Prahova. My friends crowded around me. We passed the article and photos around.

Kenna was oddly excited. "Maybe this place really is haunted. Maybe Bram really did travel here. You should take some notes, Alex. We could use this for the movie—"

Not only was this a very weird thing to say. The *way* she said it. Like an actress doing a really bad table read. Like she was thrilled that we were trapped and alone in a haunted castle.

Hazel's face contorted in a mixture of annoyance and confusion. "What are you talking about? This doesn't make any sense. And what does it have to do with the movie?"

Kenna made a frown with her newly redone red lips. "I'm just saying—"

Another clap of thunder cut her off.

Reagan entered the music room just as it fell quiet.

Apparently having forgotten about the newspaper article, Kenna turned the full force of her attention to Reagan. "Well? Did you figure it out?" she said in the same voice that she might use to demand to see the manager.

I tucked the newspaper clipping into the pocket of my jeans.

Reagan returned her annoyed look. "Well, I walked through most of this wing. It's enormous, by the way. And I did find the one spot that seems to get a cell signal. If you take the stairs down, you get to a bunch more bedrooms, like the ones up here. If you go into the room at the very end of the hall and press your body into the corner, and hold your hand high above your head, you can get one bar." When no one immediately said anything, he added, "You're welcome."

Maddie put down a large makeup brush. "But did you find out—"

Reagan bit his lower lip. "I haven't found out anything new. The money was transferred to an account at a web-based bank. Did . . . did anyone give out our username and password?"

The question mainly seemed to be addressed to Kenna.

"No," she said.

"Well. Then. We've been hacked," Reagan said with a grim finality.

I thought for a second. "We never figured out who the donor was in the first place. Maybe whoever it was took the money back."

"That's not what happened," Kenna snapped.

"How do you know?" Carter asked.

"GoFundMe doesn't really work like that," Reagan said.

"We should call the police," Maddie said.

Carter stuffed his hands in the pockets of his jeans. "What police? The Paradise Valley police? What good would that do?"

"We should call our parents," Maddie said.

Reagan shrugged. "I sent a request for help to GoFundMe, and I disputed the transfer. I think that's all we can really do right now."

"We have to do something," Kenna said, wringing her hands. She was in full makeup and a red crushed-velvet dress that Maddie had made for the scene. She looked like she was rehearsing for a goth soap opera.

"What can we do?" I asked her. "It's pouring rain outside. The caretaker still isn't back. There's next to no cell phone service here. We can't leave right now, and it would be hard to contact anyone. Reagan's already done everything we can about the money. Let's at least try to film the scene."

As I spoke, an uneasy feeling settled in the pit of my stomach. I sounded so uncaring. Like I didn't care if she was upset. I wanted to take my words back.

But Jax said, "Alex is right. Let's get a couple of shots in tonight. In the morning, we'll take another vote. If everyone still wants to call our parents, we will."

That settled the matter, and we got back to work. Maddie helped Reagan get dressed in the black cloak and white mask. We were able to run through the scene several times. Something about Kenna's frayed nerves actually improved her performance.

On the fourth take, just as Reagan whispered, "Maybe what you want is dangerous," a series of doors slammed downstairs.

At first, I froze, but cheerful, indistinct chatter traveled up the staircase, and I realized that Raul Stoica must have returned with the housekeeper and the cook. I could tell that we all felt better with adults in the castle.

"I hope we'll get some food soon," Carter said.

"You're always thinking with your stomach," Maddie murmured.

Everyone else hustled down the stairs to see what was going on, but Maddie and I remained in the music room. I helped her put away her makeup kit and clean her brushes.

"What's up with Kenna?" I asked. Both Kenna and Maddie were weirdly interested in what had become of the GoFundMe money. And Kenna was almost thrilled to find out that locals believed there were real vampires hanging around the castle.

"Kenna always takes care of herself." Maddie hesitated before continuing on slowly. "You remember what we talked about before, right? Well. You know what I think? Alex, I think Kenna is a swan."

She left her kit stacked neatly on the box.

Together, we headed toward the wide doors of the music room.

I paused at the small statue of Vlad Dracul. The small kilij it had been holding was gone. "Wasn't that thing holding a sword earlier?" I asked.

Maddie ignored my question. She stopped to look over her shoulder, her gaze lingering on the chandelier for a moment, and she said, "Alex? What if . . . what if the worst monsters are the ones we brought along with us?"

The large music room windows showed a black abyss outside.

I stared out the window for a minute before returning my attention to Maddie's face.

"We're stuck here for tonight," Maddie said. "But in the morning, we need to make decisions. We should try to figure out how to use our phones. To call our parents. Or maybe try to call that rehab place where Catrinel is. I don't think we should be here, Alex."

Maddie stood very close to me.

The little hairs on the back of my neck stood up.

"I don't think we're meant to be here," she said.

General Directorate for Criminal Investigations

Alexandra Elaine Rush—Transcript—Tape 1 [CONT.]

Inspector Skutnik: What do you think Maddie meant by that?

Alex: I . . . [cough] [inaudible] she . . . Maddie was kind of an . . . intuitive person . . . Like she believed in psychics and tarot cards and stuff.

Inspector Skutnik: And Reagan Wozniak? We couldn't find any record of him, or anyone, contacting GoFundMe.

Alex: Well . . . I only know what he told us.

Inspector Skutnik: Do you think he lied?

Alex: I don't know. And at the time, I was more concerned about Kenna.

Inspector Skutnik: But Maddie was very interested in the missing money as well.

Alex: Yeah. And I found out why. And then the storm came.

Three days ago

INT. SECOND-FLOOR HALLWAY—DAY

For the next twelve hours, it seemed like everything would work out fine. Raul had showed up with the housekeeper and cook. They were a mother and daughter team. The mother, Ana-Maria, baked these cheese pastries called branzoaice that made the entire castle smell amazing, while her daughter, Ioana, took on the thankless task of trying to clear the cobwebs off the chandeliers. Over dinner, served in the east wing's formal dining room, we agreed on a plan.

The next day, we'd do some of the filler shots first thing, mostly in the castle and on the terrace. If it continued to rain, we'd *have* to stay inside. If the weather improved, we would try to shoot outside. But the rain meant mud, and mud meant that we had to be careful where we put our equipment. At lunch, we would make a decision about our parents and the GoFundMe.

After dinner, I unpacked my clothes into a lovely gold-trimmed wardrobe. My old, faded stuff looked even worse on the castle's silk hangers than they did at home. And . . . nothing eventful happened between me and Jax either. While I returned from the shower, I found that he had tucked himself under the purple velvet comforter and was snoring softly.

We got going around eight the next morning. Everything went as planned. Even the weather initially cooperated. By ten, we'd had breakfast and gotten some good stuff on film. Mainly shots of Reagan as the Dracula character peering around corners, lingering in the shadows, peeking out from behind the drapes. Stuff we could cut in to heighten tension.

Then things started to go wrong.

We wanted to do a makeup and wardrobe test for scene four.

But we couldn't find Kenna.

She had wandered off while we were all busy dragging our equipment inside from the terrace. More clouds pushed in from the west, and I didn't want our cameras outside if it rained again. I sent Maddie to look for Kenna. After a half an hour, neither of them came back. Finally, I went myself and found Maddie in the hallway that led from the sitting room to the kitchen with her ear pressed to the door.

"What—" I started to say. Before I could get the rest of my words out, Maddie waved her hands to silence me.

She was wearing a short, white silk dress, and she had her long, dark hair hung up in a curled ponytail. Her appearance was oddly elegant.

Inside the kitchen, an argument was in progress.

Between Kenna . . . and Raul Stoica.

"No. No," Kenna said. "You can't do this."

"Miss McKee, what is it that you think I *cannot* do? I will tell you what I *cannot* do. I cannot make them stay if they wish to go. And they wish to go," Raul answered.

The slamming of a door immediately followed this statement. Footsteps approached us, and Maddie jumped back to get out of the way as the kitchen door swung open. Kenna was rubbing her tearstained face.

"What was that all about?" I asked.

Kenna tried to appear calm. She was still dressed in her

costume. "Ana-Maria and Ioana have to go back to town. Raul is driving them there now."

I frowned. Was she casually revealing that we were going to be alone again in the castle? "Back to town? Why?"

"Um . . ." Kenna stammered. "Um. I showed them that article. They . . . ah . . . they think the castle is haunted."

That article was still in the pocket of my jeans from yesterday. She was obviously lying.

"Um . . . what?" I asked.

"Why would you do that, Kenna?" Maddie demanded.

Before Kenna could answer, a new set of footsteps sounded on the tile. A second later, Hazel was in the hallway with us. "Alex," she said. "The boys are downstairs in the smoking room. They think that's a good place to shoot for now. Maybe you want to—"

"I'll go check it out," Kenna said before any of the rest of us could respond.

Hazel and I were about to follow when Maddie stepped in front of us. "We need to talk. And there's something you need to see." She motioned for us to follow her to the sitting room, where the huge windows were filled with almost-black storm clouds moving in at a fast clip.

Her ponytail swung from side to side as she moved. "Look at that storm. I don't think that Raul guy plans on coming back," she said.

I stared out the window. "Well. The storm is coming in really fast—"

"I know it's coming in fast, Alex," she snapped. "Raul knew

that too! He knows what the weather is like out there way better than we do. He went out there knowing full well that it would be difficult, maybe even impossible, to get back today. You didn't hear what he was telling Kenna when they were in the kitchen."

No, I did not.

Maddie picked at a loose silk thread on her sleeve and gave me an impatient sigh. "He was telling her all kind of things. Like what to do if the power goes out. Or water floods the terrace. Or if we need to build a fire in one of the fireplaces. Not only is telling Kenna stuff like that totally useless, but it was pretty obvious that he wanted to get away from here."

Suddenly I did too.

But also.

If Raul was gone and a storm was coming, then . . .

"What do you think we should do?" Hazel asked, wrapping her arms around herself.

Maddie's anger deflated. She grabbed the sleeve of my sweater and pulled me into the hall. "Come on. You have to see this."

Hazel and I exchanged a tense look, but we both followed her. She flipped the switch to turn the staircase lights on and marched up the second floor. We passed my room first, and since it was so near the stairs, I hadn't really been down this hallway. It seemed impossibly long and was dimly lit by an occasional crystal light fixture hanging from the tin ceiling or a few wall sconces that probably once held candles but had been modified to contain lightbulbs. More of the expensive tile was covered by an odd assortment of expensive rugs.

Maddie pulled on the next door we passed, but it remained

shut. "There are a bunch of locked doors up here too." Some of the doors had elaborate but tarnished brass knockers, and others had what looked like peepholes. She stopped in front of a small painting hanging on the dark paneled wall. She pulled her cell phone from her dress pocket and used it as a flashlight to cast a beam across the image of a young boy with dark brown hair. "Do you have any idea what this is? Do you even know?"

I shook my head and looked at Hazel, who also had a bewildered expression on her face.

Maddie didn't even wait for us to respond.

"It's the lost Raphael. I'd bet money on it," she said.

I could see the time on her phone screen. It was a little before noon. It was getting late and I didn't know who Raphael was and I had no idea that he was lost. "Okay. But so what?"

Maddie approached the painting, reaching out, almost letting her fingers graze the oil, regarding it with reverence. "So *what*? This is one of the most famous paintings on the planet. It was stolen by the Nazis. No one has seen it since World War II. It's worth a fortune."

The three of us stared at the innocent face in the frame. His opulent furs and floppy hat.

"It could be a copy," Hazel suggested.

"It could be." She pulled on my arm again. "But . . . there's something else."

We kept walking, past more doors.

"This is our room," Maddie commented, pointing to a large door on our right. "But this is what I want to show you." The hallway ended at a wall constructed from sharp, primitive gray stone. She pointed her phone's light at the ceiling. A bunch of cables erupted from a few small holes in the stone wall before quickly being tucked into one of the ceiling tiles.

Hazel sucked in a deep breath and ran her palms on yet another pair of yoga pants. "Somewhere in this place must have cable TV. Or internet access."

I brushed my fingers across the rough rocks. "Maybe," I said, not really wanting to think about what it would mean if Raul had lied.

In the other corner, a glass case contained a headless mannequin in an old black cloak that was very similar to the one shown on the Vlad Dracul statue outside.

Hazel had the map. She had ripped it out of the folio and folded it up and put it in her pocket. She unfolded it and held it out for us to see. "There's nothing beyond the wall. This stone looks like it's hundreds of years old." She pointed to a spot on the paper. "The courtyard should be on the other side. But if so, where do these cables go?"

I fought the urge to cough as I waited for an answer.

Maddie just stared at me. She turned off her phone light.

"What do we do?" I asked once again.

"I don't know," Maddie said. Her shoulders slumped. "Alex, there's something . . . bad . . . going on here. Wikipedia says that this place has been under construction for years, but look how run-down most of it is. There's millions of dollars in art in here. Raul Stoica took off, and he probably isn't coming back. There are locked doors. Hallways that go nowhere. Something's not right."

It was Hazel who answered. Her face had gone as gray as the stone of the castle walls. "We . . . we need to get out of here," she said. "I should have said something before. Back at the airport. But . . . I just . . . I just . . ."

"What?" I asked.

Hazel rounded her lips into a distressed pucker. "You remember when Ms. Weiland was trying to sell that script about a Russian crime family?" She snapped her fingers. "She kept pitching it as a Tony Soprano and Vladimir Putin buddy movie? Like *John Wick* meets *Pineapple Express*? And she offered extra credit to anyone who'd watch true crime shows and hand in watch reports?"

Maddie and I both nodded. Hazel was probably the only one who did it.

Hazel was having trouble breathing. "Well, I had a C in Screenwriting, so . . . Anyway, I watched, like, four documentaries that were about the international manhunt for this Romanian gangster named Yuri Stoica. He . . . he ran some kind of drug cartel. Interpol thinks he personally killed, like, forty people. There were all kinds of law enforcement agencies trying to track his movements. He supposedly died in a car accident."

Maddie stood very still.

"And I think . . . I think . . . that the reason there's so much stolen art in here . . . and the reason that the castle is decorated the way that it is . . . and . . ." Hazel stammered.

I understood what she was getting at. My blood ran cold. "This castle used to belong to him. And the construction. It's fake. It's really a way of keeping tourists out of here."

Hazel avoided looking right at me. "The caretaker must be related to Yuri Stoica in some way. Maybe his son?"

"He's gonna kill us! We need to get out of here," Maddie said in a high-pitched voice.

"We don't know that Raul is a killer just because his father was. But. We have to call our parents," Hazel said.

I wanted to remain calm. "I don't think Catrinel Bloom would send us to some drug dealer's lair," I said.

"*I think* Catrinel Bloom has got some bats in the belfry," Maddie snapped.

We walked back to the staircase. The chandelier was dull and dark even though I knew we'd turned the lights on when we came up the stairs.

I started to say something, but Hazel had somehow managed to get her brain back in organizing mode. "The first thing we need to do is to tell everyone else what's going on," she said. "I'll go downstairs and get them. Let's all meet in the sitting room."

Maddie nodded, and we went in that direction. Once we were alone in the sitting room, the first thing she did was turn the record player on. The album that Carter had left playing stuttered and scratched, and then jazz overtook the silence.

"There's something else," I said, coming to stand in front of the window, much in the same way I had right after we arrived. I wasn't quite sure why I waited for Hazel to leave before mentioning Kenna's lies. But I needed someone to know. "Kenna lied back there. That newspaper article we found last night? It's still upstairs in my room. She didn't show it to anyone. I don't know why the cook left, but it's not because this place is haunted."

Maddie joined me by the window. She was an oddly glamorous figure. Tall. Statuesque. When she came closer to me, I caught a whiff of some expensive spray that smelled like sea salt and honeysuckles.

"Kenna is a liar, Alex," Maddie said in a hard voice. "You heard her in the kitchen with Raul Stoica. She's probably going to say that I stole our money."

I suddenly felt exhausted. "Why would she say that?"

Thunder cracked and rain poured down and beat against the glass.

I turned around to face Maddie.

She flopped down onto the sofa, leaving me alone at the window. She spoke slowly and used the same words as she had when we were back in my room. "You remember when I told everyone that I was visiting my grandparents in Wisconsin over Christmas?"

This was what she had been trying to tell me that afternoon in my room when Catrinel Bloom showed up. I nodded and waited for Maddie to go on.

She bit her lower lip. "You know my grandparents own this resort on Birchwood Lake. Well, my dad was supposed to be helping them manage their accounting. But my dad is an artist, and what does he know . . . and the gallery is doing bad. My dad invested in some art. It isn't selling. While we were in Hayward, it came out that there's money missing. A lot of money. My aunts and uncles are gonna go to the police if we can't replace it. I asked Kenna if we could use the GoFundMe money to help him. And then it went missing. She all but accused me of taking it."

"But you didn't?" I turned back to the window. "Did you?"

Another round of thunder made the glass tremor.

While I waited for her to answer, I scanned the forest land-scape. Huge trees in deep shades of green rocked back and forth under the force of a heavy wind. Off in the distance, the spruce swayed at the tree line where the forest met the river.

Water poured onto the terrace down below.

"Alex, I think Kenna took the money, and tomorrow I need you to help me find it," Maddie said. She was on the verge of tears. "I can't let my dad go to jail. I need that money."

This time *I* didn't answer her. I thought about my own dad. He got cancer. He hadn't done anything wrong. He didn't steal money for art and galleries. And I wasn't asking Maddie to give *me* five hundred grand to help him.

I ran my fingertips over the cool glass. And then.

My gaze landed on something out of place.

An outline of a dark figure in a long cloak.

A man in a mask. A white mask exactly like the ones we used for filming. Rounding the corner of the terrace, heading in the direction of the stairs that led to the kitchen.

Terror whipped through me just like the wind traveled through the twisted tree trunks.

I think someone's out there.

I tried to find my voice to whisper this. Or scream it.

But I blinked. And the man was gone.

General Directorate for Criminal Investigations

Alexandra Elaine Rush—Transcript—Tape 1 [CONT.]

Inspector Skutnik: Maddie didn't answer you?

Alex: No.

Inspector Skutnik: You had no idea why the staff that Raul Stoica had hired really left Prahova?

Alex: No. Not until much later.

Inspector Skutnik: And Hazel believed that Prahova had been the base of operations for Yuri Stoica's criminal activities?

Alex: Yeah. That's what she thought.

Inspector Skutnik: Did you know that Raul was Yuri's son?

Alex: We assumed they were related in some way.

Inspector Skutnik: What did you do then?

Alex: I just prayed that we would make it through the night.

Three days ago

INT. THE MUSIC ROOM—NIGHT

I whirled around. It must have been the shock on my face, but Maddie got right up and joined me at the large windows.

"There's someone down there," I said.

She swiveled her head all around. "Where? I don't see anything."

I tried pointing to the spot where I had seen the masked man, where I had seen the Dracula. But the terrace was empty. I wondered if there had been anyone there at all.

Soon everyone was back in the sitting room. They seemed to buy the idea that the housekeeper and the cook had been chased off by stories of vampires. Maddie didn't mention the masked man, and I didn't say anything about her father and the missing money. We had made a tacit agreement to keep secrets.

Maybe because we were stuck at Castle Prahova for the night.

There was no need to make it worse.

We spent the rest of the afternoon arguing. Roaming around the castle, checking to see if anyone had any cell service. Debating going into the storm. Eating whatever food we could find. Hazel told them all about Yuri Stoica. We took turns staring out the window. Most everyone was on the lookout for Raul. We couldn't decide whether we wanted him to come back.

Or wanted him to stay away.

I was watching for the man in the mask.

We managed to build a fire in the sitting room, and we lingered by the fireplace well into the night. When the fire had died down, when silence fell over all of us, we really had no choice but to go to our rooms upstairs. We went as a group, wearing identical nervous expressions.

The light to the lower staircase was back on again. The old crystal chandelier flickered as we passed.

Maybe I *was* going crazy. Because I'd swear that light was off earlier.

Reagan hesitated at the door to his room with an odd look on his face. We stared at each other until Jax came inside and closed and locked the bedroom door.

I exhaled. We were together, and I knew Jax would keep me safe. And really, nothing had happened. The housekeeper and the cook went back to town. Hazel had a hunch about the castle from some homework assignment. I was under a lot of stress. I was making a *Dracula* movie. So it made sense that I was seeing Dracula when I was scared.

Even though I had no service, I plugged my phone into the charger. The routine felt reassuring.

One thing was for sure. There was nothing romantic about what was going on. Jax fell asleep right away. The guy could sleep anywhere. I lay awake listening to the rain hit the window while he snored softly.

After a while I managed to doze off.

I was awakened to the slow, moaning creak of the wooden floorboards.

Bolting up to a sitting position, I watched in horror as a shadow traveled slowly across the gap between the bedroom door and the floor.

Someone was in the hallway.

I fumbled around on the nightstand next to the bed.

The clock told me that it was a bit after midnight.

I poked Jax a few times, but he just mumbled stuff like "Wuzz-goinon" and "Ten more minutes" and "It's okay, Alex." That, at least, was normal. I once snapped a director's clapboard right in his face when he fell asleep at film camp, and he didn't wake up. I swear, he could sleep through a nuclear bomb. There was no telling how long it would take me to get him up.

"Jax! Jax!" I whispered again.

He rolled over on his side, turning away from me, snoring even louder.

I unplugged my phone from the charger and crept to the door. I unlocked it and opened it slowly, peering out in all directions through a narrow slit.

The hallway was empty.

And the only sound was that of my own heavy breathing.

I took a step into the hall, mainly seeking to reassure myself that no one was out there.

No one was out there. I was alone, the long red rug underneath my feet.

I was about to return to bed.

When.

A beam of light poured into the hall. Coming from the music room.

It was followed by the sharp, metallic tinkles of the Celesta.

I relaxed. Carter was probably in there playing the piano. But I was kind of pissed too. With everything going on, this wasn't exactly the best time to be writing music.

"Carter? Carter?" I called as I walked toward the music room and the staircase at the end of the hall. The chandelier over the staircase landing swung slightly from side to side. The golden yellow light coming from the music room grew brighter and fluttered along with my pulse as I approached. The music continued, sounding more and more like a way-too-loud busted music box. I had to admit, it would be perfect for the film.

I took out my phone to get some footage of Carter playing in case it came in handy later. After pressing record, I moved through the wide double doorway.

The music immediately stopped. Carter had lit the two white taper candles that sat on top of the Celesta. He had stepped back from the instrument and was silhouetted in the corner of the room. "Don't stop playing on my account," I said.

I zoomed in close on the candleholders.

When the white mask filled my phone screen.

I screamed.

A heavy breath blew the candles out, leaving the music room dark and cavernous.

I felt my phone slide out of my sweaty grip. It landed glass side down and slid in the direction of the harp.

I clambered to my knees and crawled toward the door.

A cool, silky cloak brushed my cheek as I moved, and I screamed again.

In a panic, not knowing if I was going toward danger or away from it, I kept scurrying along until I was back in the hall. I almost ran into Kenna. She was coming up the stairs in her fitted knit pajamas. She had her phone out and was using it as a flashlight and carried a bottle of water in her other hand.

Kenna was breathing hard. "What's going on?"

Doors up and down the hallway were opening and closing, everyone else coming into the hall. Reagan darted toward me, wearing only a pair of plaid pajama bottoms. "Alex!" He helped me to my feet. "What the hell . . ." he said.

I broke out in sobs. "I came in here . . . Some of the instruments were . . . making noise. And there was someone in here," I said.

By that time, Jax and Carter were also in the hall.

"Alex saw something," Kenna told them, in an oddly upbeat tone of voice.

Reagan glared at her.

Maddie shook her head to wake herself up. "We're here now, Alex." She put her arm around me.

Jax used his phone to find the music room's overhead lights, and then checked the room. "This candle wax is warm," he said.

Carter made a skeptical face. "But if someone was in here, where did they go?"

I hobbled back into the room and searched the floor until I located my phone. My hands shook and I nearly dropped it again, but I was able to get the video loaded. I played it for them, and everyone gasped when the white mask appeared on the screen.

"But where did he go?" Carter asked again. That time, he sounded terrified.

"Check the windows," I said.

Carter and Jax went around the room opening all the drapes, looking for the man in the mask or some kind of clue or a door through which the Dracula might have escaped. When we were certain that we were alone in the music room, Hazel and the boys returned to the hall to search the other rooms on the second floor.

Kenna, Maddie, and I stood clustered together. I opened my mouth to speak, but I couldn't make sense of things. I couldn't put the tightness in my chest into words.

Maddie stepped back from Kenna. She stared right at me. "We have to get out of here. We have to go. Now."

The storm outside was getting worse, and we were having to talk louder to be heard over the steady beat of the rain and the thunder that pounded with increasing frequency.

We had already discussed that. But Maddie had this expression on her face. Like she was about to run.

"We agreed that it's not safe to go out," I said in alarm. "It's the middle of the night. There's a terrible storm. Our phones don't work. We can't just head out into that murder forest and hope for the best." I tried to steady myself. "Let's get the boys. We'll—"

Another clap of thunder cut me off.

The chandeliers overhead wobbled and then went out.

I took a few deep breaths to remain calm in the darkness.

Kenna's hands clamped around my shoulders. "I'm here."

From the hallway, we could hear what sounded like Reagan crashing into all the furniture and swearing loudly.

"Maddie? Maddie?" I called. I got the sense she wasn't with us anymore.

I was able to get the flashlight on my phone turned on. I shined it every which way, finding only Kenna's face and the otherwise empty music room.

A minute or so later, the overhead lights came on. Somehow, they seemed dimmer than before. But at least we had power again. I turned the light on my phone off.

"Where's Maddie?" I asked Kenna.

The blank look on Kenna's face told me that she didn't know either.

Fast steps pounded down the staircase.

Maddie was freaking out. She'd really lost it.

She was going outside.

In the rain. In her bare feet and pajamas.

Kenna began shouting for Carter. But he didn't answer. I had no choice but to go after my friend. I ran into the hall and took the steps down to the first floor as fast as I could. The rain was coming down even harder, creating noise that echoed all through the hallway. The lights pulsed with more regularity, as if the power was being affected by the storm.

Oh crap.

The downstairs chandelier light was off. I *knew* it was on when we came up.

There was a pool of water near the first-floor landing, and I grabbed on to the carved, twisted bannister to stop myself from being hurled like a pinball down the tile. The first floor had an odd smell, a kind of smoky and woody smell. It was like a distinguished old British guy with a monocle had been pacing the hall with his pipe and left behind the odor of cloves and sulfur and tobacco. My feet pattered on the floor as I tried to get my footing.

I slid off in the wrong direction, toward where the hallway ended at the mysterious locked door. As I collided with the wood, I noticed a shiny silver key jutting from the lock. Jax had spent, like, five minutes messing with that door and wasn't able to get it open. Now it had a key stuck in the lock.

Whoever was screwing with us had a set of keys.

Maddie was at the other end of the hall, heading toward the sitting room, probably intending to leave through the kitchen door.

"Maddie! Maddie!" I called as loud as I could.

A new, dizzy panic threatened to overwhelm me. I fell, and it took me a minute to get back up. When I finally arrived in the kitchen, the wooden door that opened to the terrace and the outside staircase was blown flush against the kitchen wall by the force of the storm. Rain poured into the room, creating a flood in the entryway and a wash over the countertops.

As I approached the door, the force of the wind sent a heavy mist over me. I continued to call for Maddie. What the hell was she doing? Why was she doing it?

I reached for the door handle to steady myself.

My palm landed on something warm and sticky. When I pulled my hand back, my fingers ran with blood.

Blood. Smelling of copper and salt. On my sweaty palm. Underneath my fingernails. Before I could do anything or even open my mouth to scream, the lights flickered one last time. And then they went out.

This time they stayed off.

Leaving me alone in the kitchen.

In darkness.

General Directorate for Criminal Investigations

Alexandra Elaine Rush—Transcript—Tape 1 [CONT.]

Inspector Skutnik: You believed that to be Maddie's blood? And you decided to go out after her.

Alex: That's what we thought. And yes. We had to find Maddie. We had to . . . go . . . out there . . .

Inspector Skutnik: Should we take a break, Alex?

Alex: [inaudible] . . . water . . . [cross talk] . . . I'm . . . I'm . . .

Inspector Skutnik: Are you okay? [noise] [inaudible]

Alex: [coughs] . . . yeah . . . yes . . .

Inspector Skutnik: At that point, did Kenna tell you what she knew? What she had been doing?

Alex: No, that was later. Much later. I'm not even sure what day that was. When we found out that . . . that . . . well . . . Right then we were focused on finding Maddie. And we did. We found her. I mean, we found her body.

Two days ago

EXT. THE TERRACE—NIGHT

Maddie was gone.

I fell to the floor.

Frantically wiping my sticky hand on my sweatpants.

The blood.

It was like it didn't come off. Like a permanent stain. A scarlet glove I would wear forever. And the metallic aroma filled the kitchen, overpowering the musty, mildewed air. The copper pots on the rack swayed and knocked into each other, creating a horrible racket. Demonic wind chimes filling the castle with unwanted music.

Through the kitchen window, menacing lightning electrified the clouds.

Rainwater pelted the tile floor.

"Maddie! Maddie!" I screamed again.

It felt like I was down there forever. By myself. Trying to make sense of what was happening. All I wanted to do was to get into film school. To make my movie. And I was in a remote castle, being hunted by some maniac, and my friend had run out into the night.

"Maddie!" I screamed again.

So loud that the window glass shook and my throat became scratchy.

I checked my phone in the silly hope that I would happen to

have service. Then I took a series of deep breaths and made myself crawl through the muddy puddles that covered the tile floor and over to the cabinet where I had seen the supplies earlier. My hands and arms trembled as I fumbled around in the small amount of light coming from my screen. After a minute or so I had found two flashlights and turned them on. This worked way better than my phone, and the first thing I did was use the beams of light to scan the kitchen.

Maddie wasn't there.

Like, I knew that she wasn't in there.

But I was stupidly hoping she would be.

The door was still open and I was alone.

I snatched up the first aid kit, grabbed a box of red disposable rain ponchos, and closed the cabinet door. I heard everyone else in the sitting room. Indistinct sounds. Friends calling out to each other. Walking into furniture. A low rumble of conversation that I couldn't quite make out. I thought about trying to get to the sink to get rid of the blood crusting on my hand. But it was so dark and the kitchen so unfamiliar that I didn't want to risk it.

Finally, Jax was in the hall, calling my name, his footsteps coming slowly closer. The occasional grunt when he hit the wall in the darkness. The door between the kitchen and the hall creaked open. I pointed one of the flashlights in that direction and waited.

Jax entered the kitchen, shielding his eyes from the light. "You found the flashlights, I see," he said, in a light tone meant to conceal the terror I knew we were all feeling. "My phone battery is almost dead. I haven't been able to charge it since we left home."

"Door . . . blood . . . Maddie . . ." I panted out.

He rushed over and kneeled alongside me. "Alex! Are you all right? Did you get hurt?" Feeling around on my bloody pajamas, he checked for wounds.

Jax took one of the flashlights from my lap and waved it all over, turning his head in every direction. Looking for the man in the mask.

"Maddie went . . . out," I told him.

He kept a firm, warm hand on my elbow as he helped me to my feet.

I could feel the air return to my lungs and some of the numbness leave my limbs. "I'm not hurt. When I came in, the door was open. I went to shut it, and the knob had blood all over it." For a second, I was grateful that it was too dark to make out the expression on Jax's face. It would have been too much to find that he was as scared as I was.

"We have to go after Maddie!" I told him.

"We will, Alex," he said, patting my back tenderly, "but we need to figure out the best way to do it. It's not going to help Maddie for us all to get lost in that storm."

I knew he was right.

Jax took some bottles of water from the fridge, and together we returned to the sitting room. The flashlights revealed our friends bumbling around, stubbing their toes on furniture and knocking the expensive artwork off the wall.

"Good. You found the flashlights," Reagan said. He was trying to start a fire in the opulent, massive fireplace that took up most of the wall near the door. He'd found more newsprint and matches.

"We can build a fire later!" I said. "We need to find Maddie. She's missing."

Reagan froze and turned to me. I saw his stricken face in the beam of my flashlight.

"What do you mean 'missing'?" Carter demanded.

"I mean she just freaked! Really fucking freaked out. By the thing with the masked guy being upstairs and . . . the gangster and . . . I think . . . I think . . ."

"Are you sure she went outside?" Carter asked. "Maybe she's downstairs. This wing is huge, and we haven't explored the whole thing yet."

I bit my lower lip. "The kitchen door was open, and there was blood on the knob."

"Oh my God," Carter moaned. "We have to find her. We have to—" He got up and tried to take the flashlight from Jax.

"We don't know if that's her blood," Kenna said. "It could be from anything . . ."

"From anything?" Reagan repeated in disbelief. "Kenna. What the hell are you talking about? How could the blood be *from anything*?"

"Whose blood do you think it is?" Carter screeched. "Jax. For fuck's sake, give me the fucking flashlight."

"No. No. We're not running around from room to room acting like tokens from a Clue board game that have come to life. We need to calm down." Jax held the flashlight away from Carter's reach and spoke in his Fred Flannigan voice.

Carter grunted in frustration. "Fine! I'll use my phone." He tried to step around Jax to get to the door.

"No. No," Jax said, blocking Carter with a maneuver he probably learned during lacrosse practice. "We need a plan. We need to build a fire and we need to get dressed. If we just run out there the way we are, we'll all get hurt. We probably won't find her."

"This room has huge windows. You can probably see them from the terrace. It'll make it easier to get back," Hazel agreed. "We're going to get Maddie back." She sounded like she was trying to convince herself.

Kenna sat on one of the armchairs, hugging her knees, saying nothing.

We worked as fast as we could to get the sitting room set up. I dropped the first aid kit on one of the end tables and joined Hazel in the corner, where we found another one of the delicate cabinets made of intricate gold filigree. It reflected the flashlight back at us and almost seemed to glow. I found a small handle in the center of the cabinet door and gave it a tug. There were jars of long matches as well as a number of crystal ashtrays and a couple of cigars. The bottom shelves were filled with partially used candles, creating the impression that the power in here went out frequently.

This was not reassuring.

They were also the same kind of candles and holders as the ones upstairs. The silver candleholders were part of a matched set. The masked man, the Dracula, might have been down here too.

We placed candles on the tables throughout the room. When we were done, the room had an almost cheerful gold glow, and the smell of juniper and saffron drifted across the wide space. Reagan had managed to build a tiny fire that was sending plumes of smoke into the sitting room.

"Nice work, Jeeves," Jax said, coughing and waving his arms at the smoke.

Hazel put tons of candles on the coffee table.

It looked like an altar.

"We just need to make the fire bigger," Reagan snapped. "When your fire's not burning hot enough, it doesn't push the smoke up the chimney."

"Who cares?" Carter demanded. He paced around on the rug. "It's plenty light in here. We're not trying to roast weenies and make s'mores. I need to find Maddie. Let's get on with it."

"He's right," Kenna said, still looming in the corner like a ghost in the shadows. It was hard not to notice that she hadn't done anything to help us.

After that, we hustled upstairs. We went room by room so that no one would be alone. In our bathroom, I scrubbed off the blood on my hand as quickly as I could. When we all had on pants, sweatshirts, and decent walking shoes, we returned to the sitting room, huddling together near the fireplace.

Hazel held her hands in front of the fire to warm them. "Let's put together some kind of a plan." She was right in her element. She probably wanted to make a spreadsheet. "We should form two teams. One group can search this wing." Carter started to object, but Hazel shook her head and kept going. "Yes, she's probably outside. But it makes sense to be methodical about the search. There are rooms we haven't even been in. The second team can go outside and search the terrace. That team should take the ponchos and the first aid kit."

"Okay, me and Carter will search outside," Jax said, leaning over and stoking the fire with a silver poker. "Um . . . Reagan and Hazel can check this wing. Alex and Kenna should wait here in case Maddie comes back."

"Why do I have to stay here?" I asked. Maddie kept trying to tell me that she was scared as hell, and I didn't do anything. I owed it to my friend to go out and look.

"I'd *prefer* to stay here with Alex," Reagan said.

"Real nice," Carter said, red-faced and puffing from his frantic pacing.

"I'm sorry," Reagan told him. "But it's not my fault *your* girlfriend ran off."

Carter froze mid-step. "I still don't understand what's happening. Alex, are you sure she didn't say anything else? Anything at all?"

I choked out a sob. "No. No. I told you. She just said that we need to get out of here and then she ran out into the storm. Why would she do this? Maddie's usually so calm." My hands shook as I spoke. "How could she . . . Why would she . . . And the rain. She went . . . *out there*! She's gone! Maddie's gone. Why would she do this?"

"I don't know, Alex," Jax answered helplessly.

"It's like a plot point in a B-movie," Reagan mumbled.

Carter clenched his fists. "Shut the hell up, Wozniak."

Hazel breezed by me where I remained near the cabinet and moved to stand by the door. "We're wasting valuable time."

We were all quiet for a minute. The flames in the fireplace rose and crackled and popped.

None of us really wanted to go outside.

Jax cleared his throat. "Which brings us right back to Hazel's plan. No more arguing. Alex, you can go with me. We'll go out-side. Carter and Hazel will do the inside. Reagan, you can stay here with Kenna."

"Does everyone have their phone?" Hazel asked.

"Hazel! Our fucking phones don't work. If they did, we could call Maddie. And fuck you, Jax, I'm going outside," Carter said. He was almost shrieking. He was losing it too.

Hazel somehow managed to stay calm. "It's for the light. And the clock. We need to set a time limit so we're not wandering around all night."

Jax nodded and turned to Carter. "We're not helping Maddie by standing around here arguing. We have our plan." He pulled his phone from his pocket and checked it. "Okay, it's 1:14 a.m. Everyone be back here in one hour." He glanced at Reagan. "You stay here. Don't leave this room."

"Yes, sir," Reagan said. He flopped down on the sofa.

Kenna was back in the armchair, picking at the hem of her sweatshirt. She said nothing and stared at the fire. Her expression was somehow confused, as if she'd been asked to solve a really difficult math problem.

Jax gave his flashlight to Hazel, and I picked up the plastic ponchos from the coffee table.

Hazel grabbed Carter's arm. "Come on," she said, giving him a tug.

"Be careful," I said as the two of them left the sitting room.

"You too," Hazel said. She had the map out again and had pointed the flashlight at it. They vanished into the hall, their con-versation and footsteps trailing off behind them. The last thing we heard was Hazel's detailed plan for searching the east wing, floor by floor, starting on the lower level with the smoking room and bathhouse.

"Okay, back to the kitchen," Jax said when it was silent again.

I tucked the flashlight under my chin and pulled a plastic poncho over my head. When Jax had his poncho on too, I turned the flashlight back on again, and we left Reagan alone with Kenna by the roaring fire. He gave me a weak smile. Kenna didn't even look up.

We returned to the hall, saying nothing as we walked down the long, dark space lit by an impossibly thin beam. Even though I had the flashlight, Jax darted out in front, like he wanted to prove that he was the most interested in finding Maddie. Most of the kitchen floor was soaked with rainwater, and we had to move slowly.

Jax took the flashlight from me and examined the doorknob, running the light over the blood that the storm hadn't washed off. "Something's not right."

The exact same words Maddie had said the last time I saw her.

"What do you mean?" I asked.

He pointed to the knob, which I could see was completely covered in deep crimson. "The blood is on the inside of the door."

"So Maddie was bleeding, then she opened the door and went outside?" I didn't really see what Jax was getting at. That some maniac had gotten to Maddie before she went outside?

Jax shook his head. "That would mean that she was injured *inside* the kitchen. But look at how much blood is here. What kind of injury would have produced this? And see how all the blood is only on the door? If Maddie was hurt in here, there should be a terrible mess everywhere. A trail everywhere she went."

He handed the flashlight back to me.

I almost dropped it. "You're saying that . . . that someone put this blood here deliberately?" What he said made a great deal of sense. I hadn't considered it before, but if somebody was really hurt, you'd expect there to be more of . . . well . . . a mess.

"Who would do that? And why?" Jax asked, putting a light, reassuring hand on my back.

Someone was trying to scare the hell out of us.

For a second, I kind of hoped maybe Maddie was playing some kind of an elaborate prank on us. That we would find her on the opposite side of the door. That we would be pissed at first and then reluctantly laugh later on.

We pushed the door open, letting rainwater flood the kitchen entryway again.

No one was on the other side.

No one I could see anyway.

The visibility was awful. Fog billowed around us like a black flag. I had the flashlight, but it provided an unhelpful pinprick of light.

We stood there for a second in the doorway.

Afraid to go out. Into the storm.

Into the night.

Jax was the first to go. Then me. Rain drenched my face. My legs and shoes were soaked the instant I set foot on the landing outside the kitchen. My flashlight was useless against the thick fog. We had to go left to get to the terrace, but if we walked too far forward we would have fallen down the sharp stone steps that led to the courtyard. Searching for Maddie in this weather seemed foolish.

And pointless. Realistically, how could we find anything in these conditions?

"Take my hand," Jax yelled over the heavy rainfall.

I let him draw me toward the terrace, trusting his judgment more than mine. We took slow but steady steps to the left, calling "Maddie!" every few seconds. Tucking the flashlight under my arm and holding on tight to Jax with one hand, I put my other arm out in front of me to guide myself. When we'd taken around fifteen or twenty steps, my fingertips grazed the rough masonry of the waist-height wall at the edge of the terrace. Jax squeezed my palm. He was thinking the same thing as I was.

"Let's follow this wall," he yelled. "It should guide us around the entire terrace."

My teeth chattered and I got a mouthful of rainwater as I called back, "Oh-oh-kay."

With slow, tiny steps, we continued forward. I pointed the flashlight at the ground in the hopes that it would keep us from tripping.

By the time we passed under what must have been the sitting room window, where only the tiniest glow of light from the candles and fire penetrated the darkness, a weight settled into my chest as I realized that we were unlikely to find anyone or anything out here.

Jax shouted into my ear. "This isn't helping. We're going to be lucky to keep track of each other in this weather."

I hated to admit that he was right. "Five more minutes," I yelled back.

We went on, arriving at the north edge of the terrace. I almost stumbled down a narrow flight of cobblestone stairs. I realized with a new jolt of terror that it was an alternate way of entering the castle from the forest. There were probably all kinds of ways around that we didn't know about. Ways to get in. Ways to get out.

"Maddie!" I called with even more urgency.

Being out in the storm felt like swimming on land. Rain soaked every inch of me not covered by the poncho. In the fog, I couldn't see more than a foot in front of me.

Something, a phantom, a streak of darkness, tore by us.

The figure knocked Jax into me. I wanted to believe it might be Maddie, so I called her name again. I wanted to believe that it was anyone other than a drug lord or a strange man in a Dracula mask. Jax was forced to release my hand, and he gave a yelp as he fell down the first few steps of the cobblestone staircase. It was so dark that I could no longer see him. The only sound I could hear was the water beating against the plastic of my poncho.

"Jax! Jax!" I yelled into the wind again and again. "Jax! Maddie?"

I stood out there in the rain. Alone. Calling into the darkness. For what felt like an eternity.

But I knew that I had to go down to the bottom of the stairs.

I had to go. To find Jax. To help. To do something. But I stood there. Like a coward. Or a frightened animal. Digging my fingers into the staircase's stone railing. Wishing the storm would wash me away or the clouds would scoop me up or the lightning would flash again and I would bolt upright and find myself at home in my own bed. That I would discover this night was nothing more than a nightmare that belonged in Bram Stoker's world.

Not in mine.

A scream sounded from somewhere down the staircase.

A horrible, haunting shriek. The kind of thing you hear and know immediately that you will never, ever be able to forget.

You have to go down there.

That's what I told myself. Jax was down there.

I made myself take the steps quickly. I slipped and slid all over, falling down hard on one of the steps near the bottom, my elbows throbbing and back aching. I wanted to cry, but how could I when the rainwater continued to cover my face? I had managed to hang on to the flashlight, and I sat there in a small bubble of light. The rest of the world was a dark blur of fog and rain and forest and clouds. There I was. Trying to breathe. Trying to stay alive.

A hand reached out of the mist and grabbed my ankle.

I screamed.

Again and again.

A figure scrambled toward me.

It was Jax. And he seemed all right. Physically okay, anyway.

He fell onto the stair next to me and wrapped me in his arms.

"Alex!" he panted. "It's okay. It's okay."

I pointed the flashlight at his face. It was covered with scrapes, and the area underneath his eye was red. He'd have quite a shiner later. Jax was hurt. It was *not* okay.

And there was something else. Something in his eyes.

He had found something.

I pushed myself to a standing position even as Jax tried to keep holding me. "Don't. No. Don't go down there," he said, speaking right into my ear. "Remember her the way she was. Don't look. Don't go."

Maddie. I had to see her.

She was my friend.

I stumbled down the last two stairs. My feet sank several inches into the muddy earth.

I slogged along, keeping the flashlight toward the ground.

I kneeled down and came closer. I continued to sink into the earth, and my lungs barely worked as cold panic again threatened to overcome me. I felt around in the mud until my fingers found skin. I made myself scan her body with the flashlight. She was crumpled up like an old discarded doll. Red scuffs and scrapes ran all up and down her forearms. But even in death, her limbs curved and arched with an artful elegance.

When I came to her face.

Green eyes. Wide open and bulging.

Skin the color of blueberries. Her lush lips frozen mid-scream.

And, oh God.

Cherry-red blood oozed from a wound on her head.

I screamed again.

General Directorate for Criminal Investigations

Alexandra Elaine Rush—Transcript—Tape 2

Inspector Skutnik: At that point, you didn't know who killed Maddie? You thought it was, perhaps, an accident?

Alex: Reagan said that he thought Raul did it.

Inspector Skutnik: You returned to the castle? You found [papers shuffling] . . . Ah . . . yes . . . I see here [inaudible] . . . you found [inaudible]? The flight manifests, printouts of . . . [inaudible] . . .

Alex: Um. Yes. And that's not all we found.

Two days ago

INT. BATHHOUSE—NIGHT

I felt Jax drag me away from Maddie's body and toward the stairs while my feet continued to sink in the mud. "Jax! We can't leave her. We can't . . ."

"Alex!" he yelled over the rain. "We'll be lucky to make it to the castle ourselves. There's no way we could carry . . ." *Maddie.* He couldn't bring himself to say her name. "We'll come back as soon as the storm lets up." Jax gave my arm another hard yank. "I promise!"

I didn't want to stay in the muddy clearing, but I didn't want to go either. There was something unspeakable about leaving our friend out there in a pool of murky rainwater and her own blood. But Jax was right. I could barely force my stiff, numb legs onto the stone steps, and my hands wouldn't stop shaking. It was still impossible to see more than a couple of feet ahead due to the fog. We'd never make it to the castle with Maddie's body.

And even if we could, then what?

As I willed myself up the stairs, between my shaking and all the water, I could no longer keep my grip on Jax's hand. Like that, he was gone again, enveloped in fog and mist. We were separated for what seemed like hours. I was so alone. Absolutely alone. Screaming Jax's name.

"Alex!" he said, emerging from the stairs with the desperate air of someone who had fought off a monster. "It's okay. When I was climbing back up . . . I think I . . . hit my head on one of the steps . . . I . . ."

I'm not even sure how we got back to the castle. Jax was disoriented, and we hobbled along together. When we finally arrived at the kitchen door, my plastic poncho was ripped to shreds and my jeans were soaked and my arms were covered with scrapes and bruises and cuts. Jax gave me a final shove into the castle interior before stumbling inside and collapsing onto one of the marble countertops.

"Oh . . . God . . ." he panted. "We made it. Now . . . we . . . we . . . have . . . to . . ."

We had to find everyone else. Find them and . . .

Tell them.

Maddie was dead.

I wanted to scream.

The sound of the water dripping off our clothes filled the kitchen.

There were no rumblings of conversation. No arguments. No pacing or footsteps on the tile flooring. It was deathly quiet. Perhaps we were the first to return. Even if we were, I would have expected Reagan and Kenna to be talking in the sitting room.

I pulled my phone from my pocket. My wet screen read 2:43 a.m. We were back late. Almost thirty minutes late.

Jax once again took my hand, and we walked through the doors that led to the hall and to the sitting room. I took deep breaths as we walked. Clutched my flashlight tightly. Tried to imagine myself saying the words out loud. Something happened to Maddie.

Maddie is dead.

Probably killed by some criminal overlord.

We found the sitting room much as we left it. An almost cheer-ful fire sizzled and popped. The candles Hazel and I had lit still cast a warm, yellowish glow across the opulent red Russian fur-nishings. The air was heavy with wax and juniper. Someone had put on another record. Probably Louis Armstrong crooning and puffing on his trumpet.

And the room was . . . empty.

"Where's Reagan?" I choked out, turning to find Jax's shocked face.

"Where's Kenna?" he asked. He stared at the armchair where she had been sitting staring out into space when we left to search for Maddie. Jax kept staring. Like if he watched the spot long enough, Kenna would appear there.

The two of us naturally gravitated toward the fireplace. We were wet and freezing and scared all to hell. Jax had a long gash on one of his cheeks, and he looked like he'd soon have a black eye. There was a large wet spot on the area rug right in front of the fire.

Jax kicked at the soggy part of the carpet. "Someone's been in here."

We had *all* been in the sitting room, and Kenna and Reagan were supposed to still be there. But I understood what he meant. Someone else had come in and been wet and had the same idea we had. To get warm in front of the fire.

I watched the flames rise. "Jax, you have to listen to me. I'm re-ally scared. Earlier, Maddie all but told me that she thought Kenna had stolen the GoFundMe money. We heard Kenna arguing with

Raul before he took off. And then Hazel said all that stuff about Yuri Stoica. And then that guy started showing up in the Dracula mask. And Maddie is dead."

"Um. Yeah. I know," Jax said. That wasn't the reaction I expected. I had basically just told Jax that the son of a psycho gang lord had pushed him down a flight of stairs where he landed on Maddie's dead body.

"Someone is after us!" I said. "We need to do something."

But my boyfriend was distracted. He was fiddling with a piece of paper caught in one of the fireplace's carved, twisted wooden curls. "Oh God."

I guess that was becoming his catchphrase.

"What?" The spot on the wall above the fireplace was bare and looked off. Like something belonged there.

"Check this out!" Jax said with an accent of mortification.

He handed me a crumpled-up piece of printer paper.

It was a boarding pass.

"So?" I said with a shrug. Printing out your boarding pass was pretty unnecessary and retro, but it was the sort of thing that Hazel would do in her quest to maintain a million levels of organization and preparedness. Maddie was dead. We were being hunted. Who cared that Hazel was totally anal? I tried to give him back the paper.

Jax put a hand on the mantel to brace himself. "Look at the date!"

I leaned closer to the fire and held the paper to my face. "Oh God." I was saying it too. The pass was dated three days ago. It was a different airline and for a flight that landed at least two days before we arrived in Romania. The part at the top, where the name should have been printed, was soaked in water and illegible. Someone else had come to Prahova and had gotten there before we arrived. I thought about my mom. How she thought maybe someone had made that enormous donation to our fundraiser to lure us here.

Lure us here to hunt us.

The piece of paper slipped through my fingers and sailed downward. Jax had to jump forward and snatch it out of the air to prevent it from being burned. He stuffed it into his pocket. His mouth hung open, no words coming out. He leaned against the mantel again.

My gaze traveled across his profile and to the wall behind him. The nasty gash on his cheek and black eye somehow managed to make him even more handsome.

A damp area was forming underneath me on the rug. After a moment of scratchy sounds from the record player, a big band broke into an upbeat rendition of "Dinah." The jaunty squawk of the saxophone was totally wrong for our circumstances. I left Jax alone by the fireplace, rubbing his eyes with his hands, and went to the corner. With the help of the flashlight, I was able to find the record player's off switch. The Louis Armstrong album skipped a few times, and then the room fell silent except for the crackle of the fireplace.

And footsteps in the hall.

"You're right! Someone is after us," Jax said. There was a hysterical edge to his voice. "What the fuck are we going to do? Where the hell is everyone else?"

I hustled back to Jax's side, intending to grab one of the swords off the wall behind him.

Then it hit me.

One.

Two.

Three.

Four?

The fourth sword was gone. There were two empty hooks where it used to hang in line with the other three ceremonial blades.

"Oh God," I said, not able to focus on his words. "The kilij is gone."

His face went even paler in the firelight. I reached out and shook him.

"The kilij! The sword! The one that belonged to Vlad Dracul!" I hissed.

"You're telling me that—" Jax said slowly. He squinted at the row of swords.

The footsteps continued to grow louder.

My body somehow managed to be weak and stiff and sore all at the same time. "Yes! That the man in the mask . . . or . . . someone . . ." I said with a wave toward the paper in Jax's pocket, "is wandering around the castle with a super-sharp sword that Count Dracula used to chop people's heads off."

Jax wobbled like he was about to fall over. He braced himself on the mantel. "Oh God."

"We have to stop saying that," I said.

The footsteps approached the door. A shadow appeared in the gap between the door and the marble tile.

Jax pulled one of the nearly useless tarnished old swords off the wall. He let the sheath fall to the floor as he motioned for me to get behind him. I pointed the flashlight at the rounded wooden door that led from the sitting room to the hallway and the stairs.

My eyes widened as the door creaked open. I could almost hear the beat of Jax's heart.

It was Reagan.

The air left my lungs with a whoosh.

Carrying one of the candles on a crystal holder, Reagan stepped into the room.

"What the hell is going on?" Jax asked.

My best friend's gaze traveled from my aggressive stance to Jax clutching the dull sword. "I had to take a piss. I decided to take one of the candles because my phone battery is almost dead. What the hell is going on with the two of you?" Reagan said.

He came forward and wrapped me in a hug that lasted a second too long.

Jax lowered the sword. "Where's Kenna?"

Reagan frowned. "Kenna?" He stepped into the center of the room, coming close to the armchair where Kenna had been sitting earlier. He seemed surprised not to find her. "We . . . went upstairs together. She said she needed a sweater. She isn't back?"

"You were supposed to stay together!" I said.

"I was going to the bathroom," Reagan said with an eye roll. "And anyway. You were gone over an hour. But in this plan of yours, you didn't tell us what to do if you didn't come back. I was hoping that I'd run into Hazel when I went upstairs."

"Did you?" Jax asked.

Reagan's shoulders slumped. "Well . . . no. Did you guys find anything?"

I turned off the flashlight. "We found Maddie."

A confused look overtook Reagan's face as he scanned the room. "Um. Is she invisible?"

"She's dead," Jax said quietly.

Reagan's head continued to swivel from side to side, as if searching for Maddie. He placed the candle down on a small table near the sofa. "That can't be right. What do you mean . . . dead?"

"He means *dead* dead," I said through clenched teeth. Reagan was standing there with his hands in his pockets, and meanwhile I couldn't stop thinking about the sight of Maddie's crumpled-up body. "It looked like she was attacked and pushed over the terrace wall . . ." I choked on a sob.

Jax patted me on the back. "Maybe she fell. You saw what it was like out there. It would have been easy to slip. And fall."

He meant to be reassuring, but we both knew that Maddie hadn't fallen. "I saw . . . I saw . . . her head wound."

"Head. Wound?" Reagan repeated in a tone that suggested that he finally understood the gravity of what was happening. Of what was going wrong. Or perhaps he thought I was going mad. He leaned against the armchair. Lost in his thoughts for another quiet minute. He opened his mouth to speak but glanced at Jax and decided to remain silent.

"The sword is gone too," Jax said.

My words from earlier came back to haunt me.

We need to stay away from that thing. It's dangerous.

I coughed. "Someone pushed Jax down the stairs."

Reagan's eyes widened, and he had the look of someone who'd been given too much information. Like a computer about to freeze up. "We need to find Carter," he finally said.

"And Kenna." I didn't intend to let Reagan forget that he had not done his job.

But he shrugged. "If I am certain of anything in this world, it's that Kenna McKee can take care of herself."

I wanted to tell Reagan about the boarding pass we'd found.

But Jax said, "We need to move."

Maybe it was for the best. There was nothing we could do for Maddie right that moment, and it really didn't matter who was chasing us. Did it really matter if it was some maniac who had followed us from home or a Romanian criminal? We still needed to find our friends.

Jax picked up one of the candles that Hazel had put on the coffee table. It was in a small sterling silver repoussé bowl. Dad loved to find repoussé at estate sales. It tended to hold its value. The sight of the old, antique silver made me miss home. I wished I could talk to my dad or call home or go home. I felt horrible for what had happened at the airport. Kenna and Maddie had wanted to call home. I should have let them.

This was supposed to be the vacation of a lifetime. Not the trip that ended all our lives.

Reagan reclaimed his candle and said, "We should use these as much as possible to save our phone batteries. Who knows when the power will come back on."

I still had the flashlight, and Jax made sure to bring the old sword, although I doubted it was very useful as a weapon. Together the three of us headed to the hall door.

"So, you went upstairs to use the bathroom?" Jax asked as we walked. "And you didn't see anyone?"

"No," Reagan said sharply. "I already told you that."

It was strangely defensive.

We arrived at the massive wooden staircase that branched off to both levels. With the power out, it was not much more than a few steps upward and downward that vanished into a dark void. "He's only asking so we can get an idea of the best place to search. If you just came from upstairs, then we should start on the lower level," I said.

"Oh. Right," he said.

It occurred to me that Reagan might be as terrified as I was.

"As long as we stay together, I think we'll be okay." I said it with a wimpy kind of flutter in my voice that was unlikely to make anyone feel safer or more secure.

Jax was better at playing a hero. "We'll be fine," he said. "I'll make sure of it."

He held his candle up high and went first, descending into the silent blackness.

Reagan and I exchanged a candlelit glance and followed Jax down.

From what I could see, the lower level had retained more of Prahova's original decor. The beam of my flashlight landed on ancient walls of jagged gray stone, and our feet found hard brick flooring that amplified the sounds of our steps. After walking down what seemed like an impossibly long hallway that ran underneath a series of tall vaulted arches, we came to a cluster of three doorways—one each to the right and left and one that went straight ahead.

"Should we . . . split up?" Reagan stammered.

"No," Jax said flatly. "Whatever happens, we stay together from now on."

Without waiting for any more debate, he shoved the door in front of us. He raised the sword in the air as the door opened slowly.

Revealing what could only have been the smoking room.

It was empty and quiet.

Candles had been lit and placed strategically throughout the large room. It was decorated much in the same style as the sitting room. More deep reds and wood paneling. There were more doors on both sides of the room. In the center, four massive leather armchairs faced a small round table. Long, low leather couches lined most of the walls. Wooden cabinets covered the wall opposite the door. There was more expensive-looking artwork all over the place, and it reminded me of Maddie. She would probably have been able to identify the stuff. She would have been able to do a lot of things.

But not anymore.

"Someone's been in here," Reagan said, barely above a whisper.

"Weren't *you* down here earlier?" I asked.

Reagan snorted impatiently. "You think I was down here lighting all these candles? Like I'm doing set decoration for *Barry Lyndon*?"

He was right. Whoever did this was familiar with the room. They knew exactly where to place the candles so that they properly lit most of the space. There was no way Reagan would've had the time to set all this up.

I came closer to the grouping of furniture in the center, finding a Romanian magazine with Catrinel Bloom on the cover tossed casually on the table next to a half-full crystal glass of whiskey and . . .

A lit cigar.

Reagan moved toward the wall, holding his candle up to a painting. "Jesus. Is that Stalin?" Reagan asked, gesturing at a massive portrait of a man puffing on a pipe.

"Jax," I said, waving a quivering hand at the smoking cigar in the silver ashtray.

He joined me at the table, placed his candle on the table next to the ashtray, picked up the thick cigar, and scowled at it. "It's a Cohiba," he said. "You can tell by the smell. Cuban cigars always smell like wet dirt and hay. Fred Flannigan is a big fan." Jax's head turned from door to door. He clearly understood that someone was down there with us.

And could come back at any minute.

"Great," Reagan said. "Glad to know that the killer has such bougie taste." He continued walking around the room.

"I think we need to get out of here," I said. The words stuck in my throat. It was such a cowardly statement. It wasn't right to want to leave Kenna and Hazel and Carter behind. But right at that moment, I wanted to make a run for it. To take my chances in the storm and fog and darkness outside.

Jax stabbed the ashtray with the cigar, snuffing it out in a blaze of embers. "I'll keep you safe, Alex. I promise."

Reagan tried to imitate Jax's self-assured air. On the other side of the room, he pulled open one of the cabinets. He came to a bar, very similar to what you'd see in an old steakhouse. Glass bottles, full of all kinds of fancy booze, rested on a shelf and sparkled in the light of his candle. A few framed photos of a man with a handlebar mustache posing with various celebrities hung behind the bar. Castle Prahova was in the background of each photo.

In one of the pictures, he was with Justin and Catrinel Bloom.

"Look at that guy," Jax said.

I leaned in closer. "It's Justin Bloom. The film director," I said.

Jax shook his head. "No. The *other* guy."

The *other guy* looked like someone who was some kind of criminal. The other guy also looked like an older version of Raul Stoica. Hazel was right. Raul was Yuri's son.

I shivered.

Jax wanted to keep us focused. "I don't suppose anyone got much of a look at the property map?" He glanced from door to door.

I shook my head. I had only managed to steal a couple of quick glances. Hazel always liked to be in charge, and that map gave her a sense of power that she wouldn't have relinquished.

"We should go right," Reagan said. "This layout must run along the same lines at the other floors. Going right should be the quickest route to get outside. Similar to how the door to the right of the stairs on the first floor leads to the terrace."

"We don't want to go to the terrace," I snapped. That was, of course, why I couldn't really run. I was too chickenshit to go back outside.

Reagan sighed again. "Well, we have to go one way or the other. Or split up."

Jax shook his head. "We're not splitting up. But going right is as good of a plan as any. So let's do it."

He always acted like a leader. Perhaps it came naturally. Or perhaps guys like him had been treated like leaders for so long that he naturally fell into that role. Considering that we didn't know what, or who, we'd find in the other rooms, I couldn't understand why he was so confident. What was he leading us to? But there wasn't any time to really analyze things. With the candles in hand, we once again trailed behind Jax as he forced the massive door to the right open.

We moved into another gloomy hallway.

Except this one was wet. And moldy. And musty.

Beads of water ran down the stone walls. It was like there was a hole in the ceiling or a leak in the castle pipes. When we had gone about twenty feet, we heard the faint sound of running water. The distant hum of a shower in use. I fell back farther behind Jax, allowing myself to be completely shielded by his muscular body. Reagan was behind me, clipping my heels several times.

This new hallway ended at yet another one of the massive wood doors. The sound of the water had grown into a rush, and whatever was making it was almost certainly on the other side of the door. Again, it fell to Jax to lead us into the next room.

The three of us came into an absolutely enormous room with a ceiling so high that it wasn't visible in the small amount of light coming from our candles and lone flashlight. The space looked and felt like a black abyss. On the floor was maybe a dark rug or more of the black marble tile. I pointed my flashlight to our left and saw a series of shower stalls. In one, the glass walls were all steamed up, and hot water gushed at full blast. As with the cigar, here was another reminder that we weren't alone.

Someone had been inside. Was probably still inside.

Only Jax was brave enough to take the ten steps or so over to the shower and check it. He pulled the glass door open fast, the way they do in cop shows on TV. I held my breath.

"It's empty," he said with a sigh of relief. He turned off the water, leaving only an occasional drip.

My shoulders relaxed a bit, and I took a few more steps into the large room. I shined my light upward at the ceiling that kept going and going, ascending almost endlessly toward the heavens. A huge mural covered the wall to my right. It showed a man, a king on a carved throne, in a red coat, as other men kneeled all around in a tiled throne room. The room in the mural reminded me of the sitting room on the first floor.

I moved forward, struck by the terror on all the faces of Vlad Dracul's cowering subjects.

"Alex! Watch out! I think that's a—"

Swimming pool.

That's how Jax would have finished his sentence had I not been underwater and unable to hear him. The giant black square in the center of the room was not a rug. It was an indoor pool. The water was warm, more the temperature of a lukewarm bath.

This was the bathhouse.

The water was unexpectedly deep. I was already barely managing to keep it together, and the fact that I was sinking to the bottom of a bottomless dark hole sent me over the edge. My jeans weighed me down, and my shoes made it hard for me to kick myself upward. I sucked in several mouthfuls of chlorinated water. I fought my way to the surface, gasping and coughing and about to throw up.

"Alex! Alex!" Reagan was frantically calling. His candle existed as a pinprick of light that I focused on as I stabilized myself and began to tread water. "The stairs are over here."

I swam in his direction as best I could. I tried to keep the flashlight out of the pool. But it was already starting to flicker. It probably had water in the battery compartment. We'd lose one of our lights. Because I was clumsy and couldn't pay attention to where I was going.

It was taking me a while to get to Reagan. He left the candle by the side of the pool and swam out to meet me, pulling me into his arms. "It's okay, Alex. It's okay."

And for a second, it seemed like it would be okay. I was with Jax and Reagan. My best friend and my boyfriend. Moving fast, Reagan scrambled out of the water and collapsed next to the candle.

Jax dropped the silver sword with a clink, and his heavy footsteps came closer as he ran around the pool without letting his candle go out. "Alex! Are you okay?"

Fumbling my way up the steps, my knees knocked against the stairs and I almost fell again into the pool. My light continued to flicker. "I . . . I think I broke the flashlight."

"It's okay," Reagan said again.

Reagan flopped over and wrapped one of his hands around my upper arm to help pull me from the water. I put my hand on the top step to brace myself.

It landed on something squishy yet firm.

I yanked my hand back and pointed the pulsing flashlight at the step.

Confusion reigned inside me for a moment as it took time to fully register what I was seeing. Blue bulging eyes, white crepe-like skin, mouth frozen open in a perpetual scream. Red-black blood that ran into the blue bathhouse water.

Oh God. Oh God. It was Carter's head.

Sunken beneath the shallow surface of the first step. Tiny waves of pool water and blood lapping over his skin.

Carter Ricci's head.

Without his fucking body.

My flashlight went out.

General Directorate for Criminal Investigations

Pending report—EXHIBIT 22

Rush, Alexandra. *Dead Boys Don't Bite*. Theatrical script.

Revised March 14

Scene 5; page 8

Lucy Westenra [running from the masked man and out of breath] [whispers to herself]: He said he loved me. I tried to tell him that I loved him. But that I loved myself more. And after . . . after that moment . . . I found myself trapped. By these stone walls. By this forest full of twisted tree trunks that tangle around my feet. Everywhere I look, there are monsters. When I look again, they are gone.

Lucy Westenra: Everywhere there are monsters. Maybe even inside of me.

Two days ago

INT. THE LOWER FLOOR—NIGHT

Oh God. Oh. God.

"It's Carter's head!" I shrieked.

Reagan leaned forward. "Oh. Fuck," he whispered.

I reflexively pushed away from the pool steps, and my dramatic motion created a small tide that sent Carter's severed head farther into the pool, where it fell from the stairs and sank into the darkness beneath me.

I felt it brush against my leg.

Carter's stubbly facial hair dragged along my ankle bone.

Reagan, lying on his stomach on the pool deck, reached into the water and gave me a sharp tug by the collar of my shirt while I made a series of disgusted noises that sounded like the combination of a cough and a spit and a retch. I am pretty sure I stepped on Carter as I returned to the steps.

Emerging like a shaking, hulking sea monster, I stumbled onto the tiled pool deck. The candle that Reagan had left by the side of the water when he ran to rescue me got drenched with water running off my jeans. Jax still carried his candle, but it lit only a few feet around him, making him look like a star against a backdrop of oppressive darkness.

Reagan felt around for my hand. It was wet and cold and clammy.

But at least I wasn't alone.

I wanted to sink into the floor, but instead I collapsed onto the tile and continued to scoot away from where I knew the water was. From the resting place of Carter's remains.

"Jax!" Reagan called. "Slow down. We should try to save that light!"

We didn't know how long our phone and flashlight batteries would hold out.

Jax was halfway across the bathhouse, still making his way over from the shower on the other side of the room. "Yeah, okay," he said. He slowed down a bit more. Jax wasn't moving that fast in the first place. Falling down all those stairs must have taken more out of him than he would admit. Cupping the candle flame with one hand, he took small, deliberate steps toward us.

Meanwhile, Reagan inched toward the pool. As Jax came closer with the light, I could see Reagan feeling around the top step. Water splashed as he moved his hand.

"Oh. God. No. Reagan . . . You're not trying to get . . ." *Carter's head.* I knew I would totally lose it if he pulled our friend's head from the water.

"No. No," he said in a weak voice. Before he could explain what he was doing, Reagan rolled over to his side so that he faced away from me. I could hear him gagging, and the acidic, sour smell of vomit washed over me. I heaved a couple of times, but I had next to nothing in my stomach to throw up.

Jax placed the candle down on the ground, several feet away from the water's edge. "Alex, I'm here," he said, easing himself to sit on the tile and wrapping his arms around me. "It's okay."

We sat there for a couple of minutes, me sobbing into Jax's shoulder and Reagan puking and Carter's head sinking farther and farther down into the blackness of the pool.

Reagan sat up and turned toward me and Jax. He was fiddling with something, and a second later a light popped on. He had fished the flashlight from the pool, dried off the batteries, and managed to fix it. Its light still flickered, but it was working.

Jax kissed me on the forehead then released me, leaving me colder and more frightened than ever. "Shine the light this way," he told Reagan.

I shivered as Jax poured the water out of Reagan's candle, dried the wick with his shirt, and successfully used his own candle to light the one I had put out.

So we were back to three lights.

Jax helped me to my feet. Reagan got up as well, and the three of us stood even closer together than before, huddling elbow to elbow.

"Should we get *it* out of there?" Reagan nervously jerked his head toward the pool.

"No," Jax answered with typical firmness. "That will be a job for the police when they get here." His thinking was so filled with certainty and optimism. As if, of course, the police would come and save us and figure everything out.

But I couldn't shake the feeling that we were utterly and completely on our own.

"There's a door right over there," Reagan said, pointing to the corner behind us.

While Jax went back to his original position near the showers for the rusty old sword, I shined my light along the blue tile. A trail of crimson blood ran from another one of the huge wooden doors to the pool. It seemed pretty obvious that the killer must have either come in or gone out that way.

I wanted to scream so loud that my distress would echo across Prahova.

Instead, I dug my fingernails into my palms.

When Reagan had his own candle back, he held out the flashlight for me to take. My hands trembled as I accepted the fluttering, pulsing light. We continued to stand there, unsure of what to do next.

"We need to find out where that door goes," Jax said in a flat voice.

I knew Jax had grown up deeply embedded in the Fred Flannigan school of Real Men Never Show Weakness, but I couldn't understand how he could stay so composed. His friend's head was bobbing around the bottom of a pool. Whoever did it was sneaking around smoking cigars and helping himself to the whiskey.

And anyway. We could make an educated guess as to where the door went. "It probably goes outside. If Reagan is right, then the route we took would lead to the lower terrace. We don't need to go out there," I said. "We should find Hazel and Kenna."

It hit me. Maggie and Carter were dead. Hazel and Kenna were missing.

There were only five of us left. I thought again of the boarding pass in Jax's pocket. Someone was picking us off one by one.

Reagan coughed, and the sound bounced off the tiled floors

189

and walls. "Yes, we do. We need to check if the door is locked and make sure no one is out there right now. We have to know . . . We have to . . ."

They were struggling to come to grips with what had happened. Just like I had needed to see Maddie's body to be able to accept that my friend was really dead. Jax was already moving in the direction of the door. Regan trailed behind.

I took a few quick steps to catch up and instantly regretted it. Carter's body rested up against the wall in the corner nearest the door, and the scene told a terrible story. There was a round splotch of crimson red about six feet up on the tiled wall. Carter's head must have hit the wall before rolling into the pool. Rivers of blood ran through the grout of the tile. Swatches of ragged, bloody tissue were littered between his headless body and the pool. Smudged footsteps were tracked to the door.

Reagan heaved and threw up again.

My breathing was becoming shallower, and I struggled to remain calm. "Jax! Jax!" I said. He was only a couple of paces from the door, and I ran to get in front of him. My pulse raced so fast that I could almost hear the rush of my own blood. "No . . . Don't . . . You can't . . ." I panted. I was slipping and sliding all around in what seemed to be a mixture of water and blood. Two of our friends were dead. We could be next. My feet skated from side to side before I fell up against the door, coming to rest in the long, gooey streaks of what was left of the footprints.

"Jax, you can't open that door," I said, barely above a whisper. "It isn't safe. I don't want to know what's out there. I don't want to know *who* is out there."

He helped me to my feet, but he was determined. "It's okay,

Alex. I won't let anything happen to you. But we have to check it out." He handed Reagan the sword.

Reagan patted my arm and then moved me behind him so that the two boys stood between me and whatever was out there in the night.

I shined the flashlight at my shoes. They were soaked in blood.

Jax wrapped his fingers around the door handle and yanked it. The door was unlocked, and it did in fact open with a creak to a small square stoop. The situation outside had not changed. A veil of storm clouds and mist completely engulfed Prahova. We could see a couple of steps from a stairway that led to the terrace but nothing beyond. Heavy rain pelted down, and water flooded into the bathhouse from the open doorway.

He took a step out, getting hit with thick raindrops, and tried to peer out into the foggy night. "Yeah. I think that's the terrace up there. We should go—"

"No!" I said with an amount of force that surprised even me. I tried to suppress my terror for a minute and turn on my logical brain. Whoever hit Jax and almost pushed into me was headed for the door by the kitchen. They must have gone to the sitting room and taken the sword. In theory, the killer could have doubled back across the terrace and to the bathhouse. But they would have run into us in the kitchen. So they must have gone downstairs and through the smoking room. That would explain the candles and the cigar.

The killer had most likely gone *out* the bathhouse door.

A fact that should have been reassuring. Except Jax seemed hell-bent on going back out there too.

"Listen to me! Hazel and Carter were supposed to be together.

If he is . . . dead, where is she?" I moved closer to the door, tugged Jax back inside. "And the killer might still be out there. We are safer inside."

I put my arms around him to try to comfort him, but he shrugged me off.

"Jax, are you . . . okay? I . . . we . . ." *We just found Carter's dead body.*

"There's a key in the lock." He knelt down to inspect the lock, squinting at the brass fixture. "Look. At some point, they must have replaced the original door locks, if there were any, with these double-cylinder dead bolts. Look at this thing. It's new but made to look old."

And he was right. Looking closer, the lock was something my dad might have ordered from a fancy hardware store back when we still had money. It blended in perfectly with the old door, and its design suggested that it would use an old-time skeleton key, but it had a more modern keyhole.

Reagan nodded. "Great. So you need a key to operate the door from either side?"

Jax stood up. "These locks look pretty secure."

The key was on our side of the door. It had been unlocked from the inside, reinforcing the theory that the killer had gone out.

But out *where*?

Outside, I could barely see two feet in front of my face.

Jax removed the key and inspected it using the light from his candle. "I think this might be a master key," he said. "I'm hoping it will work on the other doors."

"Um . . . yeah . . . good," I stammered.

"Let's find Hazel," he said in a lifeless tone.

Jax used the key to lock the door to the outside landing and took the old sword back from Reagan. We then retraced our steps, leaving the bathhouse and returning to the long, musty hallway. I couldn't help but notice that I was leaving a trail of cherry red footprints behind us. Perfect imprints of the soles of my shoes remained etched in Carter's blood. A couple minutes later, we arrived in the smoking room. But it wasn't as we left it. All the candles had been blown out.

The room was completely dark except for the lights we had with us.

And the cigar was gone.

I shivered and grabbed Jax's arm. He tucked the sword under his arm and held my hand.

"What the fuck is even happening?" Reagan asked.

"Maybe the candles blew out when we opened the door back there?" Jax suggested.

"And what? The cigar evaporated?" Reagan returned.

No one bothered stating the obvious. Someone else had been in the smoking room.

"Hazel? Hazel?" I called out into the dark room, feeling foolish when no one replied.

We pressed on. Reagan and I were a couple of small steps behind Jax. He led us back to the point where the hallway broke off into two directions. This time we took the door to the left, coming into a long, massive library with floor-to-ceiling bookshelves lining every wall. I waved my flashlights at the books. They looked old and were mostly in Romanian or possibly Russian. It seemed like whoever did the castle decor hadn't done nearly as much remodeling in this room as elsewhere in the castle. There were rough wooden benches and a few basic writing tables here and there. The room lacked the posh rugs, and in the corners, there were more tattered mannequins in medieval garments, similar to the one at the end of the second-floor hallway.

Our footsteps were heavy and loud on the uncarpeted wood as we moved through the library, which ended at yet another interior door. Jax opened it, and we found ourselves in a hallway almost identical to the one upstairs. It even had some of the same rugs. Reagan was clearly right. The layout for both floors was the same.

Reagan closed the library door behind us, and the instant we were in the dark hall, I began to call out, "Hazel! Hazel!" while Jax and Reagan frowned at me.

Somewhere farther up the hallway, one of the doors began to jiggle, and we heard Hazel's muffled, frantic voice. "Alex! Jax! Is that you?"

For a couple of moments, it was pretty chaotic. Jax released my hand, and the three of us ran around the hallway, trying to figure out where the noise was coming from. Hazel's shouts came from the last room at the end of the hall. And even when we found the correct door, we had another problem.

Someone had wedged several silver ashtrays under the door to keep it from opening. I had the smallest fingers, so I put my flashlight down on the floor, lay down on the dusty rug, and pried them loose. Or tried to. Whoever put them there did a good job. It took me a while to dig them out so we could open the door.

The instant that we did, Hazel almost fell from the room. Jax caught her with the arm he wasn't using to hold the candle.

I ended up with a stack of ashtrays in my hand. And I recognized them.

From the smoking room.

"What the hell happened to you?" Jax asked. He rested the sword against the wall and helped Hazel stand normally.

Her hair was a mess, but otherwise she looked okay. She had her phone in one hand and was clutching the castle map in the other, holding on to it like her life depended on it.

"What happened to *you*?" The candlelight flickered in Hazel's light brown eyes. "Where is Kenna?"

Behind her, I could see that she had been trapped in a completely dark bedroom with another one of the four-poster beds that we all had. Even though I desperately wanted to know how she had gotten separated from Carter and who had gone through all the trouble of locking her in there, I had to admit that our little party looked downright frightening. Jax was beat all to hell, my shoes were covered in blood, our clothes were ripped, and we were all soaking wet. We'd need to explain before we got any answers out of her.

The four of us lingered in the hallway. Jax did most of the talking. About how we found Maddie's body outside. That maybe she fell. Or was pushed. About our trip through the smoking room. Hazel had to brace herself on the doorframe when we came to the part about Carter's head. Reagan had to explain that he lost track of Kenna when he left the sitting room.

"So you haven't seen Kenna?" Hazel said in a low voice.

I glanced at Jax to see if he planned to show the boarding pass we had found.

"Okay. Now. What happened to you?" Reagan prompted.

Hazel sighed. "We went upstairs—"

"I thought you guys decided to check the lower floor first," I interrupted. The power had been off for a while, and it was getting cold down here. I wrapped my arms around myself.

Hazel nodded. "I wanted to. I thought that was more logical, but Carter was adamant . . . that he wanted to search for Maddie outside. He thought maybe we'd be able to see her from one of the windows on the second floor. He wasn't being . . . rational."

She sniffed before going on. "He thought she might have stolen the money. He thought she might try to do something to herself." She paused, staring for a second at the light of Reagan's candle.

"Stolen the money?" Reagan repeated.

"Her dad is in some kind of trouble. Maddie said he stole some money from her grandparents, and her family is threatening to go to the police. But she thought Kenna is the one who hacked our GoFundMe," I said.

Reagan's temper flared. "When were you planning on telling me this? I—"

"Reagan," Jax cut through him. "We've been pretty busy running for our goddamn lives." He turned back to Hazel and motioned at the bedroom. "But how did you get in there?"

Hazel drew in a breath. "We had searched most of this floor. When we were in here, Carter said he heard something in one of the other rooms. He was . . . Well . . . you saw him upstairs.

He wanted to go outside and look for Maddie. He was totally pissed at Jax. I tried to stop him. I mean . . . that wasn't the plan. When we came down this hallway, he grabbed the flashlight and pushed me in here."

"You're saying Carter locked you in there?" Reagan asked.

"He jammed the door with these," I said, holding up the ashtrays.

Hazel's shoulders fell. "Carter was obsessed with going outside to search. He kept saying that if anyone should be out . . . there . . . it should have been him. That he should have taken better care of Maddie. Looked out for her better." She paused for a second and then held up her phone. "Reagan, is this the room where you got a cell signal yesterday? I tried for a couple of minutes before my battery died, and I didn't get anything."

We *were* in the room that Reagan had mentioned.

"Is that why you came in here?" I asked.

Jax put an arm around me. "Alex, you're freezing."

Before Hazel could answer, Reagan shot Jax a disgruntled look and said flatly, "It's probably the storm. And the signal wasn't great to begin with."

Jax's frown sank deeper, his perfect-boyfriend mask in danger of falling away. "We should get back upstairs."

With Hazel and the map, we made quick time back to the grand staircase. We were mostly quiet and lost in our own thoughts. I knew it was my imagination, but it felt like there were more stairs than before.

"Did Carter light a cigar when you were with him?" Reagan asked.

"A cigar? No," Hazel said. "Why would he?"

I had run out of ways to feel terrified. I was cold and numb.

We arrived on the first floor, exhausted and panting.

Jax hesitated near the stairs. He began to pull the soggy, crumpled boarding pass from his pocket. "We found something that you need to see."

But Hazel didn't wait for him to produce the paper. "So did we," she said. "Follow me."

She grabbed my flashlight and took off up the stairs.

General Directorate for Criminal Investigations

Pending report—EXHIBIT 61

INTERPOL—Background—Yuri Stoica

Skutnik's note: Translated summary of criminal file.

We do not know a lot about his early years. There is some indication that he may have served in the Central Intelligence Division during the Soviet area. He may have been born in Brasov. This much is known. In the early nineties, he went to the police academy in east Georgia. He only briefly served as an officer before being arrested for corruption. After that first arrest, he broke a window in the jail and jumped out a second-story window and fled to Moscow. At first, he worked as a hitman, until he finally started his own cartel around 2001. He could fire a gun with either hand. He once won a fight in the prison yard against twelve other inmates, and he would kill anyone. Women. Children. Politicians. Police. Anyone. Or have them killed.

The last few years of his life, he was on Interpol's Most Wanted List. The old officers called him the Likho. The spirit of misfortune. Because when he came for you, he destroyed everything. Your family, your house, your friend. Everything.

Two days ago

INT. THE END OF THE HALLWAY— NIGHT

If being trapped for an hour in total darkness had gotten to Hazel, she didn't let it show. And she hadn't seen any of the . . . bodies . . . that we had seen. Or fallen down the stairs or tumbled into a pool with Carter's severed head. She moved fast, climbing the steps to the second floor and then taking off down the long hallway that led to our bedrooms. The rest of us were at least ten paces back. The boys were making a show of going slow to keep their candles from blowing out. But I knew the truth.

We were exhausted. And terrified.

Water squeaked out of my shoes and squirted onto the antique hall rugs.

I wished Hazel had at least *asked* me before taking my flashlight. She left me the only person without a light. I guess I could have turned on my phone, but Reagan kept saying we had to save the batteries. So a ring of darkness existed around only me.

We passed by our rooms, and my thoughts briefly went back to earlier in the trip when my biggest problem had been worrying about whether or not Jax would see me in my underwear. Hazel kept walking past our bedroom, and this too had echoes of the evening—when Maddie had told me to follow *her* down the hall. The four us walked by the lost Raphael.

Hazel paused at the very end of the hallway, in front of the mannequin in the Vlad Dracul costume, where Maddie and I had seen the wires that ran from the ceiling and disappeared into the stone wall. I could still see them, and I was flooded with relief. It was stupid. But I needed the reassurance. That I wasn't going mad after all.

I pointed up. "Look. That's the cable we saw earlier."

Hazel nodded. "I'll get to that in a second." She froze with her hand on the doorknob of the last room on the left. Waiting.

There was something wrong with the way she was going about everything. We were fighting for our very lives. But Hazel . . . it's like she wanted to maximize our suspense. Give us time to recognize that she was the smartest person in any room. It reminded me of the way she always paused in class before answering a question. She needed everyone's full attention before she gave us all the solution.

I was about to say as much when she started speaking first.

"Okay," she said, with a certain amount of melodrama. "Carter and I were going down the hall checking each room. We mostly didn't find anything. Until we got here. Look."

She flung the door open.

And we *did* all let out identical shocked gasps.

The room contained yet another variation of a four-poster bed. But there was something else. A small table rested up against the one wall that was made of stone. The table was home to a gorgeous lamp with a red crystal shade.

The light was on.

The power had been out since Maddie ran off.

But *this light* was on and sending a cheerful orange glow across the room.

Jax knelt down and inspected the lamp. It was plugged

into an outlet on the wall. "Shit. Oh shit. So. The power isn't really out."

Hazel's arms fell slack against her body. "No. I don't think it is. After we found this, we went back to each room. We checked all the lights and all the outlets that we could see. Only this wall has power. Which would seem to suggest that—"

"That someone turned the power off deliberately," Jax finished. "Probably at a breaker box. But *this* wall must be connected to a different switch."

"Wait. What?" Reagan asked, almost dropping his candle. "Are you saying what I think you're saying?"

"The cable terminates at that wall too," I said.

Hazel looked almost pleased. Like my deductive reasoning had passed her test. "Yeah, exactly. I think you're right. That cable probably connects to a phone or a computer. And it most likely has power."

"Wait. Wait," Reagan said again. His voice rose to a high, hysterical pitch. "You're saying . . . you're saying that someone deliberately turned off the power. To make it easier to . . ."

"Kill us," I said, closing my hands into fists to keep them from shaking.

Hazel bit her lower lip. "Carter's theory was that . . . Kenna had done it. Not to kill us. But for some other reason. Because earlier . . . her pajamas were wet. And when we were upstairs in the music room . . . when the lights came back on . . . when you were chasing after Maddie . . . she wasn't with me."

"That's just not possible," I said. "If Kenna wanted to turn off the power, not only would she have to know where the breaker box was, she would need to flip all the switches in the breaker box. Because she would have no way of knowing which switches powered which lights. Leaving one on would be too risky."

It was silent for a moment.

"Show her the boarding pass," I told Jax.

Jax drew the crumpled-up paper from his pocket.

"Oh. Shit," Hazel said. She stared at the paper. Reading and rereading it.

"Is there anything else I don't know?" Reagan asked, with a look of betrayal.

I put my hand lightly on his back. "I'm sorry. I'm so sorry . . . I . . . We just . . . We had just found Maddie and . . ." Everyone else seemed to be so strong. But I couldn't help it. I hated myself for being the one to break, but I couldn't stop the tears from forming in the corners of my eyes and running down my cheeks.

Reagan's expression softened. "I know. It's okay, Alex."

Hazel stared at me. "Someone really came here to hunt us? All the way from Phoenix?"

"Yes," I said with a sniff. I began to shake. Maybe from the cold. Or from shock.

Jax gave me a reassuring look. "We need to change our clothes and get back down to the fire. There's no use freezing to death on top of everything else."

It felt somehow disloyal to Carter and Maddie to be concerned about my own comfort. But I appreciated Jax's suggestion. I was wet and cold straight through to the bone.

"Well," Reagan said. "If we get desperate, we can always charge our phones in here."

"I don't want to come back to this creepy room," I said with a shiver.

We left the lit room and returned to the dark hall.

The four of us came to a stop in front of the door to Reagan's room.

Hazel wrung her hands. "I don't want to wait out here by myself."

"Come with me," Reagan said. "I'll change in the bathroom. At least you won't be alone out here."

The two of them went into Reagan's room. Jax and I continued down the hall until we got to our own bedroom. Jax put the candle down on the room's writing desk, and it did a reasonably good job of lighting the room. I didn't recognize my own reflection in the long oval mirror. I had cuts and scrapes all over my face and neck. My left eye was swollen and puffy, and I couldn't even see the color of my shoes. They were covered in too much blood.

Jax went to the wardrobe where I had put all my clothes earlier. He handed me a pair of sweats, a T-shirt, and a cardigan sweater. "We should dress warm."

I nodded but had to go over to the wardrobe myself for a clean bra and panties. All of my clothes were soaked in blood and rainwater too. Leaving him searching for his own clothes, I went into the bathroom connected to our room. I couldn't close the door because I needed the light from the candle to see. Even though I desperately wanted to take a shower, I did my best to clean myself off with a wet towel. Reagan and Hazel would be waiting.

And we still needed to find Kenna.

After tossing my old clothes and shoes into the bathtub, I crept back into our room. When I came out, Jax was dressed in his own sweats and rugby shirt and sat on the bed, staring out into space. He must have picked up the old sword at some point, and it rested on the bed next to him. But he left it there, and together, we opened the door to find Reagan and Hazel standing in the hallway.

"Okay," Jax said brusquely as he tried to renew his authority. "Let's go to the sitting room and check on the fire. Then we'll make a sweep for Kenna."

No one said anything. I don't think any of us wanted to go back to the lower floor.

"Can I have my flashlight back?" I asked Hazel.

She hesitated and reluctantly handed it over. I pointed the light ahead, shining it at the empty landing of the staircase.

We followed Jax down the stairs. The wood creaked more than it did before.

I tried to tell myself that it was my imagination.

"You have the key, right?" Reagan asked Jax.

Jax nodded as we continued downward.

"What key?" Hazel said in a whisper.

"We found a key stuck in one of the doors in the bathhouse," I said. "We think it might be a master that could work on the exterior doors."

We arrived on the ground floor, and I was first onto the tile. In what was becoming a horrible pattern, I nearly tripped and fell again. Both Hazel and Reagan gave me stern looks when I dropped the flashlight.

It rolled across the tiled floor through a splotch of thick, fresh mud.

A track of small, smeared footprints led from the door to the terrace in the direction of the sitting room. "No way those were there before," Reagan said.

I grabbed the flashlight from the floor and strained to listen for any kind of sound. But there were no footsteps.

"Shit," Jax whispered. "I left the sword in our room."

The old sword was a dull piece of crap that was probably useless anyway.

It wasn't the kilij.

But at least it was something.

We moved in a tight huddle, closer and closer to the sitting room door.

Step.

By.

Step.

Jax pushed the door open with so much force that it actually bounced off the sitting room wall and slammed shut. He had to open it again, and we all jumped into the room, landing in various poses like silly cartoon superheroes.

The room was empty. Except for.

Kenna McKee.

She sat on the couch near the fire, clad in a crimson crushed-velvet track suit that somehow managed to be both casual and ridiculous. She had a book on her lap, and her mouth was stuck in a surprised O as she took in our appearance. "Where the hell have you guys been?" she asked.

A pair of small, muddy Adidas shoes were tossed casually in a pile near the sofa.

Kenna had clearly made the footprints.

What if Carter had been right?

"Where have *you* been?" Reagan demanded. "You said you were going to your room for a sweater. And then you didn't come back."

Kenna squinted at him. "What are you talking about? I told you that I was going outside to look for Alex and Jax. They were gone over an hour."

Reagan shook his head slowly from side to side.

"I *told* you that's what I was doing when I saw you upstairs," Kenna insisted.

Reagan froze. Because we had been friends for so long, I could tell that this conversation was unnerving him. "I didn't see anyone when I went upstairs."

Kenna rolled her eyes. "I came out of my room and passed you in the hall. You said you were going to the bathroom. I told you that no one was back yet and that I was going out on the terrace to try to spot someone."

"That did *not* happen," Reagan snapped. But his face was uncertain.

"*You* were going down to the basement," she went on with a snort. "To look for Carter."

Reagan took a seat opposite the sofa. He curled his fingers tight around the arms of the chair. "Why are you lying?"

She closed her book with a dramatic snap. "I don't lie."

Hazel's attention snapped from Reagan to Kenna. Watching carefully. Taking mental notes. Like she planned on scoring the debate later on.

Reagan ran his hand through his hair, which was more curly

than usual. "Kenna, we all *know* that there are lots of things that you're not telling the truth about."

"Pot calling kettle, Reagan," Kenna said as she adjusted her sweatpants. "We've all got our little secrets. But I know what I saw."

Reagan glanced at me and then looked away.

"You don't seem very wet," Hazel commented, coming to stand in front of the fire.

Kenna shrugged. "I wore one of the ponchos and used my umbrella. And I wasn't out there very long. I mean . . . it's a mess out there. It was obvious that I wouldn't be able to find you."

Jax and I joined Hazel at the fireplace, and I warmed my hands. Kenna's umbrella rested in the corner nearest to the door to the kitchen. It was bone dry and didn't look like it had been used since she went out earlier to do her vlog.

Also, it wasn't particularly muddy on the terrace.

But there *was* mud in the clearing where we found Maddie's body.

We were all lost in our thoughts until Kenna prompted, "So . . . where's Maddie and Carter? Were they downstairs helping themselves to the whiskey?"

She had a wistful smile on her face. Like she expected good news.

"They're dead," Hazel said flatly.

Kenna's mouth fell open. She initially didn't want to believe us. It fell to Jax to explain how we found Maddie in the clearing and Carter in the bathhouse. Kenna's face went pale as he spoke and she pressed her arms into her own body, like she wanted to take up as little space as possible.

The room fell silent.

"What are we going to do?" Kenna asked in a small, girlish voice.

Jax turned his back to her and watched the fire. "We're going to stay in this room until morning. At first light, we're going for help."

Where would we go? Who would help us?

And what would we do about the monster hunting us?

Jax was busy playing the part of fearless leader. But there were things to be afraid of.

Kenna glanced at her phone. It was like the enormity of what was going on finally hit her. "It's barely three. It won't be light for hours. Maddie and Carter . . . What will we tell people when we get home? Who will tell their parents? What are we going to do? What am . . . I . . . I . . ."

Reagan stared at me for a minute. "Is anyone else thinking what I'm thinking?" Without waiting for us to answer, he continued. "What if it's Catrinel Bloom?"

Hazel's face scrunched in confusion. "She's a major movie star. So. Um. No. I was not thinking that."

"If it weren't for her, we wouldn't even be here," Reagan said in an accent of frustration. "She helped us raise the money. She chose this location. She's supposed to be with us but isn't. That creepy caretaker, who also took off, is her cousin. And there's a picture downstairs of her with a reputed crime boss."

"Who is probably another one of her relatives," Hazel agreed.

Reagan nodded. "What if, after everything she went through with Justin Bloom, that she's a few Froot Loops shy of a full bowl?"

I frowned at Reagan. "Justin Bloom is a sexual harasser so his wife must be insane?"

"We can't worry about that now," Jax said in a voice as dull as the blade of the sword that we'd left upstairs. I realized that we were all dependent on him for leadership.

"Let's focus on . . . surviving," he said.

Kenna gave him a single jerky nod.

After that, we moved furniture to block both of the sitting room doors. Jax put more wood on the fire, and we made ourselves as comfortable as possible.

"You can rest," Jax told me. "I'll stay awake."

I wanted to say that I would stay awake with him. That I would be there for him. Instead, I curled up in one of the oversize chairs. My eyes fluttered, and a few minutes later I fell into a fitful sleep. I'm not sure exactly what time it was when I woke up, but the day had broken. White-gray light streamed in from the massive windows that made up one whole wall of the sitting room.

Jax was asleep in the chair across from me. Everyone was sleeping.

Kenna was on the sofa. I watched her yawn.

For a moment she lay there, a sleeping beauty in a castle tower.

Then she bolted upright.

And let out a blood-curdling scream.

General Directorate for Criminal Investigations

Pending report—EXHIBIT 42

Transcript of TED Talk by Justin Bloom

For me, when making a horror film, the setting is as important as the characters. In many ways, setting is a character. A castle, for instance, is commonly understood to be a symbol of wealth or of power. It's the seat of the crown. The home of the ruler. You start with that. But it's walled, enclosed, often corrupt. Often an inescapable environment. It might be the home of Prince Charming. It might be inhabited by a monster. The monster and the prince might be one and the same.

You never know. And that is its power.

Two days ago

INTERCUT, SITTING ROOM, THE GARDEN—DAY

Jax sat up fast, creating a yellow-gold streak with his messy pompadour. "Um. What? What's happening?"

Kenna appeared to be moaning "Oh God" over and over and over. With her hands covering her face, she made an awful wheezing noise that woke Hazel.

"Geez. Kenna. What . . . the . . ." Hazel murmured between yawns.

"Dead . . . dead . . ." Kenna whispered.

Kenna must have been having a nightmare about Carter and Maddie. Hazel scooted over on the sofa. She patted Kenna's back. "It's okay. It's over. We'll find a way out of here today." But Hazel didn't sound sure.

She sounded like she wanted to convince herself.

"It's gonna be okay, Kenna," Jax said, also trying to be reassuring.

For a second, I tried to remember the version of reality where we were going to make a film. The boxes of equipment were still tossed in a pile in the corner of the music room. The copies of my script were still upstairs.

That version of reality no longer existed.

We'd be lucky to escape with our lives.

Jax stood up and went to the window.

The room was still warm from the remains of the fire, and

gray light flooded in through the giant window, creating an environment that suggested a gloomy nineteenth-century romance. Outside, low-hanging misty clouds drifted above the tall, verdant forest trees. We were alive and relatively safe. And Jax. My Jonathan Harker. Tall, controlled, muscled arms that seemed like they could support the weight of the world. There he was, overlooking the scene below, the model of a brooding gothic hero.

"The weather is a bit better today," he said.

Kenna coughed a few times.

I glanced at her. Carter had thought Kenna had some role in what was happening. She and Reagan told different stories about what happened upstairs. I didn't think she had it in her to chop Carter's head off with an antique sword. But she stretched the truth in the best of times, and I had the feeling that there was something important that she wasn't telling us.

"You need to have some water," Hazel said. She picked up a bottle from the coffee table and offered it to Kenna.

My gaze landed on Hazel, who was also staring at me. I had spent enough time in class with her to know that she was doing a similar analysis and coming to the same conclusions.

I rubbed my fingers on the plush upholstery of the sitting room chair. Hazel continued to clutch the bottle of water like it was a potion that she could neither take nor release. Kenna wrapped her arms around herself and formed a tight ball. The large clock ticked, and occasionally an ember from the dying fire popped. Otherwise, the sitting room was silent.

After a few minutes, Jax returned from the window and sat down again. "We need to get our stuff together. Pack up what supplies we can find and get out of here."

Reagan stood and went to the fireplace, eyeing the spot on the wall where the swords used to hang. "I don't know, Jax."

"Oh, great. Now we're gonna argue about whether or not it still makes sense to leave Prahova," Hazel guessed. Her yoga ensemble still looked fresh, and her bob was even relatively smooth. Like she could lead a production meeting on a moment's notice.

Reagan snorted. "Spoiler alert. It does *not* make sense."

Jax gripped the back of my chair. "Someone is basically hunting us, Reagan. No one is coming to help us. Our best bet is to head out and contact the police."

"You said the weather is better." Kenna croaked out the words. "Maybe that Raul guy will come back."

Yeah. That sounded great. "For all we know, he's the one who killed Maddie and Carter."

"It's at least forty kilometers to the nearest town. Which is tiny and might not even have a dedicated police force. This is tough territory. We don't speak Romanian, and we don't have maps or gear," Reagan said.

"But once we get to the road, our cell phones will work," I pointed out.

Reagan let out a dramatic sigh. "*If* we get to the road, they *might* work. It was an hour walk, Alex. Out there in the open. If the man in the mask, or Dracula, or whatever you want to call him, can pick us off in the castle, imagine how much easier it will be to kill us in that dark, creepy forest."

"We could just stay here," Kenna suggested. "Fortify a few rooms as best we can. Maybe someone will show up. Maybe help will come."

"Someone will show up?" I repeated in disbelief. Who would just *show up* at a cliffside castle in a dense Romanian forest?

"Eventually our parents would send someone to look for us," Kenna said.

"We would run out of food and water long before that happened," Hazel snapped.

Kenna sighed. "There's plenty of food. And there's a well in the garden."

My insides ran cold. "You're thinking we wait? And hope that someone shows up? Or that Raul Stoica comes back? Oh, and that he's not the killer?"

Hazel pivoted on the designer rug, spinning on the pads of her feet. "Look. There might be a working phone here. Or a computer. That's what we decided last night. You all saw the cable."

"Might be?" Jax echoed.

"'Let's check the castle grounds for a phone' sounds like a much better plan than 'Let's frolic through the haunted forest,'" Reagan said.

Always logical, Hazel said, "We should do both. Form two groups. One group looks for the phone. The other makes a break for the road."

I dropped my stiff hands into my lap and let out a little hiccup. "No. No. No. We need to stop splitting up. We're becoming a horror movie cliché. Splitting up cost Carter his head and got you locked into a bedroom on the lower level. We should stay together."

It was silent for a few minutes.

"Look, we need to think logically here," Hazel said. "The boarding pass was only for one person, so let's assume there's a single killer. If we're going to do this, the second team should go for the phone right away. It increases our odds, since the killer can't chase all of us at the same time. For the record, I think we should stay together and go to the road. But if we are going to split up, we should make it mean something."

"I'm not going to the fucking road," Reagan said. He had his back to me and was watching what was left of the fire.

Hazel glanced at Kenna. "If the castle has a phone, we can call 112. The police could be here before sunset."

"112?" Kenna asked.

"It's the Eurozone's emergency number," Hazel said. When Kenna made no effort to indicate that she understood, Hazel tried again. "It's like 911 in Romania."

Of course Hazel would know that.

"It'll be better for the girls to look for the phone. Alex and Hazel are good with maps and directions," Jax said. He was trying to make me feel like hiding required more valor than fighting.

"That was Cat5 cable that we saw. It's more likely connected to a computer and not a phone. That's my department. I'm the geek here, remember. Can anyone else code in fourteen languages? Has anyone else set up a PBX box? I'm not going to the road," Reagan said again. This time he choked it out. Like he was on the verge of tears. He wouldn't look at me.

"I'll go," I said. "I'll go to the road."

Everyone stared at me. I wished that Reagan would change his mind and that I could remain in the sitting room until the boys came back with the police. But no one else was going to volunteer, and sending Jax out alone was almost taunting the killer to a hunt.

We spent the next half hour packing whatever supplies we could find and listening to Hazel detail her exact plan. She still had the castle map from earlier and tapped the location where cables terminated at the western wall of the wing we were in. She intended to follow the terrace around to end up on the exterior side of the wall. Her theory was that the cable would be attached to a pole or there at least would be some kind of hint or clue to follow.

I ended up with a backpack full of bottled water, cereal bars, an umbrella, a couple of the disposable ponchos, and a notebook and pen. Jax and Reagan grabbed sweatshirts, and the five of us left the castle together through the kitchen door. From the looks of things, we were in a brief period of calm weather. The clouds overhead were fluffy and white, but above the forest, a darker, black-gray storm was about to roll in.

I looked back.

We had left a trail of muddy, chaotic footprints on the terrace floor.

Although we stayed as a group down the stone steps, when we arrived at the garden, Reagan charged ahead through the tall grass, coming to an uneasy rest near the headless statue of Vlad the Impaler. Jax lingered near the base of the staircase. He and Hazel were preoccupied with helping Kenna down the stairs. She looked like a celebrity being released from rehab. She staggered around, frail and fragile and thin and brittle.

I kept moving and ended up by Reagan.

Standing in the shadow of the decapitated Dracula.

"You think I'm a pussy, right?" he asked me.

"No," I told him. And it was true. I was no braver than he was.

A cool breeze rattled the long grass. A couple of red-breasted geese poked around the courtyard. They made a sound like puckered lips kissing.

He kneeled down and opened his backpack. "Good. Because I'm not." His words were barely above a whisper. "I have no idea what is happening around here. But whatever it is, I think Kenna is behind it. And I told you before, Alex, I have to keep you safe."

I glanced at Kenna, about twenty feet away, doing her damsel in distress routine. She was keeping us from criticizing her by acting like a wilted flower. She almost appeared to faint as she took the last step and finally arrived in the courtyard. She swooned and nearly collapsed into Jax's arms. Hazel made a disgruntled face and wrapped her arm around Kenna's back, and the two hobbled on together.

Right at that moment, there was nothing threatening about Kenna McKee.

But looks could be deceiving.

I turned my attention back to Reagan, who was pressing something into my hand.

A hammer.

"It was the only thing that I could find that even resembled a weapon," he told me with a solemn expression. His hair created a red crown around his face.

I stared at the rusted metal head and claw.

It wasn't silver and would never polish up.

Kenna, Jax, and Hazel were coming closer.

"Maybe you should keep it," I said. "Maybe . . ."

Maybe Maddie was right. Kenna *was* a swan. Beautiful but deadly.

"I have a plan," Reagan said firmly, motioning for me to put the hammer away in my own backpack. "Keep yourself safe, okay. Get Jax to come back as soon as you can. You have to know, the whole *going to the road* thing isn't going to work. Even if you make it there . . ."

"It might," I said stubbornly. But it was more of a whisper. "Reagan, I'm worried about you. Kenna is lying. Keeping secrets. You think I'm in danger. But I think you are."

He shook his head at me, leaving me no choice other than take the hammer and put it in my pack. But he looked unnerved.

Jax was close to us, and he reached out for my hand.

"Come back as soon as you can," Reagan said so that everyone could hear. "We're heading west."

I took Jax's hand and gave it a squeeze. We stood there in the courtyard. Watching Reagan and Hazel shuffle away with Kenna.

"I hope we see them again," I said after they had rounded the castle's corner and were out of earshot.

"Don't worry, Alex," Jax told me with a half smile. "We'll all be fine."

Except we weren't fine. Two people were dead.

We'd never be fine again,

"I hope so," I said.

The two of us needed to retrace the path we'd followed when we arrived. Past the courtyard, down the dirt path, through the forest, and back to the spot where Marius, the bus driver, had dropped us off.

We turned to face the path to the forest. It stretched out before us. A rough, rocky trail that passed underneath Prahova's stone arch and extended about fifty feet or so before plunging into the thick web of impossibly tall trees. A new storm was rolling in, and the sky was already slightly darker than before.

We began to walk.

General Directorate for Criminal Investigations

Alexandra Elaine Rush—Transcript—Tape 2 [CONT.]

Inspector Skutnik: You and Jax left Prahova's east wing via the footpath to the south of the castle? You believed that you would be able to make calls once you reached the main road. Who did you intend to call?

Alex: I don't know. The police? Our parents, maybe? But then . . . then . . . [inaudible] we . . . he . . . [inaudible] . . .

Inspector Skutnik: Alex, do you need a break? Alex?

Two days ago

EXT. THE LABYRINTH—DAY

Only a few steps into the forest, we found ourselves under a cool, gloomy canopy of green, following the narrow path through the twisted, textured trunks of beech and gray alder trees. It had been a slog getting up to the castle. Going back to the road was mostly downhill. Which should have been a relief.

Instead, it felt like we were on a conveyor belt at a meat processing plant, being hurled toward a fate both inevitable and terrible.

We walked on in silence, crossing the bridge that extended over the river.

We'd been going for around twenty minutes when Jax suggested that we stop for some water. He reached in his pack for a bottle, opened it, and handed it to me to take a sip. His gaze traveled across the foliage, and he squinted as he found the treetops blocking our view of the morning sky. Beetles buzzed and hummed. The rush of the river water could still be heard.

"In spite of everything," he said, placing his foot on a rotting, moss-covered log that had fallen near the edge of the path, "it's pretty."

Yeah. But I knew I would be pretty happy to never see that forest again.

Jax touched my cheek. "When this is all over, I want things to be different."

"Um. Okay," I said, scanning the forest for . . . well . . . Dracula . . . as stupid as that sounded.

"I mean it, Alex."

I wasn't sure what he meant. Was he breaking up with me when we were running for our lives? The tree branches swayed and rattled, and it almost seemed to be getting darker as we stood there.

A gorgeous bird with a teal head and fire-red feathers hopped around on the branches behind Jax. It cocked its head and stared right at me for a minute before moving on.

"Jax . . . I don't know what you mean . . ."

He grabbed me by the shoulders with a startling amount of force. "After what we've been through . . . I think . . . I see things differently. I don't want to go home."

I almost dropped the bottle of water. "Wait. What? We have to finish school, and you're supposed to start at USC in August."

"Yeah, well, I don't want to," he said.

I stared into his blue eyes. "Is this because you're worried that I won't get in? Because even if I don't, I can go to ASU and maybe try to transfer in later." I was starting to feel that my mom was right. That there were worse things than not getting into film school.

Much worse.

He ran his hand through the crest of his perfect hair. "No. I mean . . . yes. I mean . . . sort of." Jax leaned down to kiss my forehead. "Tarantino didn't finish high school or go to film school. Neither did Christopher Nolan." He released me, leaving me feeling cold and exhausted. "I think what I really need is more life experience."

Life experience?

The longer that we lingered in the forest, the shorter our lives might get.

"Jax, you're not thinking straight. We'll get home . . . figure things out . . . Things will go back to normal. Things will be fine."

Except. We were isolated and alone and a killer was out there.

"That's what I'm trying to tell you," Jax said softly. "I think I want things to be . . ."

Overhead, a light mist was falling. My guess was that it would soon be raining again.

I took a couple of steps forward to hopefully get us moving again. When he remained still, I added, "Listen, we have all the rest of our lives to discuss this."

At least, I hoped we did.

Jax said what I was thinking.

He hustled to get in front of me. "Do we though?"

Except he meant something different. He really thought that we'd get to the road and get away from the maniac who was out to get us. He thought there was a future for him beyond the horrors of Prahova, but also that he was in control of his own destiny. He believed in happy endings. Guys like him usually got them.

"After everything we've been through in the last twenty-four hours . . . we don't know how much time any of us really has," he said. "We have to make it count. After the police come, when we're all safe, I want to stay here."

My heart dropped. Air laced with the scent of dew and wild mint hit me in the face. "Here? At Castle Creepy?"

Jax sighed. "Here in Europe. We can take our share of the money—"

"Our share? Of the money that's been stolen?"

"—and spend some time figuring things out and—"

His blue eyes were hazy and unfocused. He had everything. The perfect face. The perfect body. Rich parents. A USC acceptance letter. The whole world was laid out at his feet, and he didn't care. He wanted to stay in the woods and watch the tree branches sway and listen to the birds chirp. And maybe that would have worked for him. The filmmaking world was full of stories about male directors who started out as theater ushers. Female directors needed perfect résumés and impressive educations and professional networks full of famous actresses if they even wanted a shot at making a feature film. Plus, there was my family.

I put my hand on his cheek and forced him to look at me. "What about my parents? Or my sister?" I said. "I have to help out with my dad's business until he can work again. We have to go home, Jackson Flannigan."

For a minute, he seemed uncertain. Like he wanted to go on arguing.

But he nodded as he glanced at the trail ahead and said, "That pack looks heavy. Let me carry it." He reached for my backpack, made even heavier with Reagan's hammer, and swung it over his right shoulder so that he carried my pack on one arm and his own on the other.

Jax was always a gentleman.

Twigs crunched under the toes of my shoe as I resumed walking on the dirt path toward the road. Jax was a few feet in front of me. A beam of sunlight burst through a gap in the trunks of the alder trees and cast a golden glow over his windblown blond hair. He looked over his shoulder at me. Gave me a small smile. Even from where I was, I could see the charming crinkle of the skin around his blue eyes. And for a second, the world was right and whole and I could picture a future where we could go home and heal and mourn and put ourselves back together. Everything was in that smile. Every kiss. Every moment. Everything.

I pulled Kenna's phone from my pocket. "Still no signal," I said.

Jax faced forward and kept walking.

Then.

The bird vanished.

The hum of the insects went quiet.

We saw it at the same time.

About twenty feet to the right of the path, peering out from a cluster of birch trees, existing almost entirely in the shadows of the thin tree trunks.

The masked, shrouded figure of Count Dracula.

The instant we saw him, he swept up his flowing cloak in a dark blur and retreated farther into the forest. Jax took off through the trees, following Dracula through the forest. Leaving me no choice but to run behind as well.

"Jax! Jax!" I screamed. Why the hell did he have to chase after that monster? Why did he have to be such a hero all the time?

I checked the phone again, desperately hoping something had changed. The display still read NO SIGNAL. My foot caught on part of a tree root that jutted out from the moist soil. Flying through the air for a few seconds, I crashed hard into a tree trunk that shimmied and blanketed me with wintergreen leaves. The bark created a deep cut along my cheek. My vision went black, and as I lay sprawled out on the damp earth, I blinked furiously, trying to recover my sight and make sense of what was happening. I struggled to remember where I was or how I got there or how much time had passed or what to do next.

Thick raindrops began to fall.

The rain washed over me and brought me back to my senses.

Jax!

I brushed the leaves off and rolled over onto all fours. The water-soaked forest came into view. My stomach heaved, and I wrapped my arms around myself. I didn't have time to throw up. I had to help Jax.

Getting up, I had to brace myself on the tree for a minute to stop the world from spinning. As soon as I could move, I took off in what I hoped was the same direction as Jax. I could no longer see or hear him. The only sounds were my heavy breathing and the low, distant whooshing of the river.

I ran.

The forest broke into a clearing.

I skidded to a stop in front of a massive iron gate flanked by two gray marble statues of a beautiful woman.

This had to be Justina's Labyrinth.

Exhausted and confused, I grasped the carved stone pillar of the statue nearest me and gazed up as I got my breathing under control. The statues were remarkably lifelike. Rock had some-how been chiseled into the soft curls of Justina Szilágy's hair and the folds of her elegant dress. I knew from my Dracula re-search that Justina was Vlad Dracul's second wife and that even though they were only married two years, they were deeply in love.

I eyed the tall hedge maze in front of me.

The garden was a tribute to the love of a monster.

Unlike the statue of her husband in the courtyard, the Justinas still had their heads. They gestured toward the garden with graceful hands. Rain ran down their faces, creating the illusion of two weeping beauties.

It seemed like a terrible idea to go into the labyrinth. The boxwood hedges were impossibly tall and in desperate need of a trim. The overgrown bushes made the path through the maze narrow and dark. I'd probably be lost in there for hours. I hadn't seen Jax go in there, and I couldn't understand why he would.

Why would he follow a killer into a such a place?

To my left, there was a cobblestone walkway that looked as if it led back to the castle. I desperately hoped that Jax had gone back to the castle. Where Reagan would talk some sense into him. Brushing the rain out of my face, I resolved to go that way.

And I heard the screams.

Awful. Horrible screams.

Jax's primal yells that would always echo through my nightmares.

The sounds were obviously coming from inside the labyrinth.

I ran into the hedge maze, not caring that the branches hit me in the face or that thorns stuck into my fingertips as I tried to push them away. The labyrinth appeared to have a circular design, and I peeked around the corners, hoping to see Jax, making the best decisions I could about which way to go.

Coming to a dead end, I stared for a moment into the wall of lance-shaped leaves, afraid to turn around because I was certain that I'd find Dracula or Vlad Dracul . . . or . . . something terrible behind me. I waited and waited. Listening to the tree branches rustle.

Another scream got me moving again.

It felt like I was in there for an eternity. It felt like I ran past the same section of turns over and over. It felt like the sky would fall.

Finally, I poked my head around a curved portion of the hedge.

I had arrived at what must have been the center of the maze.

A marble replica of Castle Prahova lay ahead.

Jax clutched one of the model's spires. Holding on for dear life.

Dracula towered over him.

With the hammer. The monster must have taken the hammer from Jax. Dracula had the hammer because my boyfriend had insisted on carrying my pack.

Pounding and swinging. Fleshy smacks. Dull thuds.

Crimson red blood splashed and splattered across the white rock.

The count's black cloak billowed like a terrible sail, flapping as he swung, its hem soaked with a horrible mixture of mud and rain and blood.

I clamped my hand over my mouth to stifle a scream.

What a coward. I was a terrible, useless coward. I did nothing. I stayed where I was. Frozen. Like a statue. Listening to the gurgling of blood. To Jax's last desperate gasps of breath. I wanted to tell myself that this was what he would want. That Jax would want me to be safe. But I would have rather died with him. I should have died.

Jax deserved better. So much better.

I remembered our first kiss. Our first film festival. The two of us deliberately letting our arms brush. The jolt that went through me at the touch of his skin. Sitting in the stands at his lacrosse games, drinking cocoa, and the sense that all was right in the world. The nights spent in a sleeping bag in his backyard. At the same time, I could feel the future shrink and deflate and pop like a balloon on the day after the party. No happy endings. It was gone.

It was all gone. We were supposed to become a Hollywood power couple.

Without him, who was I?

I waited there. On the ground.

Shaking and heaving. Refusing to release the sobs trapped inside me.

Even when I heard the footsteps trail off, I didn't move. I dug my fingernails into the palms of my hands and let the rain wash over me. Part of me wished that the killer would come back and knock the life out of me with that hammer. I wished he would. I almost prayed for that.

The sky was black and furious and dark when I finally crawled over to the miniature castle. As I came closer, I realized that the castle model was actually a fountain. Just like the real castle was surrounded by a river, its doppelganger had its own mini moat.

I moved through the sludge of mud and blood and mildew and moss. I cradled what was left of Jax's head in my lap. Half of his face was bashed in. His beautiful, beautiful face destroyed. His cheekbone crushed. Half his skull caved. A single blue eye stared up at me. Glassy and accusing. His blood soaked through my sweats. A coldness settled deep inside me.

I would never be warm again.

Dracula had discarded the hammer near the base of the castle. I don't know why, but I reached for it. I held it in my hands for a second, horrified, thinking that if I could only get rid of the hammer Jax would be fine, and like magic, he'd recover. He'd wake up like something from a dark fairy tale. With a jolt, I realized what I was holding. I dropped the hammer into the algae-filled fountain.

The rain poured down.

I began to scream. *Help. Help. Help me.*

Even though I knew it was hopeless.

Help. Help. Help. Help. Help. Help.

Even though I knew no help was coming.

I continued to scream.

General Directorate for Criminal Investigations

Pending report—EXHIBIT 98

McKee, K. [@KennaDressedInBlack] (January 4)

Skutnik's note: Typical social media post by Kenna McKee on American horror film culture. Video shows a young girl in a long, black lace dress with heavy gothic makeup holding a black Ouija board.

People want to be afraid. They like being scared. From a position of safety. In real life, there's a lot of stuff to be afraid of. Getting old. Climate change. Spiders and car accidents and your dad getting your credit card bill. We don't like to think of those things, so we turn to horror and we let ourselves be afraid of the unreal. The monster in the basement. The ax murderer hiding in the garage. The vampire coming for your blood. But then again. Maybe ghosts are real. Maybe the house is really haunted. Are you afraid of the spirits? Afraid of what they might say?

Two days ago

INT. THE GRAND HALL—DAY

I'm not sure how long I waited there.

Ice-cold. Frozen. Letting the rain and blood run over me. Hoping that the killer would return. Fearing that he would. Unsure of what to do next. Should I go back to the castle? Try to find my way back to the road by myself? It was Jax who always knew what to do.

He was the hero.

I don't know why, but at that moment, finding Reagan and Hazel seemed like the best idea. Maybe that's natural. People need each other. If I had made it to the road, Jax's death would have meant something. If I could have called for help, he would have died for a reason. Part of me felt like I was betraying him by leaving his crumpled body there by the fountain. But I didn't want to be alone.

By some miracle, I found my way out of the maze, arriving at the exit on the opposite side. There were no statues there. Instead, a series of pointed iron arches covered with wisteria in late bloom lined a cobblestone path that extended in the direction of the castle. I dragged myself underneath them. The rain had let up to a light drizzle, and the dangling strands of purple plants provided some cover. Tiny petals sailed down from the archways as I passed underneath, getting stuck on my sticky, bloodstained sweater.

As I walked, I continued to strain my ears for any sound from the killer, but things had returned to normal. It sounded normal anyway. Tweeting birds. Rustling leaves. The patter of the rain. The scuffle of my shoes in the dirt.

The path ended in a wide square between two of Prahova's buildings. Little to no renovation had been done in this area. But there were remnants of old world luxury. A few broken marble tiles. A scratched-up, faded mural on one of the stone walls. Smashed-up ceramic pots that must have held plants. Part of a carved wooden bench, rotted and gnawed on by the things that go bump in the night. I nearly tripped over tangled weeds that concealed chunks of stone. At one time, there must have been more statues out there, because a few half-pulverized pillars stuck out from the long grass that was in desperate need of a mow. But trampled sections of grass crisscrossed the area, and there was a well-worn path from where I stood to another series of garden arches on the opposite side.

Someone had been there recently.

Someone traveled through this square frequently.

On my right, I spotted the wall of the courtyard of the east wing and, farther in the distance, the steps up to the kitchen where we had entered yesterday. To my left, I found a dilapidated stone structure. What was left of the grand hall. According to what Reagan told me, this was where I should find him. From where I was standing, I could see the outer wall of the east wing. If he and Hazel had been looking for the cable that ended at that wall, they should have been there.

But I was alone in the square.

I was unsure of what to do. I regretted my decisions. All of them. The decision to leave Jax in the maze. My choice not to try to make it to the road. The trip to Romania. All the times I let people talk me into things. All the times I left everything to Jax.

The sorrow weighed me down. An anchor that kept me rooted in the square. Perhaps if I stayed still long enough, I would become a statue and someone would put me up on one of the empty pillars. And there were practical issues too. I guess I assumed that I'd return to the castle and just run into Reagan and Hazel. It was beginning to dawn on me how silly that notion was. The castle grounds were extensive. There was no telling where the search for the mystery phone or computer had taken my friends.

Or even if they were still alive.

What if Dracula . . . or whoever . . . had killed them before coming for Jax . . . and me. What if I was all alone? What if I was the next and final item on the killer's to-do list?

Plus, they had Kenna with them. Who the hell knew what was up with her?

What little sunlight there was appeared to be coming from the western part of the sky. Half the day was gone. The night would come.

Thunder clapped and the wind picked up.

The clouds overhead were pitch-black again, and I knew we were in for another storm. Like last night. It would be dark. And again, we would be trapped. Still, I continued to stand there. Listening to the wind whisper through the grass. Jax's blood drying, forming a crust over me. My feet sinking slowly into the mud.

I would probably still be standing there.

Except I heard a scream.

A high-pitched, girlish scream.

And then another . . . and another.

Coming from the direction of the grand hall.

My pulse raced even as I hesitated. But I decided to go in. I mean, I had to. How many people was I going to let die? How could I live with myself if I did nothing? Again. I told my feet to move and they obeyed. I ran in the direction of the grand hall, my footsteps landing heavy and splashing mud as I went.

It took me a minute or so to get over there, during which time the screaming stopped. I arrived at the remnants of an enormous stone arch and what was left of another one of the massive wooden doors that we'd seen all throughout the castle. Someone had made a half-hearted attempt to board up the entrance, but I was able to climb through a gaping hole between two planks of water-rotted wood. As I forced my way inside, thunder clapped again and rain began to rush from the sky, pouring down like water from a broken pipe.

Inside the hall, it was almost completely dark. Between the storm and the wooden planks that covered what were probably windows, the visibility was poor. There were a few places where the roof sagged or boards didn't cover the windows, but these provided only a few dull spotlights. I reached into my pocket for my phone and turned on the flashlight. My phone wasn't in the best of shape, and the light pulsed as it extended a little glow around me.

There wasn't enough light for me to be able to see the dimensions of the room, but it felt like a massive, cavernous place. I could tell that the building had enormously tall ceilings. Rain filtered in through large and small gouges in the roof. Occasionally, I got a glimpse of the gray-black storm clouds.

It smelled of mildew and musky fur and like a bunch of cats called the place home.

From beyond my little circle of light, I could hear water drops pelt wood and metal surfaces and land with little smacks in the mud.

And the light flutter of wings.

I shivered.

Moving farther away from the door, trying to shine my light in all directions as I walked, I stepped over discarded wooden beams and broken mosaic titles, similar to those in the bathhouse, and odd piles of trash. Potato chip bags. Candy bar wrappers. Condom wrappers. A discarded pack of chewing gum. Who on earth needed to come in *here* and chew gum?

My breathing felt too heavy. Too fast.

"Reagan?" I whispered. Not really loud enough for anyone to hear.

I didn't see or hear anyone, but I couldn't shake the feeling that I wasn't alone.

"Reagan?" I said again. More in my regular speaking voice.

Continuing to creep along, searching for Reagan, and whoever was screaming, I very nearly crashed into a tall stack of boxes. Someone must have intended to restore this part of the castle at some point, because there were stacks and stacks of building supplies. I pointed my flashlight at labels that said things like R-13 INSULATION AND PORCELAIN TILE. There was also a whole pallet of concrete mix. But the stuff had been there for a while. The boxes were dusty and water soaked, and rats, or something, had been nibbling on the plastic that covered the concrete.

The piles of rotting supplies created aisles and corners and even darker spaces.

Perfect places for someone to hide.

The flapping paper sounds grew louder and closer, and they were accompanied by a weird chirping and sucking, like small suction cups being pulled off a glass pane. An odd breeze traveled in my direction, and too late, I realized what was happening.

Bats.

The place was utterly infested with bats.

They whipped over my head, grazing my hair and brushing my cheeks with their furry bodies. Too grossed out to even scream, I found myself ducking in between two stacks of boxes, where I flopped onto the ground and curled up, pressing my face between my knees. I panted and gasped and ran my hands over my body in the places where the bats brushed by me, trying to rid myself of the creepy sensations. The bats were trying hard to find a place to settle, but the storm raged on outside and I was messing things up for them in the grand hall. I held the light of my phone against my body, hoping that if it was dark again they'd go back to being quiet and still.

And then footsteps seemed to come from every direction.

Until.

I was forcefully tackled and dragged by the collar of my sweater and tossed out from between the rows of boxes, rolling to a stop in a pile of tile fragments. I coughed out a mouthful of dust.

"Ahhhhh!" said a familiar voice as a bright light dazed me.

It was Reagan.

He lowered the light. "Alex?" he said. "Oh . . . thank God. What are you doing here?"

It took everything I had not to burst into tears. "I . . . I was looking for you . . . Something terrible happened . . . The man in the mask . . . he . . . he . . ."

Reagan reached out to help me up off the ground. "I followed him in here."

"The Dracula?" I asked in an accent of dread. "He . . . he killed Jax."

Reagan was silent for a second. In the darkness, I couldn't make out the horror that I knew filled his face. "Oh, Alex. I'm so sorry. I . . . I . . . The man in the mask . . . he tailed us from the east wing. I slipped away from Hazel and circled around him. When he noticed I was behind him, he ran in here."

Something about that didn't make a lot of sense. The Dracula couldn't be following Reagan at the same time that he was chasing me and Jax through the forest.

"We need to get out of here," I said, reaching out to tug on his sleeve. "We should go back to the road. Jax was right. Calling for help is our best shot."

"No," Reagan said flatly. "It's either us or him, Alex. We won't survive if he does."

"Reagan! Reagan," I said, desperate to convince him to get out of the grand hall. "Where are Hazel and Kenna? We need to get out of here. I heard someone scream."

I could see for the first time that he had the last working flashlight with him and it was casting a much more powerful beam across the area. The space was, indeed, great and large and mostly filled with construction materials.

"Hmm. What?" Reagan said absently as he scanned the room. His light briefly grazed over a wall with the remains of a mural similar to the ones we'd seen in the east wing. "Kenna threw a fit and went back to the castle the instant you and Jax took off. Hazel and I . . . well . . . we found something . . . strange . . . on the north side. She's over there now."

"You left her there?" I repeated in a screech.

"Shh!" Reagan said, listening intently. His head snapped to the left, like he'd heard something. "She's fine," he went on in a whisper. "You want to worry about someone? Worry about us. We're the ones trapped in—"

This time I heard it too.

The scuffle of feet and the thud of falling boxes. In the far corner to our left side, the cloaked Dracula figure climbed a tall stack of boxes, attempting to make it to a large, high window, pushing supplies to the floor. Iron pipes and plumbing fixtures and a waterfall of nails came crashing down as we watched.

"Come on!" Reagan yelled.

I wanted to tell him *NO.* That I had already chased down the man in the Dracula mask once today, and it ended with Jax's terrible murder. I wanted to grab Reagan and drag him out of there and get us somewhere safe. But he was already gone. Leaving me no choice but to follow behind.

Running to the corner, I joined Reagan in frantically pulling boxes to destabilize the figure climbing toward the window. Even as the bats circled and fled the grand hall through the narrow opening, the Dracula continued to climb. He was almost to the very top. His fingers curled around the lone plank of rotting wood nailed to the window frame. In a few seconds, he would vanish. And be free to regroup. To restart the hunt.

The Dracula dropped something small. It bounced off a couple of the boxes before hitting the ground with the sound of cracking plastic. Reagan groaned in frustration, let out a guttural yell, and charged the stack of supplies with as much force as he could manage. The tower rocked, and Dracula struggled to keep his balance. Relief briefly surged through me.

Until.

The figure fell from the stack.

Letting out a high, horror-movie scream as . . . he fell.

Gracefully careening down and coming to a terrible end. The black silk waving like a pirate's flag. The sickening sound of tearing flesh. One final, sharp scream, piercing through me. More blood. Forming small streams that run down the wooden pole and onto the dirt and smashed-up porcelain tile.

The body of the Dracula.

Impaled by a fallen, jagged wooden beam that had broken free from the roof.

Cut in two by the remains of the crumbling castle.

"Oh . . . oh . . . shit," Reagan said. The beam of the flashlight bounced up and down as he shook and nearly dropped it. "I had to . . . You saw . . . what happened . . . I had to. You know that I had to do it. At least it's over."

His voice trembled when he said this last part.

Because we both already knew.

It was *not* over.

It was a girl's scream that we heard. Reagan took my hand in his, and as we approached the bloody, bent body, we could both see that it was small. Way too small to have been the person I saw in the maze pounding the life out of Jax. Way too petite to have overpowered a star lacrosse player. Even as we stepped forward, my well of dread was refilling.

This wasn't Jax's killer, and that meant there were two of them.

Or more. This wasn't the end of anything.

It was the beginning of a new hunt.

When we were a couple of feet away from the cloaked figure with the ragged pole stuck through her heart, Reagan dropped my hand and continued on alone. He moved slowly. Like someone approaching a venomous snake. Like he'd rather be anywhere else, doing anything else.

He reached out and slowly pulled off the Dracula mask.

I could see that it was exactly the same as the ones Maddie had made.

Maddie had made the mask.

I wanted to throw up.

"Reagan," I said. "What the fuck is happening?"

General Directorate for Criminal Investigations

Pending report—EXHIBIT 34

Skutnik's note: Message saved as draft in Kenna McKee's email. The message is incomplete as the Prahova satellite dish went down before Kenna sent it.

To: justin@bloomhousestudios.com
Subject: What the HELL?

I don't know what to do. Or who to contact. Raul
turned the power off. Our cell phones don't work. I just
found out. I don't know. I don't know how you could
have done this to us. You must have known that the
castle was owned by Yuri Stoica. That he was Cat's
uncle. I think that he's—

Two days ago

EXT. THE NORTH WING—DAY

It was Kenna McKee.

And she was dead.

Reagan dropped the Dracula mask onto the rough floor of the grand hall and backed away from the grisly scene. "Alex! What does this mean? What . . . what . . . You saw what I saw! Right? It was an accident and I thought she was the . . . the killer. Is Kenna McKee the killer?"

My brain sputtered along with Reagan's words. I had a hard time believing that Kenna would kill anyone. But why did she have the mask? Why was she dressed up in the Dracula costume? Why had she lied to get us here?

I clung to Reagan. "Did you check her pulse? Is she breathing? We need help . . . We need to call . . ." Who? We couldn't call for help. We were all alone. "What are we going to do? We're all gonna die. He's gonna kill us all."

In some strange way, Kenna's death hit harder than Jax's. It was as if watching Jax die had pierced my heart, but seeing Kenna ripped my chest wide open. I guess she was a liar. But she was *our* liar. Our fabulist. When Reagan returned to my side, I leaned into him; the weight of all the world felt like it was going to pound me into dust.

I also noticed that he didn't bother to contradict me.

There were only three of us left.

Maddie. Carter. Jax. Kenna. All dead.

The killer was still out there.

Waiting for us.

"We have to get out of here," Reagan said, repeating what I'd said earlier.

I nodded but released his arm. Kenna had dropped something, and it felt important to determine what it was. Using my phone's flashlight, I scanned all around until I spotted a small black object that had landed a few feet from Kenna's body.

I took slow steps and approached it cautiously.

"It's a camera," I told Reagan as I picked it up.

"I see it," he said. And then more sharply, "We *have* to go."

He gave Kenna's body one last glance, as if to check that it was really her and that she was really dead, before taking my hand and leading me back to the grand hall door.

Through the gaps in the wooden planks covering the doorway, we could see the rain still coming down hard outside. I hesitated before going into the storm and inspected Kenna's tiny high-definition camera. It was nicer than her old model and had a small built-in microphone. It wasn't the one we had rented from the camera shop. I pressed the power key and unfolded the viewfinder. An image of Jax, Reagan, and me in the smoking room appeared on the screen. Reagan was inspecting the lit cigar. It was taken the prior night when we were searching for Carter. Kenna must have been hiding.

I held it out for Reagan to see. "What do you think this is? What does it mean?"

Why was Kenna filming *us* as we explored the castle?

Reagan turned the camera off, leaving me with a blank screen in my hand, squeezed through the rotting boards, and left the grand hall. I shoved the camera underneath my sweater to protect it and followed behind him.

When I emerged, he put a light hand on my upper arm. "Alex, if we make it. If we survive tonight, I have to know that you have my back. Otherwise, people might think that . . ."

Otherwise, he might go to jail.

"It's okay, Reagan. I'll protect you," I told him.

We'd only been outside the hall for a minute or so, but we were already soaked again.

I tried to grab his arm. "We should go to the road," I said.

Reagan shook his head of wet, red hair. "No. We have to get to Hazel. Tell her what happened. Make sure she's still . . ."

Alive.

At least Reagan seemed to have a sense of where he was going. We headed west, away from the grand hall, leaving the maze and gardens behind, charging ahead toward the unkempt grounds and the part of Prahova that lay in ruins. His wet sweatpants stuck to his stick-skinny legs, and rainwater flattened his red hair to his scalp.

The farther we got from the east wing, the slower we were forced to walk. If there were ever cobblestone walkways on this part of the grounds, they were long gone. My feet sank deep into the mud with each step. We came closer to what I thought, based on my memory of the map, was the north wing. A tall, ragged tower loomed over what was left of a squarish building with holes punched into its walls. The forest grew closer to the castle on this side. Close enough for long, twisted branches to poke the red roof tiles and scrape the stone walls. I kept my eyes on the shuddering trees, watching for any sign of the other Dracula. The one who had killed Jax.

Reagan led us underneath a stone arch between the two structures, through an outdoor hallway of sorts. There were a few doorways on each side of us, but the doors themselves were missing, leaving darkened, rotting spaces that would be perfect for a psycho killer to hide in.

We came to another of the castle's many buildings. This one was in better shape and had an intact door with a modern silver lock like the ones in the east wing. Reagan must have gotten the master key from Jax because he fished it from the pocket of his sweatpants and opened the door, cautiously kicking the wood with the toe of his shoe. It swung slowly.

Revealing a room furnished like a fairly generic office.

And it had electricity.

So the theory that someone had deliberately turned off the power in the east wing appeared to be correct.

The room was painted an ugly, corporate gray color made worse by the fluorescent lights hanging by exposed wires from the ancient ceiling. There were several metal desks, similar to the ones that the teachers used in school. A few of them contained old beige computers that looked like they hadn't been used since the first *Scream* movie came out. The floors were dusty but had several recent sets of mud tracked across them. Detailed paper maps with markings and writings in Romanian. A modern laptop, covered with stickers, was on one of the desks.

It was Kenna's computer.

"Hazel?" Reagan called out. An expression of alarm crossed

his face. Like he was regretting his decision to leave her alone in there.

I tensed at the sound of something moving under one of the desks.

But Hazel's face appeared a second later. "Oh, thank God. You can't even believe what I found. I am going to *kill* Kenna McKee," she said as she pushed a frayed leather chair forward and climbed out.

"Too late," Reagan said in a dull voice.

Hazel stood up and brushed the dust from the floor off her yoga pants. She froze with her mouth hanging open. "What do you mean?" Her eyes met mine. "Where's Jax? And Kenna? Oh. God. Whose blood is that? Alex? What . . . what . . . what . . ."

I should have told her what happened to Jax. What a special person he was. How I couldn't imagine going on without him. Instead, I blurted out, "That maniac who's been hunting us beat him to death with a hammer. While I watched . . . and . . . you . . . the last thing that happened was . . ."

That he said he wanted to run away to Europe. I burst into tears.

Hazel sank into the desk chair.

I sobbed into my blood-crusted sleeve. Had I pushed him too hard when I should have made him feel like he *was* perfect even if he wasn't dreaming about being Jerry Bruckheimer? "He was mine and I should have known. We didn't make it to the road. And now . . . we're all gonna die. We shouldn't have split up. Hazel, I told you, and you never listen! You think you know everything. You think . . . you think . . ."

Reagan let out a frustrated sigh. "This isn't helping, Alex."

"Please," Hazel said, on the verge of tears herself. "Tell me what's happening?"

Reagan stood between where I lingered at the door and Hazel's desk, as if unsure of what to do. He remained where he was. "You know that . . . um . . . person we saw in the Dracula costume? Well, that was Kenna. While I was following her, the real killer murdered Jax."

Hazel shook her head slowly in confusion. "Jax? But. You said Kenna was . . . dead?"

Glancing at me, Reagan answered, "She had an accident in the grand hall. And she fell onto a . . . a wooden beam and . . ."

"That's enough," Hazel said in a whisper.

Kenna fell? I guess that was the story we planned to go with. Reagan gave me a sideways glance that was laced with a silent plea not to contradict him. Taking a couple of steps into the room, I sat on the top of one of the metal desks and dropped the camera. It landed on the metal with a clang. It was silent for a minute, and I tried to register where I was. I never paid much attention in geography and couldn't speak Romanian, so I didn't know what to make of all the maps. But the place had the feel of a call center. There were a few supply cabinets, an old copy machine, and a bunch of old-timey corded phones on a few of the desks.

I pointed to the camera. "She was filming us."

Hazel nodded, and a bit of color returned to her face. No doubt she was relieved to have a puzzle or an immediate problem to resolve. "Oh, I know." She stared at my bloody sweater for a second before continuing. "Her stuff is in here. She was making a movie."

As Hazel held up a stack of papers, Reagan went over to the desk and stood so that he could read over her shoulder. "Everyone knows that. We came here to make a movie."

Hazel handed him a file folder. "Kenna was doing something else. It's kind of meta actually. She and her father pitched the idea to Justin Bloom. It looks like Justin Bloom might have DM'd her after Catrinel boosted our fundraiser. Basically, we thought we were making *Dead Boys Don't Bite*, but *she* hired a crew to scare the hell out of *us* and record our responses. It's supposed to be . . . gritty. A horror movie with an authentic feel."

"A crew?" I repeated. So, there were any number of people roaming around in the woods trying to terrify us? Or worse?

"Don't they, like, need our consent to film us?" Reagan asked.

Hazel motioned for him to keep flipping pages. "Yeah. But I think she forged our names. There are release forms in there for all of us."

"She probably figured she'd be able to talk us into it in the end. The way she did with everything," I said, finding that I desperately missed my friends. I missed Jax. I even missed Kenna's manipulation.

"So where is this crew?" I watched the door as if someone might bust in at any second.

"And how was she going to pay them?" Reagan asked.

But even as he said those words, a look of comprehension crossed his face. "The money. The half a million dollars came from Justin Bloom."

"Yeah," Hazel said, opening the laptop. "And according to some of his messages, he's pretty pissed that it's missing. I was able to get into Kenna's email. Up until the storm, this place actually *did* have internet access from a satellite dish that must have been knocked out. I think the crew are stuck in Braşov because of the weather."

Everyone knew Kenna's password was *$toker*.

"What makes you think there was a satellite dish?" Reagan asked.

Hazel made a tap on the trackpad. "She was able to access a Wi-Fi network called PravovaCryptoSigna."

"That's a Romanian satellite internet provider, yes." Reagan's eyes scanned the papers. "Holy shit. You're telling me that Kenna ran all over the castle, locking and unlocking doors, and . . . the boarding pass . . . the newspaper articles . . . and the blood . . . She planted all of that?"

A clap of thunder loud enough to send vibrations through the metal desk.

Hazel shuddered at the noise but went on. "Yeah. Her and Raul Stoica. According to the production notes, he's the one who turned off the power. The last email that Kenna got was a message from the director she'd hired. This guy named Florian Ioveanu. He said that they couldn't get transportation until tomorrow. He told her to use Raul and the handheld cameras and do they best they could for a couple of days. It looks like after Maddie took off, Kenna started frantically trying to contact people, but none of her messages went through. You remember when she lied about seeing Reagan upstairs? I think she was really outside trying to find Raul and call the whole thing off."

"So that's why she wanted to hole up in the castle and wait?

She knew someone was coming?" I frowned in confusion. "But. If she was trying to call it off with Raul, why was she still going around wearing the costume?"

"Well . . ." Hazel said as she squirmed in her chair.

Reagan cut through her angrily. "That was Kenna! I mean, if we have to die, why not do it on camera? She probably thought our murders would make good pre-film buzz."

It felt wrong, somehow, to criticize Kenna when we had just witnessed her death. I cleared my throat. "Were they hoping we wouldn't notice the arrival of an entire film crew?"

Hazel too seemed relieved to change the subject. "It was a small team. They have more detailed maps of Prahova in here." She waved her hands at the paper covering the walls. "There are underground tunnels that they planned to use to move people and equipment. There's a loading dock somewhere. And . . . um . . . the maid and the cook were supposed to be part of it. I guess they went home when Kenna couldn't pay them." Hazel made a couple of taps on the laptop's trackpad. "They had scripted lines and everything. Besides them, there was only going to be the director, um, an audio engineer, and some kind of an assistant. And Raul."

My heartbeat slowed almost to a stop. "So . . . you're saying . . . Raul is the killer?"

Something like relief washed over Reagan's face. But if it *was* Raul, and we were stuck at Prahova without help for at least another day, there was nothing to be *relieved* about. He was familiar with the castle and had already killed three of us. We'd already tried to make it to the road to make a call without success.

At the rate he was picking us off, there wouldn't be anyone left tomorrow for the crew to find.

But Hazel didn't answer. At least, not right away.

I checked the clock on the laptop. It was around three. In a few hours, it would be dark again. We needed to come up with a plan if we wanted to survive the night. "What did they do with the footage they shot?"

"I think Kenna was uploading it to this laptop. It's probably in that folder." Hazel pointed to the screen. "But it's password protected. I tried all of her usuals, and nothing worked."

Reagan squinted at the screen of Kenna's laptop. "I guess that's my department."

Hazel hesitated again. Doing that thing that she did. Where she opened her mouth and closed it over and over again while she tried to figure out what to say.

A new wave of adrenaline dread ran through me. "What? What are you not telling us?"

We could hear the outside rain coming down even harder than before. Thunder shook the walls and the power flickered.

What little color that had returned to Hazel's cheeks vanished, and she was even paler than before. "You asked if Raul is the killer . . . Well . . . the thing is . . . I found something else."

Reagan and I stared at her as she wrapped her arms around herself.

Hazel sighed. She clicked on another file folder on Kenna's laptop. This one was labeled *YURI STOICA*.

"And there's something you need to see."

Alexandra Elaine Rush—Transcript—Tape 3

Alex: The other officers had a lot of stories about Yuri Stoica.

Inspector Skutnik: Yes. He is something of a legend in international law enforcement. The gentleman's thief-in-law.

Alex: Bram Stoker wanted his Dracula to represent complete moral decay. He was everything wrong with the world. Other people only existed to be his victims. To be useful to him. Maybe if there's a modern version of Count Dracula, Yuri Stoica is it. A drug dealer who takes what he wants and hurts everyone he can.

Inspector Skutnik: Perhaps [beeping noise]. One of his favorite schemes was art theft.

Alex: Maddie suspected that.

Inspector Skutnik: Three years ago, Interpol pursued him into Bucharest. He was killed during a high-speed car crash. We, of course, have monitored his son, Raul, on and off. But it seems as if you are saying that Yuri Stoica is not dead?

Alex: He's not dead. He was at Prahova. With us.

Two days ago

INT. THE OFFICE—DAY

We leaned in closer to the laptop screen as Hazel made a couple of clicks. A window opened, and a piece of black-and-white video began to play. It was from some kind of a security camera, and it showed the very room we were standing in. I glanced around and didn't see a camera anywhere.

Reagan must've been having similar thoughts, because his eyes scanned the room. He turned around and pointed to the corner behind us and to our left. "I think the camera must be over there. Yeah," he said, nodding with his own statement. "Concealed in plain sight by that huge map of the forest."

I gasped in shock at the image of a tall, strangely handsome older man emerging from a trapdoor neatly concealed by wooden floorboards. He puffed on a lit cigar as he traveled across the screen. A man who looked exactly like the one in the photographs in the smoking room was on the laptop screen exiting the room via the wooden door.

The man was Yuri Stoica. Who was supposed to be dead.

"Maybe that's an old piece of footage that Kenna got somehow?" Reagan suggested.

Hazel tapped the screen. "Look," she said. "That's part of Kenna's backpack in the shot. And then . . . wait for it . . ."

A couple of seconds later, Raul Stoica emerged from the trapdoor. He was clad in the flowy black cloak and had something white in his hand. Probably one of the Dracula masks. I couldn't understand why he was after us. But that didn't change the fact that he was.

Hazel handed me a file folder. "This is from in there," she said, pointing at one of the steel cabinets. "Someone was keeping a file full of the cartel's press clippings."

I thumbed through cut-out scraps of newspaper and printed internet articles. Most of them were in Russian and Romanian. But the pictures of bodies facedown in the street were pretty easy to understand. Occasionally, there was something in English. The FBI was hunting for the mob's criminal associates. The US government was working with Interpol to find drug money. There wasn't anything in the file about Raul Stoica. Authorities didn't appear to believe that the son was like his father.

My best friend shrugged. "What better explanation is there for what's going on? Yuri Stoica has killed a small army of people, what difference does a few more teenagers make?"

And Raul wasn't just working for Kenna. He was with his father.

But if Yuri Stoica was in hiding, why had he risked returning to the castle?

Hazel was still talking. "This is from *after* we arrived. I went through the production notes in Kenna's backpack. There's an old network of security cameras that runs through the castle, and she planned to use some of that footage. But then she saw Yuri Stoica. There's a message in her drafts folder with her trying to send this footage to an email address I don't recognize. It's from this morning, and she must have known it wouldn't send, but . . ."

She wanted someone to find it.

Kenna McKee knew that we were all dead.

And she had been trying to leave behind evidence of our killer.

"What? What?" I asked, unable to catch my breath. "You're saying that . . . a Romanian crime lord is strolling around? That . . . that there's a . . . a . . . a . . . system of tunnels running beneath the buildings that lead to *this* room?" It took everything I had to fight my instinct to run. But I also understood Kenna's behavior. Sort of. "The Dracula costume was a disguise. She was wearing it to buy time. So if Yuri Stoica saw her, he might mistake her for his son and not . . . not . . ." Pound her to death with a hammer.

"I think so too." Hazel nodded and continued to watch the screen. Like if the gangsters vanished from the screen, they would be no threat to us in real life.

My pulse picked up, and I stared at the floorboards, looking all over for the trapdoor.

Sensing my thoughts, Hazel said, "I pushed a desk on top of the spot. It should make it pretty tough for anyone to come in that way," Hazel said, hesitating for a second. "There's something else. Alex. There's a lot of stuff about you in the notes that Kenna sent to Justin Bloom. They thought of you as the Lucy Westenra character. They wrote character arcs for us. Bloom really liked this idea of a horror writer who starts seeing monsters everywhere. They kind of targeted you. Wanted to make sure that you saw all the really scary stuff."

Reagan patted my back. "Sorry. I'm sorry."

"It's okay . . . but I'm wondering . . . where was Kenna going?" I asked.

Reagan shifted his weight from foot to foot and avoided my gaze.

It fell to Hazel to answer. "She was leaving this room. That's how we found it."

Reagan's shoulders slumped. "And then I chased after . . . the Dracula. I mean, I thought that's what I was doing."

But he was chasing Kenna.

I put my hand on Reagan's arm. "She should have told us what was going on."

"Yeah. But. How do you admit to something like that?" Hazel said, picking at a loose thread hanging from her sweatshirt. "Oh. Gee. Sorry, guys. I've been running around scaring the hell out of you. And *now* a bloodthirsty criminal mastermind is hunting us all down one by one."

Reagan frowned. "Yeah. But why is Yuri Stoica trying to kill *us*? This whole time, we've been assuming it was someone who followed us here. Or even one of us."

"One of those articles said that he killed his barber when he didn't like his haircut. Why did he do *that*?" I asked, trying to remain still. Whenever I moved, the smell of Jax's blood that drenched my sweater hit me. Sickly sweet. Slightly salty. Rusted metal.

Reagan's eyes met mine. "Alex, let's get you out of that shirt." He was already shrugging out of his own sweatshirt, revealing that he had a lacrosse team tee on underneath. He gently gripped the collar of my cardigan and slid it off my shoulders. My own T-shirt was drenched in blood too, but I quickly put on Reagan's sweatshirt. He took my bloody sweater and tossed it underneath the desk where I had left Kenna's camera.

He squeezed my hand. "That's a little better," he said. "Alex, I'm sorry. I . . ."

I rested my head on his shoulder. "I know," I answered in a whisper.

Hazel cleared her throat. "Alex is right," she said. Which may have been the first time that she had ever uttered that particular sentence. "Stoica is a psycho. He doesn't need much of a reason to kill us."

"There has to be more to it," Reagan insisted.

Hazel shrugged. "I don't know. Maybe."

But then it hit me. "Kenna had seen Stoica. No one is supposed to know where he is. She had seen this piece of video footage. After that . . ."

"Right. She had to go," Hazel finished. "We all did."

"Okay," Reagan said slowly. "But why did Stoica risk coming back here at all?"

To me, it felt like we were wasting our time trying to second-guess the thought process of a man like Yuri Stoica. It was quiet for a second. We were all lost in our thoughts. I was trying to come to terms with the fact that these were most likely the final moments of our lives. I had always assumed that I'd die with Jax. That we'd die of old age at the exact same moment. Then they'd give us matching posthumous lifetime achievement Oscars.

Instead, I was probably going to be beaten to death so I wouldn't be able to tell the world that a gangster was hanging out in the tunnels beneath a creepy castle.

Reagan slapped his forehead with his palm. "Oh God. I'm so stupid. That building? The grand hall? It overlooks a clearing and doesn't have anything blocking its view. That must be where the satellite dish is. That's where I would put a dish. Kenna was probably trying to fix it."

"How would Kenna know how to fix a satellite dish?" Hazel asked.

I suspected that Reagan was right. "She might have thought she could do it. Plus, she clearly was trying to avoid telling us what was going on at all costs."

Hazel sighed. "It would have been far more logical to get Reagan to do it."

"Except that Kenna was never logical," I said. And there was something else. There was a desperation in her behavior. Like she didn't involve any of us because she didn't expect the plan to work.

"We're going to have to go into the tunnels," Hazel said in a low, grim voice.

Cold dread pulsed through me. "What? No. No." After everything we'd been through, going into the tunnels sounded like the worst idea I'd ever heard of. "Hazel, we just saw concrete proof that Yuri fucking Stoica is right at home down there. We should go to the road. Jax wanted me to go to the road and try to get a cell signal."

Kenna's phone suddenly felt hot in my pocket. I'd never be able to give it back to her.

Reagan sighed and tried to smile. "Alex. Don't you see? This is good. The dish has been knocked down. Or it's out of alignment or something. But I can probably put it back up, reboot the system, and we could have a working phone. Or working internet. Or both." His smile faded. "But . . . Hazel is right. According to the map, the security and control rooms are in the tunnels. We'll have to go there. After we get the dish back up and . . ." He trailed off.

I was sure that he was right. The satellite dish had to be connected to something. A computer. A router. A network box. We would have to find it. It was logical for it to be in one of the areas we hadn't been able to access. But even if he was right, anyone who went out into that storm wasn't coming back.

I stepped away from Reagan. A lump formed in my throat, and I fought off another round of sobs. "Please. *Please.* That tunnel scares the absolute shit out of me."

"Me too," Hazel said in a small voice. Her hand shook as she closed Kenna's laptop. She glanced at Reagan.

"But I don't want to go out there either . . ." Raul or Yuri Stoica or the Dracula, or whoever, was out there. I couldn't go back outside. "We shouldn't split up. But. I . . . I . . . I guess Hazel and I could go into the tunnel and look for the control room." Even as I said those words, the feelings of shame that I had when I left Jax in the maze returned. I was a coward. Going into the tunnels sounded like a terrible idea. But it felt safer than going outside.

Hazel clutched the book holding the map a little tighter. "I don't know . . ."

"They killed Jax!" I said in a shriek that echoed off the walls. "And Maddie . . . and . . ."

Reagan closed the distance between us and patted my back. "We have to hope there's some amount of strength in numbers. We need to stay together from here on out."

Hazel sprang into action. Planning was her superpower. "Look around," she said. "Let's take anything that could be used as a weapon."

Reagan nodded. "And tools." He avoided looking at me. I knew we were both thinking of the hammer.

We spent about fifteen minutes running around the room, throwing open cabinets and searching for supplies. The office contained an odd mishmash of stuff. Ordinary business items like staplers and pads of Post-it notes were on shelves alongside old, yellowing, half-drunk bottles of Haski vodka. Hazel came across a set of screwdrivers. Reagan muttered to himself about wanting a level or a compass. I moved from desk to desk, rifling through the drawers until I came across a little unpolished silver sword—a tiny kilij, actually. It was about twelve inches long, and I recognized it from the statue outside the music room. Raul or Kenna must have taken it from the castle when they were messing with us and brought it in here.

"Ew, gross," Hazel said. She dropped a dust-covered metal lunch box on the ground. Something brown and gooey and puckered slid out and rolled across the wooden floor. Hazel rubbed her hands on her yoga pants. "I think that apple is older than I am."

Continuing to inspect the small kilij, I said, "This might come in handy." I added the silver sword to our little pile of gear that included the screwdriver set, a cigarette lighter, a fire extinguisher, and an empty glass vodka bottle.

I stood up from the desk I was sitting at and went to search the last cabinet. It was full of some seriously old wall paint, brushes, and turpentine. It looked like someone must have painted this room a long time ago and it was time for them to come back and do it again. But unless we wanted to smack Raul in the face with a paint roller, nothing in there was much help.

In total silence, we stared at our stash for a minute. The sad little pile of stuff wouldn't be enough for three teenagers to fight off a gangster and his henchman.

"I . . . I . . . I'm not sure about this," I stammered, hoping Reagan would suggest that Hazel and I stay behind. And then hating myself for thinking like that.

We distributed the gear in our backpacks. Reagan took the tools. Hazel had the bottle, the lighter, and the map. I ended up with a package of emergency flares, a really old plastic bottle of water, and the sword. We thought we would be coming right back, so we left Kenna's laptop and camera on the metal desks.

Reagan kissed my forehead. Exactly as Jax had done a few hours earlier. "It's going to be dark soon, Alex," he said. "Our only hope is to get that dish working and make contact with the police. I know you. You're tougher than you think you are. Tougher than you seem. All you have to do is stay alive for another hour. You can do that. We can all do that."

Hazel had her hands balled up into little fists.

Stay alive. Stay alive.

I whispered that to myself.

Reagan crept to the door that led to the grounds.

Thunder rolled as the wood door swung open.

Outside, the heavy rain had created a shallow, muddy river that flowed between the old buildings. Water ran down Prahova's stone exterior, as if the castle itself was crying. I glanced over my shoulder at Hazel's face, gone ashen and gray.

"We can do this," Reagan said.

Maybe he was trying to convince me. Or himself.

He put one foot out into the storm and almost immediately slipped on the cobblestones, which were slick with water and dirt.

I couldn't help but think that Reagan was lying.

That we were already dead.

General Directorate for Criminal Investigations

Pending report—EXHIBIT 22

Rush, Alexandra. _Dead Boys Don't Bite_. Theatrical script.

Revised March 14

Scene 7; page 12

Lucy Westenra: You must transform your imagination. But to do so, you must first ask yourself a simple question. Why do I terrify you? Why does any woman acting in her own self-interest frighten you? You think you are Atlas with the world on your shoulders.

[Lucy reaches her arms out as if to embrace someone who isn't there. Someone lingering in the shadows beyond her view.]

Lucy Westenra [sobs]: But you don't understand. This world has never belonged to you.

Two days ago

EXT. THE ROOF—DAY

Reagan and I tried to retrace our steps back to the grand hall, but we got lost almost immediately. It had gotten a lot darker since we went into the office, and everything seemed different. Grayer. Fog began to roll in again, rising up from the river that surrounded Prahova and enveloping the castle in a gauzy mist. The narrow spaces between the buildings had become black voids where monsters surely lurked.

I pulled my phone out of my pocket. It was around four. We had an hour. Or less. Before darkness and the storm would completely overtake the castle. We all knew we couldn't survive another night. Four of us were already dead.

There were only three of us left.

We went around in the same circle several times, walking in single file, occasionally pausing under one of the narrow stone arches to avoid being hit in the face with rain for a few seconds. The water pounded on the stone, and that sound echoed off the walls of the castle's buildings. Hazel didn't want to take the map out. She thought it would be ruined by the storm. While the rain pelted me, making my sweats stick to my legs and my shoes heavy and gummy, I thought about my parents and my sister. They were at home. Sorting silver. Or watching TV. Were they thinking about me? Were they worried about whether or not they'd ever see me again? If I lived, I told myself that I'd stop complaining about our crappy car and my sister doing barre rises all day and night. I would be a better daughter, sister, and friend.

I stayed as close to Reagan as possible. He was muttering "I think we've been here before" over and over, and it really wasn't helpful.

Hazel tried to identify the buildings as we walked, calling out things like, "I think that pathway leads to the west wing" and "There's the route to the river."

Honestly, I wished she had given the map to me. There might have been options we didn't discuss. Supposedly, there was a loading dock somewhere. And Raul had said that there was a car. If he hadn't actually left Prahova, perhaps the car hadn't either. Anything was better than being soaking wet, slipping in the mud, out there, exposed and waiting for Dracula, whatever, to come and kill us. But Hazel always wanted to control the plan. So she folded the map up and stuffed it up her sweatshirt.

Water ran into my mouth as I said, "We should go back." Loud enough to be heard over the storm. Reagan turned and gave me a look. But I didn't care if he thought I was a chickenshit. We had no idea where we were going. There was very little chance this plan would work.

A burst of white lightning temporarily lit up the sky.

It felt like the mother of all clichés when Reagan then said, "I know where to go."

And he kind of did. At least we were walking with some kind of purpose. We passed by what I thought was the door to the office, which meant that we'd been walking in the wrong direction for a while. But after a couple of minutes, I recognized the path that we were on. I grabbed Reagan's shirttail to keep us together, and Hazel followed behind. She was falling behind. Checking over my shoulder, Hazel had a thoughtful look on her face that didn't match the terror of our present situation. She was slowing down. Taking smaller steps.

Hazel was clearly still stuck on this thing with Yuri Stoica. It was a problem she couldn't solve, and I was sure that was driving her nuts. But Reagan was right. We needed to focus on staying alive. If we did, we'd have all the rest of our lives for true crime retrospectives.

"Hazel! Come *on*!" I called over another clap of thunder.

She nodded and quickened her pace just as we rounded the corner into the wide courtyard between the grand hall and the east wing. I wanted to force myself not to look at the path that led to the hedge maze where Jax's body lay lifeless and crumpled. Still, I couldn't help but glance that way. Where the purple wisteria that covered the entrance arches sagged and drooped under the weight of the rain and wind. I stared, wishing more than anything else that I would wake up from this nightmare and Jax would walk out of the maze. Perfect. Like he always was.

Like he always *had been*.

Reagan turned around. His eyes flashed with a hopeful excitement. "I think I see it!"

In fact, he was a little too excited. His odd behavior was the inverse of Hazel's. I'd seen this panicked energy before also. In circumstances that weren't good. Our little group was falling apart, and if I was the only one acting halfway rationally, we were in even worse trouble.

We hurried along, faster than before, to the east wall of the grand hall. Thanks to all the rain, the courtyard was even muddier than before, and my feet sank deep with each step. It felt like even the earth itself was working against us.

Reagan was the first to arrive at the stone exterior wall. I came next, huffing and puffing from the difficult walk. Hazel almost sauntered up. Kind of casually. Still lost in her thoughts. I put my hand on the wall to brace myself, but immediately yanked it back and shivered. Kenna's body was on the other side. Death was everywhere. All around us.

"See!" Reagan pointed upward at a portion of the roof.

I did see. An extremely large gray satellite dish had been mounted to the corner of the grand hall's roof and had partially broken off of a steel mount. The wind pushed against it, and it swung around slowly, like a door on a hinge. The dish was much larger than the small versions that cable TV companies went around putting on all the roofs in the Phoenix suburbs. It looked like it weighed a ton, and like even if you got a whole set of Craftsman tools for Christmas, you'd need all day to get it back into place again.

"This is good," Reagan said. "I was hoping for something like this. Once I get up there, I'll probably be able to see how it was positioned before and . . ."

I squinted at the broken dish. "And what? We don't have any replacement parts." Plus, the roof was at least twenty feet tall. It was the *grand* hall, after all. "How are you even going to get up there?"

Reagan pointed again. "The roof tapers down in that direction. Let's see if it comes low enough that I can climb up."

Hazel nodded distractedly, and it was enough to convince Reagan that this was a super-terrific idea. We followed behind him again, walking along the cobblestone path to the east of the grand hall, tracing the sloping roof to where the grand hall met a service hall that was a more average height. He tossed his backpack up, and it landed on the roof with a splash of water and muddy leaves.

"Give me a boost," Reagan said.

I clasped my hands together and held them out for him to put his muddy shoe in and hoisted him up as best I could. He grabbed onto the edge of the roof. He pulled and I pushed, and after a minute or so he was wriggling his way onto the roof.

Hazel leaned against the wall, watching me as I regained my composure.

"Alex?" she said, wiping her face with the sleeve of her sweatshirt. Which was ridiculous because her shirt was soaking wet and there was no getting away from the rain. "What do you think really happened to the GoFundMe money? I was assuming that Kenna took it. That she was acting so strange because she took it. But from the stuff on her computer . . . well . . . she seemed shocked that it was gone."

I blinked the water out of my face. This seemed like a pretty crappy time to discuss our fundraising. Reagan's skinny legs dangled like icicles off the side of the roof as he struggled to hoist himself up the rest of the way. We were outside in a fairly exposed location. The same spot where Raul or Yuri Stoica or Dracula or whoever had been running around a few hours earlier.

"Um. Well," I said. "Reagan said that we were hacked . . ."

Above us, Reagan seemed to be slipping downward while I watched. "Reagan? Are you okay?" I turned to Hazel and took in her small form. "Maybe I should try to boost you up? You're smaller than me, and you could get up there and—"

Hazel wasn't listening at all. Or paying the slightest bit of attention to what Reagan was doing. She stared at me and knelt down and removed the vodka bottle from her backpack. Like she'd come up with some new plan and hadn't bothered to share it with anyone. I didn't know what to do. I wanted to help Reagan, but also Hazel was on the verge of a major malfunction. She was used to being such a genius, but finally her supercomputer of a brain needed a reboot.

"Hazel. What the hell are you doing?" I asked her.

She backed away from me. "I . . . I understand everything now. I . . . I . . . Jax was right. I have to get to the road. It's my only chance."

"What?" I shrieked, unable to keep the alarm out of my voice. My words bounced off the stone walls. "Jax is dead! And you're the one who said going to the road would get us killed! It's at least a mile from here, and soon it will be dark."

Hazel swung her backpack over her shoulder. She was going to make a run for it.

Reagan's legs disappeared. He'd managed to fully get on the roof.

"Hazel! We have to stay together. You can't leave Reagan up there alone!" But by that time, I was talking to myself. Hazel was about ten feet away, running across the courtyard, brandishing the vodka bottle like a weapon. I could no longer see Reagan, which meant that he was making progress on getting to the satellite dish.

"Reagan! Reagan!" I screamed, wringing my hands helplessly. "Hazel took off and I'm down here by myself and . . . and . . . and . . ." It was stupid to keep going. Reagan couldn't hear me and Hazel wasn't listening and I was making a bunch of noise that could attract all the wrong kind of attention. I had to make a decision.

I wanted to stay there and wait for Reagan to come back down and let him tell me what we would do next. But I had let Jax die. Stood and watched as he was murdered. Whatever else happened, I could not have a repeat of that situation. I had to do something. I had to help Hazel.

Fog had begun to fill the courtyard and had risen up to my ankles. If I waited much longer, I wouldn't be able to find Hazel even if I wanted to. I could no longer see the sun or get much of a sense of where the sun was *supposed* to be. I jumped at the sound of another roll of loud thunder.

After grabbing my own backpack, I started to run.

Sticking close to the wall of the grand hall to avoid being seen, I did my best to go the same way Hazel had gone. If she was going to the road, the only route we knew of was through the courtyard, past the east wing, and to the path into the forest. As I moved through the courtyard, I couldn't see Hazel, but I could hear her sloshing footsteps in the mud growing fainter. I quickened my pace.

When I came to the entrance to the east wing garden, I froze. Hazel was inside the small enclosed yard.

But so was Raul Stoica.

I mean, I guess it was him. Hazel was backing away from someone in the Dracula mask. She shook the vodka bottle at a tall, thin figure whose drenched black silk cloak bore the faded stains of Jax's blood.

Backing up. Step by step. Past the headless statue of Vlad Dracul. Toward the open well.

I could already see what was going to happen.

Hazel was slipping and sliding around in front of the rough stone structure. "Don't! Don't come any closer," she said in a shrill voice. She almost lost her footing as she tried to give the bottle an intimidating wave.

My blood ran cold with shock and adrenaline.

The Dracula wasn't even going to have to do much to get Hazel in the well. She might just fall in there herself. She trembled, and her feet couldn't find traction on the long, wet grass. Her shoes were sinking into the mud. I remembered the well from when we arrived. It was made of stone for the first ten feet or so and then dirt all the rest of the way down. The water level had been relatively low.

If Hazel went down, she wouldn't be coming back up.

I remained under the stone arch. Wavering in my resolve, about to give in to my fear. I could run and hide. Run and find Reagan. Run to the road like Hazel was trying to do.

I remembered Jax. And then Bram Stoker.

He might kill me, but death now seems the happier choice of evils.

Dropping my backpack on the ground, I knelt down and pulled

out the miniature kilij from the castle office. I had to help Hazel if I could. I counted to five in my head and then made myself stand up. The muscles in my arms and legs tensed as I gripped the small sword and charged at Raul.

I was not an athlete nor a particularly good runner, and it took way longer than I hoped to make it to the well. As I approached the scene, Hazel screamed and threw the bottle at Raul. As I came close to him, he raised his arm to cover his face, and the bottle smashed into his elbow. Who knew how old that vodka bottle was or how long it had been in the castle. It was brittle and broke into thousands of tiny pieces that rained over me and got stuck in my scalp.

Raul groaned and muttered something in Romanian before taking a large, menacing step toward Hazel. I skidded into him, and he fell forward as I bounced off, falling onto my butt and spinning across the flattened grass. The combination of both actions sent Hazel flying back, her legs flailing and her hands making dramatic grasping motions as she searched, in vain, for something to grab on to. Hazel's head hit the stone bank with a muted thud before she slumped over like a lifeless doll and collapsed into the well. A few seconds later, I struggled to hear a light splash over the beat of the heavy rain. I spit out a mouthful of rainwater and wet dirt.

Crawling on all fours, still dazed from the fall and the glass in my scalp, I scrambled over to the well and stuck my head over the side. Although, thanks to the storm, there was more water in there than before, the darkness extended down and down. I couldn't see Hazel, but I could sense that she was below, way beyond my reach.

"Hazel? Hazel!" I called out. My words reverberated off the stone, and my own voice seemed to surround me.

"Alex . . . Alex . . ." she moaned. "Oh, no . . ."

A sharp tug of the ribbing around the neck of my sweatshirt pulled me away from the well, and a hand tossed me sharply onto the ground. I found myself on my back facing the costumed Dracula figure as he towered over me and water poured down, my vision nothing but surreal streaks of gray clouds and black silk. Somehow, I had managed to keep my grip on the silver miniature kilij.

I knew what I had to do.

Flipping over, I crawled toward the pair of men's leather shoes poking out from the wild grass and made long slashing motions with the knife across his cloak-covered legs. Raul made an impatient noise before kicking me hard in the stomach.

My abdomen seared with hot pain, and I struggled to get air into my lungs. Hazel was down in the well and was no longer calling my name. Time was running out to save her.

And myself.

Knowing I only had one last chance, I got up and ran at Raul with every ounce of energy I had left, and using my momentum, I shoved the sword into his belly as hard as I could. He stumbled back a few paces and fell down, sliding along the grass and crashing into the statue of Vlad Dracul. Raul made a series of shocked gasps and panted as he felt around for the knife concealed by the folds of wet, black material. Dark red blood flowed like a river down his arms and onto the earth.

The statue, having already been vandalized and beheaded, rocked back and forth on its crumbling pedestal before falling forward. Raul was mostly able to move out of the way before Vlad Dracul came crashing down, but he wasn't quite fast enough. He left out a howl as the heavy stone landed across his left leg and effectively pinned him there on the other side of the garden.

Holding my stomach, I hobbled over to the well and used the flashlight on my phone to see into the well. It was about half-way full of black water. I spotted Hazel's head of brown hair bobbing around and she appeared to be paddling, but she was at least thirty feet below, and there was no way that I'd be able to reach her. I spun around, scanning the garden for something—a rope, a piece of wood—something, anything that I could use to get her out.

Other than broken rocks and the occasional piece of trash, the garden was empty.

"Shit. Shit. Shit," I muttered to myself.

Raul moaned again. He finally removed the Dracula mask, revealing his real face, and said in English, "You . . . you . . . evil . . . evil girl."

The son of a gangster who had murdered my friends was calling *me* evil. A fury raged inside me, and I thought of picking up one of the sharp rocks and finishing Raul's life of crime forever. But . . . but that would have made me like him in a way, and no matter what happened, I didn't want to become something dark. Vlad Dracul. Count Dracula. Yuri Stoica. Another monster to haunt Prahova. I wanted to be the good person that Jax believed I was.

So focus.

That's what I told myself. I had to help Hazel.

I was going to have to leave the garden and search for something that I could lower into the well. With Raul panting and trying to free his leg, I ran from the garden. I decided to go in the direction of the grand hall. While I hated the idea of going back into that place, where I'd have to face Kenna's body, there had been lots of construction supplies in there, and it seemed possible that I would find some rope or even a ladder.

Moving as quickly as I could given the storm that raged on, I headed down the path toward the center of the castle grounds. When I turned the corner to enter the courtyard, my heart nearly stopped as I ran into a solid figure. A second later, I registered Reagan's shock of red hair. I had run right into my best friend. My legs wobbled and almost gave out.

"Thanks for nothing," he said, reaching out a hand to steady me. He was limping and had a pained expression on his face. "I had to jump off the fucking roof, Alex! Where the hell were you? I called and called and called."

"I was . . . I was . . ." I struggled to get out the words.

He waved his hands to cut me off, sending even more water into my face. "Never mind. We don't have much time. I was able to kind of rig the dish in place. But with this storm, it won't last. We have to find the control room *now* and . . ." He glanced behind me. "Oh fuck. Where is Hazel?"

I didn't know how to summarize everything that had happened. My words came out in a rush. "She went nuts and took off and Raul pushed her in the well and she hit her head and we have to find something to get her out and . . ."

A clap of thunder boomed across the landscape, and several

jagged lines of lightning appeared off in the distance, giving the forest a foreboding, otherworldly glow.

The remaining color drained from Reagan's face. I tried to grab his arm and pull him in the direction of the grand hall. He remained there. Standing on his one good leg. Still as a statue. Water running down his freckled face.

"Come on! I need your help!" I said.

He shook his head very slowly. "Alex. Did you hear me?" He leaned toward me and spoke right into my ear. "I can barely walk. That dish is wedged into place with a screwdriver and some duct tape. If we have any hope of contacting anyone, any hope at all, we have *maybe* ten minutes to do it."

I stared into his blue eyes.

He was saying that we had to leave Hazel for dead.

But he didn't understand.

"Raul is pinned underneath that messed-up statue of Vlad the Impaler. So he's pretty much no threat. I can help you walk," I said, hoping to better explain the situation. "Together we might be able to save Hazel. I mean, we should at least try." Plus, out of the three of us, Hazel was the smartest by far. We needed her to get out of Prahova alive.

He remained impassive as I came to his side, and he wrapped his arm around my shoulder.

"Alex," he said more sharply. "When I was on the roof . . . I saw Yuri Stoica."

I froze.

"And if I could see *him*," Reagan said, and let out an exhale. "He could see *me*."

General Directorate for Criminal Investigations

Alexandra Elaine Rush—Transcript—Tape 4

Alex: Did you [cross talk] . . . find her? Hazel? In the well?

Inspector Skutnik: Yes . . . [inaudible] . . .

Alex: I think about that. The darkness in the well.

Inspector Skutnik: Yes. Well. I . . . see. So . . . Reagan was able to repair the satellite dish?

Alex: Yeah. I guess. I mean, it worked for about a minute. But . . .

Inspector Skutnik: You had to enter the tunnels?

Alex: Yeah. And then . . . we understood. We understood why Yuri Stoica had to return to Prahova.

Two days ago

INT. THE TUNNEL—NIGHT

It was night by the time we found the office again.

We traveled through the blue of twilight. Across what would have been romantic or beguiling in another time. We'd come here to make a film, and here was the ideal backdrop.

But it was too late. Those dreams were gone. Along with our friends.

There we were. In the exact situation we'd been hoping to avoid. At Prahova after dark.

Waiting for our turn to be murdered.

Reagan's ankle was probably broken, or at the very least, it was a bad sprain. The two of us moved slowly, and every time the sagging beams of the castle creaked under the weight of the rain or water pounded the stone in a new rhythm or there was another round of thunder, we stopped walking and ducked into the shadowed spaces within the building.

Where we huddled together, craning our necks every which way.

Searching for any sign of Yuri Stoica.

I was out of breath when I finally stepped into the office. Shouldering half of Reagan's weight had taken more out of me than I expected. Water flowed off our clothing, creating large puddles on the wood floor. The temperature was dropping as night fell. I shivered.

Although I wanted to collapse into one of the office chairs and stay there until I melted into oblivion, I moved the desk that covered the trapdoor. Reagan kneeled down, somehow managing to balance on his uninjured ankle, felt around until his fingers found a groove, and gave the wood a tug. The heavy door opened and made a sound like a dying man sucking in a final gasp.

With the door ajar, we could hear the floorboards creak underneath our weight. I stared into the pitch-black hole, into the veins that ran beneath Prahova.

Reagan hesitated. "What if Yuri Stoica followed us here? What if he's coming? What if we get down there and . . . what . . . what . . ." His hand shook and his eyes darted all around. "We have to make sure. I have to take care of you. You need to be safe." He stood up and hopped around the office until he came to the cabinet where the paint supplies were. "Perfect. Perfect."

I remained where I was, unable to take my eyes off the darkness below. I really did not want to go down there, and Reagan's manic energy was making things even worse.

"Reagan," I said in an unsteady voice. "You don't have to take care of me." I couldn't look away from the void below. Take my eyes off the tunnels that whispered and moaned.

But his frantic, jerky movements stopped as he answered. "Alex. Now is not the time for us to debate the patriarchy. Everything is going to be fine."

That comment, more than anything else, sent a shiver through my spine. Because whatever things would be, they would never be *fine* again, and I feared my best friend was losing his grip on reality. I made myself raise my head and really see Reagan.

He was near the office door. His arms full of tin containers of paint thinner and dirty rags and bits of used paper. Leaning against the wall to keep himself standing. The lighter we found earlier in his right hand. He was going to start a fucking fire.

"Reagan! Reagan! No!" I said. "This is a terrible plan!"

He gave me an exasperated sigh. "Alex, according to the map, there are only four or five entrance points to the tunnel."

The map. He'd gotten a better look at it than I had. The map was at the bottom of the well. With Hazel.

Reagan was still talking. Fast. ". . . to the south is basically inaccessible and two of them are in the east wing, which is a long walk from here. If we block the trapdoor here, we reduce the chance that Stoica can follow us and . . ."

I guess that sounded rational.

Except fires were unpredictable. And hard to control.

He waved me off as I moved in his direction. "Stand back," he said.

I shook my head. He couldn't even walk. I didn't think we should light the room on fire. But if we were really going to do it, I should be the one to torch the place.

Reagan made another motion with his hands. "The fumes!" And he was right. As he poured the paint thinner along the wall where the exterior door was found, the whole room began to reek of an odor like rotten eggs and gasoline. He coughed a few times and pulled his T-shirt up to cover his face. My eyes teared up and burned.

"What if the whole castle catches on fire?" I said in a high-pitched voice.

He shrugged and coughed again. "Not all the buildings are connected. And it's raining buckets out there. Get ready."

I sat down on the wood floor and got ready to enter the trap-door. My legs dangled into the cool, cavernous space. Every muscle in my body ached with tension. "I don't think this is a good idea," I said again.

"Alex!" he almost yelled. "Do you need me to explain it to you again? I think I fixed the satellite. But we still need to get to the control room to reboot it. Once it's up and running, we can call for help. But we need to make sure that Stoica isn't following us."

"Yes, but—" I tried to argue.

Reagan had made up his mind. It's like he was trying to become Jax.

Trying to become the hero.

He struck the lighter and dropped it onto the wood floor.

It worked a bit better than he expected, and red-orange flames erupted and quickly covered the wall. He hadn't yanked his arm away fast enough, and he screamed and fell to the floor as the flames singed his wrist. The blaze traveled along the wooden floorboards, and I could see the rubber soles of his shoes soften-ing and melting. Smoke almost instantly filled the small office.

Crawling on all fours, I came to Reagan's side. His hand was burned bad, and I almost retched at the smell of his gooey, charred flesh. "Come on . . . come on," I panted. I had to pretty much drag him to the trapdoor. In a few more seconds, the whole room would be covered in flames and thick with smoke. There was no time to really think about what we might find in the tunnels. I pushed Reagan down and went through the open hole myself.

Together we tumbled down about ten feet and landed hard on the cobblestones below.

Reagan mostly broke my fall, but my arm hit the stone at full force. He moaned and my shoulder throbbed and I found myself, once again, breaking into sobs. Above us, the fire raged on. The red flames had spread through the office, and they flickered across the opening above our heads. One of the things that we hadn't planned on was that the tunnel would be so tall. We couldn't reach the trapdoor to close it. Noxious smoke streamed through the opening. Soon it would be hard to breathe down here too.

A yellow-red glow lit Reagan's face. His eyes found mine, and he reached out to touch my cheek. He quickly yanked his burned hand back but said, "We're okay. We'll be okay. Someday we'll be far away from here. We'll be safe. This will be our worst memory."

We waited for a minute to recover, but it had grown smokier in the tunnel, and I knew we had to move. I helped Reagan to his feet and turned on my phone's flashlight. My legs shook like Jell-O as we stumbled along the stone.

I pointed my flashlight all around. "I think we're alone down here." We were in a wide hallway constructed of extremely rough, yellowish stones with a rounded ceiling. Every ten feet or so, dingy lightbulbs jutted out from the rocks. It suggested that there were lights down here, but they were turned off.

Reagan wrapped his arm around my shoulder, and we began to move. We didn't have the map, but he did his best to guide us from memory. He was getting tired and kicking up dust as he dragged his feet. The farther we traveled from the trapdoor, the more that the smoke was replaced by the smell of mold and decaying wood. We took several wrong turns that ended in impassable walls constructed of ancient rocks.

After retracing our steps, we arrived at a different hallway.

In that part of the tunnel, the lights were on.

I squeezed Reagan's arm. He seemed to be relaxing. The tension fell from his shoulders. Like it was a positive development to find a hospitable-looking room. But if the lights were on, someone must have flipped the switch.

Someone like Yuri Stoica.

What if *we* were following *him*?

Reagan moved even closer to me, and together we crept so slowly toward the lit room. I held my breath, wanting to make as little noise as possible. I slid my body inch by inch toward the doorframe, the rocks of the tunnel scraping my face, and poked one eye into the room. It was an extremely long, well-lit space with more desks and supply cabinets. It was clearly the control room. The size of it reminded me of our basement, and if I had to guess, I would have said that we were underneath the grand hall. A console, with dozens of TV screens, covered the wall opposite the doorway.

"I think it's empty," I whispered.

The two of us almost jumped into the room, as if we could stun Yuri Stoica if our entrance was dramatic enough. But as far as we could see, the room was empty. Reagan stood on one foot but slumped over and put his hands on his knees, bracing himself to keep from collapsing.

I continued on toward the far wall. The area looked like a security guard setup from an old 1980s movie. Several tables rested in front of the TV monitors, and each contained an odd array of outdated equipment like table microphones and enormous headsets. The screens displayed areas all over the castle. As Reagan had suggested, there was clearly a network of cameras that covered all of Prahova. I could see our empty bedrooms in the east wing, along with views of all over the castle grounds. Most of the outdoor cameras were getting pelted with rain or swaying in the force of the wind. I pressed my fingertips up to the monitor that showed Jax's body lying still at the base of the fountain in the center of the maze.

"The cameras still work," I said.

"That's good, I guess," Reagan answered. He continued to make his way around the room, searching for something else. "The cameras are probably hardwired and don't require a network or internet access." He continued on with his analysis. "Which makes sense. The castle is remote. The security systems were probably installed a long time ago . . ."

A few feet from the old security systems and monitors sat another cluster of desks that contained several more modern flat-panel screens and computer towers. "Oh, here we go," Reagan said. "We're in business."

I joined him at the desk and stared at a large monitor that had a CryptoSign logo splashed across the screen along with text in several languages. In English it said, *The satellite signal has been lost. Press any key to retry.* Reagan slid into the chair in front of the desk.

"Okay. I can make this work," he murmured to himself.

I left him there, muttering about versions of Windows and localization and passwords, and returned to inspecting the area. A wide doorway opened up to another space that was almost as wide as the one we were in. It looked like the control room and this space had, at one time, been a single, massive space that ran underneath the grand hall. But someone had divided them with modern Sheetrock and particleboard. As I stepped into the new room, the sound of Reagan's furious typing grew fainter. This huge room was full of row after row of black metal supply cabinets. Most of them had their doors thrown open, but a few were still closed. They were shorter than me, allowing me to see over their tops. My gaze traveled over the tops of the fortyish cabinets, searching for a face or an out-of-place shadow. Here and there, I spotted some moving supplies like dollies and hand trucks. As far as I could see, I was alone in this room too. Greenish fluorescent lights hung from the rocky ceiling, and a light breeze blew across me. Like the tunnel made its own weather.

Something just seemed off about the whole place. It was a storage room. But storage of what? What would someone want to store in the difficult-to-access underbelly of a remote and ramshackle castle? I moved with hesitation, like I expected to find goblins or actual vampires in those closed cabinets. My heart thudded in my chest as I approached one of the cabinets and gave it a tug. The metal hinges squealed to reveal a series of wide shelves. Full of stacks and stacks of yellowing powder wrapped tightly in cellophane.

I'd seen *Scarface* a zillion times, and I was pretty sure that this was cocaine.

A lot of it. It was the kind of thing you'd see in your news feed under a headline that said something like *Authorities Seize Historic Amount of Drugs during Raid.*

I wrapped my arms around myself to stop from shaking.

Stoica *had* to come back here. He needed his merchandise.

I left the cabinet open and stumbled back into the control room. "Reagan. We have a big problem. A serious problem."

"I know," he said in a voice that shook with a terror that matched what I felt inside.

But he hadn't even seen the drugs.

He still sat at the desk staring at the screens in front of him.

I was afraid to go over there. Afraid of whatever he was afraid of. So I stayed where I was. Bracing myself in the wide doorframe between the two rooms. "What's wrong? Doesn't the satellite dish work?"

Reagan's shoulders fell. "I think it will. In a minute or so. The system is still rebooting. But." He hesitated for a moment, and then all the words tumbled out fast and furious. "There's a file server over there." He waved his arm toward the corner to his left. "It's got a lot of the drug cartel's financials. Information about their suppliers. The system is pretty sophisticated. I mean, for, like, five years ago. There's an old SAP enterprise system, and believe it or not, they're using PeopleSoft to track their dealers and . . ."

He was about to really go down a computer science rabbit hole. But that was Reagan. He could totally forget that our lives were in mortal peril and spend an hour talking about the history of Atari or something.

I struggled to remain calm. Not only were we in a room where a gangster was storing his drugs, Reagan was sitting at the terminal that had access to all the files of the cartel's criminal network. "Oh my God. Reagan. What's this got to do with the satellite dish?"

He shook off his monologue. "Oh, nothing. I'm just saying

that it's incriminating stuff. And . . . and . . . it's also serving as a backup for the security cameras. It's got all the video from the last thirty days." He made a couple more clicks and froze.

I took a few steps in his direction, standing between the desks full of modern computers and the old ones. On one of the screens, an image of the castle terrace appeared. Water pelted the camera lens, but it was a night vision camera, and I recognized the forms. Long and lanky Reagan and curvy, statuesque Maddie. They were out in the storm. Fighting.

It was *last* night.

Reagan had killed Maddie.

I choked out a sob. "Oh, Jesus. Reagan. What did you do?"

"Alex," Reagan said, his face so totally white that his freckles looked like dots on a domino. "You have to believe me. You have to understand."

As he said this, a blur of motion appeared on one of the monitors. One of the outdoor cameras registered a grainy image of Yuri Stoica smoking a cigar and pacing in front of a large truck in what was probably the loading dock. The area was covered but open to the outside, where it was totally black except for the occasional glint of the falling rain.

I didn't have time to process the fact that my best friend was a killer.

He remained at the desk. Like he was unsure of what to do.

My mouth fell open in horror as Stoica's image vanished from the screen, only to appear a couple of seconds later on another monitor. He had entered one of the tunnels.

He was inside.

With us.

"Reagan! We have to get out of here."

A message appeared on the large flat screen near Reagan's right elbow. SYSTEM READY. It was quickly replaced by a soccer game where teams in blue and green uniforms ran behind a ball in motion. The satellite dish was working. But would we be able to stay down here long enough to even use it?

Before Reagan could answer me, the fluorescent lights flickered and went out.

Maddie once told me that in art, black was defined as the total absence of light.

I might have been inside one of her tubes of black oil paint.

The control room became a dimension of darkness and silence.

And then we heard the footsteps.

General Directorate for Criminal Investigations

Alexandra Elaine Rush—Transcript—Tape 5

Inspector Skutnik: So Kenna's laptop and computer were destroyed in the fire?

Alex: Yeah . . . I mean, I think . . . I think so.

Inspector Skutnik: But that still doesn't explain all your injuries. Alex, how did you get those marks on your neck?

Alex: Well . . . [inaudible] . . . I . . . I . . .

Inspector Skutnik: Alex?

Alex: You have to understand. It wasn't his fault. He thought he was doing it all for me.

EXT. THE LOADING DOCK—NIGHT

"Reagan? Reagan?" I whispered. My arms reached through the air, waving and grasping for my best friend. Or anyone else who might be there.

The wheels of his chair squealed and his wet sneakers squeaked as he got up from the desk. I could sense him moving around, but he didn't answer me. I called out to him again. This time more frantic.

I was about to exhale a small sigh of relief when his long fingers wrapped around my throat and gave it a tight squeeze. Reagan was stronger than I thought, and even though his foot was injured, he was able to push me toward the doorway to the control room. My head knocked into the rocky wall, and stars exploded in my field of vision. I wanted to cry, but I was running out of air.

Reagan had really lost it. I was relieved that I couldn't see his face. I'm sure his expression would have given me a heart attack. He was going to kill me. Like he had killed Maddie.

"Reagan!" I choked out. "It's me. It's me. Alex. Your . . . friend. Remember?"

Tears squirted out of the corners of my eyes and ran down my cheeks onto Reagan's strained fingers. "Remember? I just saved you from the fire? You know me. You know."

I could feel his warm breath on my cheek.

"I . . . love you . . . Alex. I did it all for you."

"What? What?"

The footsteps were coming closer. They were precise clicks on the cobblestone. The walk of a man with a purpose and a plan. The tunnels were winding and twisted, but Yuri had spent years at Prahova. He would probably make much better time down here than we would.

Step. By. Step.

The memories flooded through me. My first kiss with Jax. Behind the old Valley Art during a break in Frightfest between *Blade* and *Let the Right One In*. The way he leaned in. How his lips tasted like chocolate. Maddie in the studio putting the finishing touches on a painting. Carter in the music room playing his guitar and how he'd always dip his fries in his chocolate shake. Kenna setting up elaborate sets for her Instagram posts. The way Hazel's face would light up when she knew exactly how to stage a shot. And through it all, Reagan being there. He loved s'mores. As he was choking the life out of me, that's what I thought about. Whenever we went camping, Reagan Wozniak made the best s'mores.

Reagan's grip continued to tighten around my throat. I could barely get the words out. "Reagan. He's . . . coming. Yuri Stoica. The real . . . Dracula."

His fingers released me, and he stepped back. "Alex. Oh my God. What am I doing?"

He backed away from me, receding into the corner of the room. Remaining in the shadows where I could no longer see his face. I reached for the sore spot on my neck where his fingers had squeezed and bruised a moment before.

"I . . . You're right . . ." he whispered from the corner. "I took the money . . . for you . . . to help your family . . . to help you."

"Reagan. No," I whispered back. "Don't say that . . . don't . . . don't . . ."

I wished he would come back into the light.

He coughed and went on. "I thought we could use it to get you into film school."

Guilt overtook me. How would stealing the money help me get into film school? What had I done to make Reagan think that going to USC was worth stealing for? Worth killing for?

But Reagan was my best friend.

"It's . . . okay . . ." I whispered. "We'll . . . we'll figure this out. We just have to survive this night. Then we'll figure it out."

"You'll stand by me, right, Alex?"

"Yes," I whispered.

Grabbing his hand, I drew him into the corridor and around the corner from the control room. His broken ankle kind of dragged, and Reagan grunted, and we made way more noise than I would have liked. We concealed ourselves behind the sharp stone wall. We couldn't go back. Reagan had set that way literally on fire. We'd have to hide and hope Stoica didn't murder us.

It was a foolish thing to hope for.

It took all the courage I had in me to peek around the corner. The beam of an industrial flashlight announced Stoica's arrival. He must have turned off the lights to make it easier to hunt us. The wide spotlight bounced across the cobblestones and rough stone of the tunnel as he cut a straight path into the control room.

I tensed as Reagan put his arms around my shoulder. It would have been a reassuring gesture. Except my friend was a killer.

Yuri Stoica was terrifying. But Reagan? He was . . .

The bouncing beam of light grew closer. Waiting for the inevitable. Yuri Stoica would find us here and kill us, and it would be all over. At least I'd be with Jax again.

But the flashlight, and the figure holding it, entered the control room. A minute or so later, we listened to a series of smashes and crashes. Cracking plastic. Broken glass. Then the creak of the opening cabinet doors.

"He's destroying everything," Reagan whispered, squeezing my shoulders.

I didn't say anything. I mean, at that point, I didn't give a damn. Yuri Stoica could trash all the computers he wanted to if he left us alone. Smoke from our fire continued its travels into the tunnel, and my eyes began to burn. Behind me, Reagan's chest kind of heaved. My heartbeat picked up as I turned around and clamped my hand over his mouth.

He coughed anyway. I was able to muffle the noise, but sound really traveled across the tunnel's hard surfaces. We froze as the racket Yuri Stoica was making abruptly stopped, and the only thing that filled the silence was our own breathing. I'm not sure how long we waited down there. It felt like hours. Or maybe even days.

Eventually, Yuri Stoica left the control room pushing a loaded cart.

My heart almost thudded to a stop. Stoica had taken care of the computers, and now he had his drugs. We stood there in the tunnel. Hoping the drug dealer would leave before the fire spread too far. Hoping that he would go in the opposite direction.

We waited and waited and waited.

For a confrontation that didn't come.

Yuri Stoica left the way he came. I assumed he went back to the loading area and his truck. Reagan and I held each other and stayed where we were. Maybe the gangster didn't know we were alive or didn't care or assumed that he'd left Raul to deal with us or felt that two idiot teenagers were no threat to him. It was the first time since we arrived at the castle that I felt anything like relief. We could let Stoica get a head start and then leave ourselves.

Even if we had to walk, we might make it.

There was a chance.

Reagan and I stayed in the tunnel as long as we could. It continued to get smokier, and eventually we *had* to leave. I turned on the flashlight on my phone and pointed it at Reagan. His ankle had gotten more swollen, and he was in more pain than before. We had to go slow. But at least it was pretty clear where to go. The smoke drifted in the direction of the exit door, and we followed it like kids chasing floating clouds.

Together, we walked on through the long tunnel that went on forever. Hazel had told us that the tunnels ran underneath the extensive castle grounds, covering several miles of territory. Eventually, it narrowed, and the rocks along the wall became sharper and more jagged. Reagan kept tripping over loose or missing stones on the walkway. Each time, he nearly took both of us down. This part of the castle was the roughest of the areas where we had been. The space came to resemble more of a cave.

There were a few spots where the tunnel must have collapsed at some point, and wood poles and planks were being used to prevent further damage. But that wood was sagging and aging and rotting away. Mildew and wood rot mingled with the smoke. I wanted to quicken our pace, but Reagan continued to limp along slowly.

We came to a white door, the same kind that could be found between our kitchen and garage back home. Large, greasy handprints covered the dingy surface and created unsettling patterns of streaks. Whoever put the door in place had done as little work as possible to create a conventional doorway out of the cave's vaulted archways. The surrounding frame was constructed of unpainted plywood, and dirt crumbled around the hinges. I was sure that the loading dock was on the other side of the door.

I let go of Reagan's arm and left him a couple of feet from the door and approached it alone. Slowly. I pressed my ear to the door. I couldn't hear anything. Reagan moved forward so that I could feel his shallow breath on the tiny hairs on the back of my neck.

It was quiet.

Reagan raised his phone. Like he thought the light might protect us.

I gave the door a jerk. Maybe because of the humidity, it didn't budge. I tugged harder, and it swung open fast. Both Reagan and I gasped. We found ourselves facing a concrete staircase without a railing that led down to an enormous, kind of dilapidated carport. I spotted several workbenches and racks of tools and stacks of tires. The stuff was old. But harmless. Beyond that an open space and the forest.

An aluminum awning covered the area for about fifty feet.

Except for the beat of the rain on the metal roof and the whoosh of the stormy winds through the forest trees off in the distance, it was quiet.

We were alone.

Stoica's truck appeared to be gone. Even better, the electric cart that Raul had told us about was out there on the right side of the garage facing the forest. If that's how he was planning to leave, it meant we could leave too.

Get away. Survive.

Reagan gave me a tiny, hopeful smile and went first through the door.

I glanced at his burned hand, which had started to ooze a greenish goo. I wanted to be reassuring, but I found myself staring at the vast, open darkness of the Prahova landscape.

As Reagan entered the doorway, a thick, capable hand reached through and grabbed my friend's sweatshirt. I watched in horror as Reagan was yanked out of the tunnel and pulled through the doorway. He let out a startled yelp.

I knew I should follow him. I knew I should have gone through the door. Summoned up some amount of courage to help my friend. But I remained planted on my side of the doorway. Watching. Listening.

A series of horrible thuds and cracks followed as Reagan tumbled down the sharp, hard staircase, his bones breaking and shattering as he went.

I wanted to scream.

"Reagan!" I whispered. "Reagan!"

With the door fully open, I caught a glimpse of the large truck. Stoica had moved it so that it was mostly out of view. The only reason that I could even see it at all was that the rain splashed off the bumper and created a silhouette.

I opened my mouth to scream.

My shoulder seared in pain as the hand grabbed it and sharply tugged. I didn't even get a good look at Yuri Stoica's face before he pulled me from the tunnel and sent me flying down the stairs. I tumbled several times and screamed at the sound of something snapping like a twig. It took me a minute or so to realize it was my own arm.

I rolled over Reagan and knocked into one of the workbenches. It shimmied and sent a red toolbox full of grimy wrenches raining down on me. I was forced to move my arm to protect my head and face, and the heavy box hit the exact spot of my break, almost like the fracture had a bull's-eye on it. I screamed again.

Reagan lay a few feet from me with his eyes closed, moaning in pain.

Heavy, booted footsteps approached. I braced myself for the end. Maybe Stoica would beat me with a hammer or a wrench. Maybe his jacket concealed a gun and I'd go quickly. I dug my fingernails into my palms and waited.

Two long legs clad in weathered blue jeans stepped right over me and kept going.

A car door opened and slammed shut, and a diesel engine

cranked to a start. A few seconds later, gravel crunched underneath tires as the truck left the castle.

Yuri Stoica was finally gone.

Using only one arm, I crawled over to Reagan's side.

He was hurt. Bad.

His red hair ran with even darker red blood.

He coughed out a mouthful of blood. "Alex . . . Alex . . . why . . . why . . ." His body fell limp.

"You'll be okay," I told him as I sobbed. "We're going to make it. We have . . . to . . . to . . . to make it. We'll go home. And everything will be fine. The same as it was. You're my friend, Reagan. I'm here for you. I'm . . . here."

I basically had to drag him over to the Bobcat. It felt like it took all night. I almost wanted to tear my own arm off. It hurt so bad, and every time I moved it I almost passed out.

His blood covered me by the time I was able to get him into the passenger seat.

Reagan's eyes fluttered open. "Alex. I wish we could go back and do everything all over again. I wish . . . I wish . . . The rain? Why is it still raining? Why can't I see the stars? Alex, why won't you let me see the stars?"

My heart shattered into a million pieces.

I glared at the storm clouds as I turned the key I found in the ignition.

When we were both in the utility vehicle, I steered us away from the castle.

As I pushed down on the gas, I said, "You have to stay awake. If you stay awake, you can see the stars." But even as I said these words, I felt Reagan's spirit slipping away. He went quiet. His body still. I had no idea where I was going or what to do.

It was only me and the falling rain and the forest that went on forever.

I was alone.

All my friends were gone.

I would always be alone.

General Directorate for Criminal Investigations

Alexandra Elaine Rush—Transcript—Tape 6

Inspector Skutnik: Reagan admitted to stealing the money from the GoFundMe? And to killing Maddie Oliver?

Alex: He said he stole the money. He never said he killed Maddie.

Inspector Skutnik: Yes. I see that here. And, Alex, why do you suppose a man like Yuri Stoica would allow you to live?

Alex: I assumed he thought I was dead. That we both were.

Inspector Skutnik: Indeed, Alex. Yet . . . you were not dead. Yuri Stoica is not known to make those types of mistakes.

Alex: When you catch him, I guess you can ask him.

Inspector Skutnik: Alex? [cross talk]

[noise] [cross talk] indistinct chatter]

Alex: Mom?

88 days later

EXT. PHOENIX SYMPHONY HALL—DAY

The usher lets me sneak into the audition even though it's supposed to be closed to the public. I slowly open the oversize door and enter the main auditorium at the Hale Theater. My sister, Meredith, takes the stage as I sink into a plush seat in the center of the near-deserted theater. One of the upsides of my newfound notoriety is that people are willing to bend the rules a bit more than they used to.

My father once told me that occasionally you find a treasure in the scrap. Somehow, after everything that happened, I have become a specialty item. Or maybe a replacement.

I watch as the music begins and Meredith shifts gracefully through the moves I recognize. Tendu. Relevé. Pas de bourrée. She's elegant in her brand-new white leotard, small skirt, and pink tights, and there's something magical in her movements that does really suggest a dream world. After a few minutes, the Tchaikovsky quiets, and a woman sitting at a table near the stage calls, "Thank you."

I meet Meredith in the dressing room as she's untying her pointe shoes.

"If they don't cast you as the Sugar Plum Fairy, I might have to kill someone," I say as I step into the long space full of chairs and lighted makeup mirrors.

"You're home!" Meredith says with a wide grin. She stands up and gives me a quick hug.

"Mom said you needed a ride, and I thought I'd catch a bit of your audition."

Since I came home, my dad has fully recovered and has even been able to hire an assistant to help out with Silver Rush. Silver prices have been soaring, and my parents have been selling a ton of stuff lately. They're swamped, and I'm happy to help get my sister to her summer ballet programs.

I tell Meredith I'll wait outside. I'm milling around, checking out posters of coming attractions and watching smiling people come and go from busy shops when a familiar face catches my eye.

Inspector Skutnik.

She looks exactly the same as she did back at the hospital in Brașov. Nondescript beige slacks. A linen blouse. A basic black bag. Her dark hair up in the neat bun. It's an outfit that's designed to appear confident but to be nonthreatening and forgettable.

A surge of adrenaline bursts through me.

What if she knows?

But my rational mind takes over. What could the inspector possibly know?

And. What could she prove?

I plaster a serene expression on my face and approach the police office. "Inspector? I'm surprised to see you."

"I thought it would be nice to attend the memorial," Inspector Skutnik says.

"Oh, good," I say with a more relaxed smile. People were sympathetic after everything that happened, and I was mostly able to raise enough money for a memorial garden. There's going to be a candlelit dedication tonight at the base of Mummy Mountain.

I have written a eulogy for my friends.

Inspector Skutnik takes a seat on one of the metal benches a few feet from the theater door. Her bland face matches mine. "Your mother said that you would be here, and I confess, I have been wanting to ask some follow-up questions for some time now."

My heart sinks, but I keep a neutral expression on my face. "Questions?"

The inspector digs around in her purse. "I called the Paradise Valley Police Department, and they said that I could use an interview room—"

I try to keep my tone friendly. "I have a lawyer now. Maybe you should talk to her first?" When I returned from Romania, my dad was contacted by a high-profile attorney from LA who agreed to represent me at no charge. So far, she's mostly written press releases and done interviews for Court TV. But I *have* a lawyer.

Her face shifts into a stern mask. She holds a small notebook and pen in one hand. "Alex, there are inconsistencies in the story you gave the CID. For instance, we did not find the map on Hazel's body when we retrieved it from the well. We haven't been able to find the truck you described in your interview. No one has seen Yuri Stoica. And if Reagan Wozniak stole the GoFundMe money, what did he do with it?"

"How would I know that?" I ask in a bewildered voice.

"Did *he* hide it, Alex?" she shoots back.

We stare at each other for a moment.

I draw in a deep breath. "I read online that you're off the case. That the LA police have arrested Justin Bloom. For reckless endangerment. Forgery. And fraud."

Her face falls. "Yes. I was removed. You see, the story of a famous film director who lured a group of teenagers to a remote castle to make a movie where they were hunted to death by a drug dealer who has returned from the dead to recover his lost bounty of drugs and secret files is far more interesting than my theory. The hunt for Yuri Stoica gets an international task force and millions of dollars in funding. The takedown of Justin Bloom has the interest of reporters from all over the globe. The idea that a pretty girl has murdered her friends for half a million dollars and a movie deal gets you removed from the case."

"I did my best to tell you what I remembered," I say.

"I think you came up with a story that everyone would want to believe."

I sighed. "What are you going to do?"

Through the theater windows, I can see Meredith making her way toward me. She's in her jeans and has a pink nylon duffel bag slung over her shoulder.

The inspector frowns. "What can I do? Forensically, the scene was useless. Every weapon either had multiple sets of prints on it, or no prints. There were muddy footprints everywhere. No witnesses. All the security camera footage from your stay at the castle was destroyed. Your friend Kenna McKee further complicated matters by planting fake blood and evidence all over." She says this last part with a tone of deep frustration. "But . . ."

"But?" I repeat, trying to slow my heartbeat. Trying to remind myself that the inspector has nothing.

"I may have caught a . . . you would say . . . a break in the case," she says.

I keep my shoulders relaxed. My face blank.

"Mr. Bloom is eager to exonerate himself. His attorney told the CID that he used to maintain a Synology device." The inspector gives me a wry smile. "I wish we had your friend Reagan Wozniak here to explain it to us. This is apparently some kind of computer, kind of like a personal cloud. He thinks the laptop he gave to Kenna McKee was backing up files until the satellite dish went down. He believes that his wife, Catrinel, is still using the Synology service. I'm on my way to seize it now."

My heart falls into my stomach. I have no idea what type of footage Kenna had managed to get. Or how it would align with the story I've told.

Inspector Skutnik turns to watch my sister. "You know, in my country we have a saying. Every bird dies by its own tongue."

She means, I suppose, that sooner or later, we all sing for the hunter. We must all confess our sins. Everyone spills their secrets eventually.

But not all birds sing. That's what Maddie had told me. A million years ago. Back in my old room. When she said that I was a swan.

"All I want is the truth," the inspector says.

"I told you," I say in a voice barely above a whisper. "The truth is messy."

Meredith steps out onto the sunny sidewalk, and we leave the inspector sitting there on the bench, staring into space as I climb behind the wheel of our family's new Tesla. We go through a Starbucks drive-through. I can't even swallow my latte.

Even though I'm pretty sure I'm about to be arrested and spend the rest of my life in jail, I continue to go through the motions. I'll end up being the subject of a true crime movie and not the director of one.

Even though it's a warm June night, all of Mummy Mountain shows up for the vigil.

The lights on the mountain are all turned off.

I talk about my friends. They'll be forever young.

Immortal. Existing always in the legends of the castle.

After the ceremony, I shake hands. I let my mascara get a little smudged. My sweater always sits a bit askew off my shoulders. I blink and sniff and carry a pack of Kleenex in my purse. I've always got the right amount of tremble in my voice.

The crowd thins. Candles are blown out. My mom kisses me on the cheek and whispers how she understands that I want some time alone in the garden.

I sit there alone on one of the donated marble benches watching the yellow flowers of the prickly pear cactus bloom. A woman takes the seat next to me.

Turning my head, I find the glamorous figure of Catrinel Bloom. As always, she's impeccably dressed in a black jersey dress that's the right amount of casual and the perfect amount of dressy. Since I had come back from Romania, we had exchanged a few texts, but I hadn't seen her.

Of course, the media had dutifully covered the fact that Castle Prahova belonged to her uncle, Yuri Stoica. But since it was her husband, Justin, who'd really convinced Mr. McKee to let us go, no one really blamed the film star. She had gotten even more sympathy than before.

Catrinel lights a cigarette. "That inspector came by the house this evening. Looking for one of my husband's old computers."

"I know," I say, wondering how I'll look in an orange jump-suit.

I crane my neck in all directions, making sure no one is around to hear. But it's me, the movie star, and an owl, hooting from some hidden location. Mummy Mountain is quiet, and I can't help but think of last Halloween. Back when all this really started.

She lets out a deep exhale. "Nice woman. Hardworking. Always good to see a face from home. He used to be quite paranoid, you know. My husband. Justin. He would not load his footage onto the cloud. He was afraid of leaks and spoilers. He spent a small fortune on this device to keep his files safe. He wanted me to use it so no one would steal my email. Like I would care if they did."

Catrinel glances at me. I wonder if she can hear the pounding of my heart.

"That computer . . . it is a dreadful, awful thing. Heavy. Difficult to move," she says, drumming her fingers on the marble, speaking in her dreamy voice. "Too bad for the dear inspector. A few days ago, I signed up for a new service . . . and converted that black box into . . . a sculpture. I even cut up some of the pieces and made a pair of earrings. I may wear them to my husband's trial."

Was she saying what I thought she was saying? That she destroyed whatever files Kenna had managed to transfer?

Tension drained out of me, and my shoulders relaxed.

Things might be okay.

"I . . . I'm sorry about Raul," I said. "I wanted to say something sooner."

Catrinel pats my arm. "Yes. Yes. Poor, poor Cousin Raul," she sniffles, and dabs the corners of her eyes with her fingertips. "Raul who told me that Uncle Yuri was dead and that he wanted to be a legitimate businessman and that the castle was a safe place for the children. Only to be working with my husband the whole time. I feel certain that one of my uncle's associates had my dear, sweet cousin killed."

Her sad expression falls away. I know I'm witnessing a dress rehearsal for future media appearances and book release parties.

She goes on in a hard voice. "Amusing, is it not? My husband threatened women. Harassed them. Maybe committed assault. And yet he may go to jail for trying to make a bad movie." Catrinel stands up. "I did tell him. I warned him. I will not always be there to clean up his messes. Maybe we finally did manage to unmask a monster, eh, Miss Rush?"

"You got the name I sent you?" she asks.

I nod.

"Good," she says. "Good. If you are going to bribe an admissions officer, you must, of course, approach the right one."

I would be headed off to USC in August.

Catrinel's shoes make a crunching sound on the gravel as she walks away. "You send me your next script, my dear Alex."

She stops and smiles. "I have a feeling you are capable of anything."

As she walks by the rows of saguaro that cast long shadows in the moonlight, she says, "This really is a lovely garden."

General Directorate for Criminal Investigations

Pending report—EXHIBIT 22

Rush, Alexandra. *Dead Boys Don't Bite.* **Theatrical script.**

Revised March 14

Scene 10; page 16

Lucy Westenra: It isn't enough to unmask the monsters. They'll simply return with more ingenious disguises. Using the language of love to hunt and haunt us. Before this night is through. Before the moon has fallen behind the turrets. Let this castle run with blood. Dead boys don't bite. Nor do the dead girls who kept themselves in finery by speaking the language of the beasts. They will cause no further problems. For the future. For us all.

209 days later

INT. TROY HALL—UNIVERSITY OF SOUTHERN CALIFORNIA—NIGHT

I've managed to forget most of what happened at Prahova. It's like an old dream. I can barely recall the details. They swirl around like a storm in my mind. Changing. Evolving. Coming in and out of focus. Reality reduced to a series of flashes.

But sometimes.

Late at night. My sheets are cool. I swim through them.

It's the details that give me nightmares.

Did I miss something? Was there a computer I didn't break or a file I forgot to destroy? Did I wipe everything down?

Late at night, I tell myself, everything will be fine. This is a world that likes a certain kind of villain. The Count Draculas and Yuri Stoicas and Justin Blooms make for better stories. People prefer that world. They'd rather that people like me operate in the shadows. They'd rather that we hide our unlikeable ambitions behind pleasant faces and friendly smiles.

But it had been hard. To engineer situations where I was alone. To make people always think that I was the victim.

Reagan told me that he needed a week. A full week to take the money. Convert it to cryptocurrency. And then to hide it in a way that couldn't be traced. Then I'd quietly find ways to get into USC. To pay my parents' bills. To get my life on track.

It was supposed to be perfect. We'd be gone during spring

break. For eight days, actually. Eight days and my future would be secure. Eight days and my parents could keep their house. Eight days and my sister could keep on dancing.

But I didn't know that some of my friends were as desperate as I was. I didn't know that desperate people recognize each other.

Maddie figured it out first. We fought. She was maybe even more desperate than I was. When I shoved her. That really was an accident. But then I knew. I had to do something. Carter wasn't going to leave that castle without figuring out what happened to his girlfriend. While we were out searching for Maddie, I knocked Jax down the terrace stairs and went for the sword. Luckily, I had made a point to pocket the key that Kenna had left in the door.

When I saw her wet pajamas, I knew that Kenna was running all around the castle. I didn't know what she had seen. I had to push her off the stack of crates.

After Carter trapped Hazel in that downstairs room, I thought I might not have to kill her. But she was smarter than I was. She knew what I had done. She figured it out.

Right before I pushed her down that well.

And Reagan. He really was in love with me. I think he began to suspect me when I made such a big show of falling in the swimming pool. If they found any of Carter's blood on me, I needed an explanation. Reagan might have gone his whole life without telling what I did. I don't think he had it in him to send me to jail. I hated to push him down those stairs. But I would've had to marry the guy, and that was its own kind of prison.

Then there was Jax.

I had to do it. Jax was a Tarantino fanboy that I'd wind up paying alimony to. He was my Justin Bloom.

But I always find myself back in that maze. With him.

Time will never erase the memory of his face.

The anger. Betrayal. Fear. Terror.

I dream about that. Always.

But what's done is done.

If I am a monster, I am my own monster.

My story will become the truth.

My story is the truth.

Acknowledgments

I continue to be endlessly grateful for readers. Thank you for picking up this book and letting us authors tell our stories.

Thanks to my marvelous agent, Chloe Seager, and everyone at the Madeleine Milburn agency, for their continuing support of my work.

I am so appreciative to the entire team at Razorbill Books. With this book, I was so thrilled to have such excellent support from Julie Rosenberg, Casey McIntyre, Simone Roberts-Payne, Krista Ahlberg, Shelby Mickler, and Sola Akinlana, who really helped me polish these pages and make them shine. To Kristie Radwilowicz and Theresa Evangelista, thank you for this eye-catching and creepy cover.

I don't know what I would do without my critique partner, Amy Trueblood, who is always up for reading my terrible first drafts and giving pitch-perfect advice. Thanks to the always amazing Kristina Pérez for being an overflowing font of wisdom.

Shout-out to the Arizona YA/MG writer community. Thank you all, especially Dusti Bowling, Stephanie Elliot, and Lorri Phillips. Our coffee dates and writing sessions are the highlights of my week.

Thanks to my early readers, including Jenny L. Howe and Nancy Richardson Fischer. Any mistakes are my own.

This year, I am celebrating my twentieth wedding anniversary with my high school sweetheart, Jim. I am so thankful for each day with my husband and am lucky to have so much support at home. My daughter, Evelyn, continues to be my inspiration and one of the reasons I am so motivated to write for younger readers. Evelyn, I am endlessly proud of the young woman you have become.